THE IMMACULATE DECEPTION

(Book Two in "The Popular Series")

BY

GARETH RUSSELL

The Immaculate Deception

Copyright © 2012 Gareth Russell

ISBN-13: 978-1481138390
ISBN: 1481138391

All rights reserved. No part of this publication may be reproduced, stored in a retrieval system, or transmitted, in any form or by any means, electronic, mechanical, photocopying, recording or otherwise, except as permitted by the UK Copyright, Designs and Patents Act 1988, without the prior permission of the publisher.

This is a work of fiction. Names, characters, businesses, places, events and incidents are either the products of the author's imagination or used in a fictitious manner. Any resemblance to actual persons, living or dead, or actual events is purely coincidental.

M
MadeGlobal Publishing

For more information on
MadeGlobal Publishing, visit our website:
www.madeglobal.com

To

*Claire Handley, Lauren Browne,
Robbie Dagher and Emma Taylor,
Who kept the faith*

THE IMMACULATE DECEPTION
- ABOUT THE AUTHOR

Gareth Russell was a student at Down High Grammar School in Northern Ireland before he went on to study Modern History at Saint Peter's College in the University of Oxford. He is the author of several plays and his first novel, *Popular*, was first published by Penguin in 2011 but updated and republished in 2012 by MadeGlobal Publishing. Since 2011, *Popular* has been adapted for the stage twice and Gareth divides his time between Belfast, London and vacations in Connecticut. His accent is best described as polymorphous, shifting with the greatest of ease from Northern Irish to English to American. This pleases him greatly. In 2012, he was invited to speak by History Tours of Britain about his forthcoming historical research. His first ever word was 'shoe' and if he had to host a dinner party with one person from history, it would be Anne Boleyn.

Contents

1. American Boy 1
2. Scheming in the Sun 7
3. On the Other Side of the World 18
4. The Mayans in Manolos 34
5. Dancing Queens 59
6. The Return of the Queen 83
7. Judgement Day 109
8. Wake Me Up 151
9. Mad Men & Loose Women 173
10. The Personal Purgatory of Blake Hartman 186
11. No such thing as a friendly game 204
12. Broken Hearts & Bromances 220
13. The Demise of Détente 237
14. By the Pricking of My Thumbs 260
15. And the truth shall set you free 274
    Author's Note 285
    Abbreviations, definitions and banter II:
    A guide to the vocab 287

'A cruel story runs on wheels and
every hand oils the wheels as they run.'
- *Marie-Louise de la Ramée (1839 – 1908)*

1
AMERICAN BOY

On the first Wednesday in July, Blake Joshua Elijah Hartman walked down the steps of the CVS Pharmacy car park in New Canaan, Connecticut, and came to a halt on the sidewalk at the bottom. He was wearing brown flip flops, a pair of green-checked cargo shorts, sunglasses and a white polo shirt with a yellow-trimmed collar. In his right hand, he was carrying a half-consumed bottle of water which he tapped absent-mindedly against his thigh. It was eighty-four degrees and Blake was already beginning to miss the air conditioning back in the pharmacy.

Walking slowly through the streets of the town he had grown up in, Blake carried himself with the natural confidence of someone who knows that they are good looking. It was not that he was necessarily arrogant about his appearance. The quiet confidence simply came from the fact that he had never had to feel particularly insecure about his looks. He had light brown hair, brown eyes, a perfect smile, which he considered to be his best feature, and that summer he had just passed six feet in height.

At the street corner, he took a right and saw the 12:27 train for New York pulling slowly out of the station. Blake's parents used to take him and his kid brother into the city on that train, with a stopover for ice cream in Stamford. Now, Blake's father was far away in Northern Ireland and his mother was preparing to move back to

Vermont. Grace had spent the last year selling the family home, packing up the last of her things and trying to face down her neighbours' confusion about what had gone wrong with her marriage. Divorce certainly happened in New Canaan, but it wasn't supposed to happen to the town's local Baptist pastor and his pretty wife.

Eighteen months earlier, when Robert and Grace Hartman had announced to their two children that Daddy would be moving to a new country, Blake knew he'd be going with him. Of his two parents, it had always been Robert who was the more organized and the more responsible. Both Robert and Grace agreed that Blake and Jack could finish out the school year in New Canaan and then join their father in his new home in Northern Ireland.

When Blake Hartman first left New Canaan High School and set foot in Belfast's Mount Olivet Grammar, he had drawn a collective gasp from most of the girls around him. And one of the boys. Alright, he hadn't been invited into the hallowed inner sanctum of Mount Olivet's Malone-bred popular crowd, but he had made friends and settled in. Had things kept going in that way, Blake would almost certainly have ended up as one of the most well-liked and respected members of Mount Olivet's fifth-year. However, fate intervened in the form of the first close relationship Blake formed in his new home.

On paper, there was almost nothing that bound Blake and the popular clique's token male, Cameron Matthews, together as friends. Blake lived in Carryduff and Cameron was the kind of person who thought the only world that mattered began at the Malone roundabout and ended somewhere near Sans Souci Park. Yet, the two boys grew closer until they ended up kissing at

Cameron's sixteenth birthday party. From that moment on, a horrified Blake had done everything in his power to avoid both Cameron's company and the questions about his own sexuality which, long suppressed, were now roaring in his head. By the time he realized that he wanted to fix things, it was too late.

Blake walked lost in thought down Elm Street. He kept worrying about his decision to entrust a highly personal letter in to the manicured and moisturized hands of Meredith Harper, the popular set's malevolent queen bee. He had been unsure about sending it to Cameron in the first place, but running into Meredith outside school on the very day he was leaving Belfast had seemed like a sign and so he impulsively handed the letter over, facing down her silent waves of hostility. Part of him had hoped that giving it to Meredith directly might partially ameliorate her wrath against him for his role in plunging her best friend into an epic crisis of distinctly unfabulous misery. However, looking back on it, there was another more sensible part of Blake's brain which now wondered if Meredith would even give the letter to Cameron or if she would simply toss it on to a fire where, if she had her way, she might not be too adverse to the idea of tossing Blake himself. It had been four days since he had handed the letter over and he had still heard nothing from either Cameron or Meredith. The first two days had been excusable, given that they had both been in transit for the clique's summer vacation in Mexico. But by day four, it was difficult to ignore mounting feelings of dread.

Clearing the main part of the town of New Canaan, Blake began walking along the side of the road, keeping to the grassy verge. A SUV sped past, driven by a soccer mom with a gaggle of children fresh from their visit to Baskin Robbins. Blake smiled a little as he heard their laughter through the car's open windows. He wondered again how much easier it would be if he could just move to Vermont with his mother. If he did that he could put everything that had happened in Belfast behind him; he could start over. It was a momentarily attractive idea, but deep down, he knew it was impossible. His father would be devastated to hear that his eldest son wasn't coming home after what was supposed be nothing more than a sudden summer visit to Connecticut and he knew that his brother Jack would be furious at being left in Belfast without him. Plus, he would never see Cameron again.

Blake opened the front door and stepped into the cool of what had once been his grandparents', and then his parents', house. For his entire childhood, this place had been home, but now, with it finally sold, the Hartman family would no longer live here. Grace would leave for Vermont in six weeks and their family's association with New Canaan and Connecticut would be gone forever. There really were only two choices left for Blake – Belfast or Vermont. Neither of them home.

He called out for his mom, but there was no answer. Perhaps she had gone into town to offer him a lift home or maybe she had gone out to buy more boxes. Either way, the house was temporarily empty and Blake had a few moments of peace. He set the empty bottle of water on the kitchen island and flicked open his laptop.

He tapped his fingers on the counter top, waiting for the computer to boot up. Through habit rather than anything else, the first thing he checked was Facebook. No one had posted anything on his wall, but he was still officially listed as being "In a Relationship" with Catherine O'Rourke. Blake grimaced as he saw it, mentally castigating himself for choosing this particular girl to silence the doubts he had felt after his kiss with Cameron. Of all the girls in school, he had decided to date the dizziest member of Meredith Harper's socialite set. If Cameron ever forgave him for his cruelty, he would still resent himself for his stupidity.

Seeing his now-meaningless relationship status on Facebook irritated him and he clicked to end it. Knowing Catherine, she was pretty likely to consider the ending of the relationship on Facebook to be as traumatic as ending it in real life had been, if not more so. Surfing over to Cameron's page, he saw that his profile picture had been changed to one of him and Imogen Dawson at the end of year ball; Cameron was smiling in to the camera and next to him Imogen had her hands draped seductively over his shoulders, winking saucily. Cameron's status read, "Cameron Matthews has finally arrived in Mexico. Phone and e-mails working! Liver, probably not."

Blake clicked out of Facebook quickly and logged into his e-mail account. His heart and stomach gave a lurch as he saw he had one new item in the inbox. It read: -

MEREDITH HARPER   **Your letter**
From: "Meredith Harper"   <sizezerois4heifers@msn.ni>
To: "Blake Hartman"   <blakejehartman@msn.ni>

Blake,

I have passed on your letter to Cameron. He read it and asked me to tell you that he has nothing to say to you about it or any of the things you brought up in it. He says he appreciates the time you took to write him an explanation (at last), but that it's far too late to fix things now. He'd rather put the whole mess of last year behind him. He wants to forget about it, and you, and move on.

I'm sure you understand.

Please do not contact him. After everything you've done to him, the very least you can do is respect his wishes and just leave him alone.

When we last spoke, you mentioned that you were considering moving back permanently to the US. Maybe that's a good idea, especially now that you realise that there is literally no reason for you to return to Belfast.

Meredith Harper

Blake sat stock-still for a moment as he tried to digest Meredith's e-mail. It was the worst possible outcome. It was actually over. Cameron never wanted to see him again. He could not even bring himself to respond to Blake personally; he had asked Meredith to do it for him. Feeling like he was about to vomit, Blake reached up his right hand and slowly pulled the laptop screen towards him. It closed with a small click and then he was left sitting alone in the silence.

2
SCHEMING IN THE SUN

Nine hours later, in a luxurious Mexican resort twenty miles south of San José del Cabo, the great love of Blake Hartman's life stepped out into the balmy evening air arm in arm with Blake's number one enemy. Standing at exactly six feet in height, trim and tall, with dark hair and blue eyes, Cameron Matthews was dressed in a purple-striped Hugo Boss shirt and white linen trousers. Next to him, with her arm looped through his, Meredith Harper cut a dramatically elegant figure in a Missoni cocktail dress, with Mont Blanc diamond studs glistening in her ears and a silver bracelet jangling lightly on her wrist. Her gorgeous brunette tresses were swept up for the evening into a cross between a messy bun and a faux bob, with its trail ends bouncing along in perfect synchronicity to the click-clack of her Louboutins as she walked across the marble. She looked like a movie star and an eighteenth-century aristocrat rolled into one. Trailing miserably behind them was Blake's ex-girlfriend, Catherine O'Rourke, looking like she would rather be anywhere on Earth than attending this dinner on the restaurant veranda of one of the most expensive and exclusive resorts in Mexico.

Weaving their way through the other diners, Cameron, Meredith and Catherine approached a circular table set for five at the far end of the veranda. Already sitting there were two blondes – Imogen Dawson and Kerry Davison. Kerry's perpetually perfect curls dangled around her head and she tossed them back as she picked up her second margarita of the evening. Opposite her, Imogen was busy stubbing out a cigarette and hooting with laughter at whatever point Kerry was making. From the table next to them, Cameron could see two young men out for dinner with their parents, trying to steal covert glances at Imogen when they thought no one was looking.

'Oh,' she said, as the other three sat down. 'I didn't think you'd be able to make it, Catherine.'

'I'm feeling a bit better,' Catherine said, with a watery smile.

'That's good,' Imogen replied, without much conviction. 'Has anyone else had the chicken?'

'Yes, I had it last night,' Meredith answered. 'It was quite nice. Too much cheese though.'

'I love cheese,' whispered Kerry, tenderly. 'Love it.'

'Cameron, you need to order a drink. It's catch-up time,' Imogen ordered.

'How many have you had?' asked Cameron.

'Three,' said Imogen, raising her margarita glass to him and winking.

'I'll go order us some from the bar then,' he said with a smile.

'Just order a round of five,' suggested Imogen, eliciting a panicked grimace from Kerry, who now practically stuck her face into her enormous cocktail glass to try and finish it before Cameron returned with another.

'This place is so beau, Meredith. Isn't it, Kerry?'

Kerry nodded at Imogen's prompt, but didn't remove her mouth from the rim of her glass. 'Isn't it?' sighed Meredith. 'Such a good idea.'

'Our holidays are the best,' agreed Imogen. 'Everyone in school was so jealous. How I cackled in their inferior faces. We'll need to go somewhere equally fabulous next year, though. Once you start this kind of thing, you can't stop.'

'Paris!' squealed Kerry, hiccupping slightly at removing herself from the margarita and trying to speak at the same time. 'J'adore.'

'We can do Paris for a weekend at Christmas,' Meredith reasoned. 'Who on earth would want to go there in the summer?'

'I would,' said Kerry. 'I said, *j'adore*.'

'Paris is hideous in the heat, Kerry,' Meredith replied, condescendingly. 'That's why all the actual Parisians leave it in August.'

Kerry regarded Meredith with sizzling dislike for a moment, before catching sight of Cameron picking up a tray with five cocktails at the bar. She hastily returned to her margarita mission.

'What about Dubai?' Imogen suggested. 'Sexy times.'

'Imogen, you will not be able to shimmy around dressed like Cleopatra,' groaned Meredith. 'We've been over this. No matter how hard you try to ignore it, the UAE has a dress code these days and you're the kind of girl who'll end up in prison because of it.'

'Jihad would not be fun, would it?'

'No, Imogen. It wouldn't.'

'What's going on?' asked Cameron, passing the drinks to his friends, including an especially pleased Kerry, who triumphantly placed her empty glass in the centre of the table.

'We're thinking about where to go next year,' Meredith informed him. 'Maybe Paris during the Christmas holidays...'

'That was my idea,' smiled Kerry.

'... but we've no idea about next summer.'

'What about a cruise?' asked Cameron.

'Oh, fun!' gasped Imogen. 'I've heard they're literally the most wonderfully tacky things in the history of humanity. We *have* to do it!'

'Well, not all of them are,' said Meredith, who had been on seven. 'It depends where you go and who you go with.'

A pale and panicked Kerry's fist slammed down on the table. 'No!'

'No, what?' asked Cameron.

'No cruise,' she answered. 'Me no likey boats.'

'They're not boats, they're ships,' he said pedantically.

'I don't care!' Kerry snapped. 'If you take me on one of those, I will go into our cabin, curl up in the bed and cry until we see land again.'

'Why do you hate boats so much?' Imogen asked, between sips.

'Have you forgotten what happened to the *Titanic*?'

'I don't really think we'll be anywhere near icebergs for our summer holiday,' Meredith said. 'And that was a long time ago. Didn't someone tell me that the *Titanic* was the last boat to sink because of an iceberg?'

'Well, it wasn't!' hissed Kerry. 'Whoever told you that was lying. Weren't they, Cameron?'

'Maybe they just made a mistake.'

'They were liars,' Kerry muttered darkly. 'One sank *very* recently.'

'Did it actually?' Meredith asked.

'Yes,' Cameron reluctantly admitted. 'But it was in the Arctic on an iceberg-viewing expedition, so it was basically asking for it if you ask me. Plus it took something like seven hours to sink and there were two other boats nearby, so everybody got off in time and everybody lived.'

'See? You've got nothing to worry about,' breezed Imogen. 'I vote for a cruise.'

'Nothing to worry about?' screeched a scandalized Kerry. 'Okay. Fine! These other boats who rescued the people, did they just happen to be in the area?'

'I think so,' said Cameron.

'And why did they pick these people up off the other boat? Out of the goodness of their hearts? What if our boat hits an iceberg and we're stuck next to some bastarding heartless captain who doesn't want any more passengers?'

'Then I'm pretty sure he'd be tried for homicide or contributory negligence or something,' shrugged Cameron.

'They'd send him to Davey Jones's locker!' Imogen interjected loudly, having now polished off her fourth margarita.

Ignoring her, Kerry pressed on relentlessly. 'Right, I understand that this is the first one to hit an iceberg and actually sink since, like, 1912, and I also understand that it took seven hours to sink, but that's just luck! How long did it take the *Titanic* to sink?'

'About two and a half hours, I think,' said Cameron.

'Oh my god,' groaned Imogen. 'The movie was longer than the actual thing.'

'I hate that movie,' added Meredith. 'Stupid, ungrateful heifer.'

'I know!' Imogen nodded. 'You could definitely have fitted two people on to that big bit of wood at the end.'

'Oh, yeah, that. Plus leaving the fiancé was super-unbelievable,' sighed Meredith. 'And how cold was the water where this boat sank in seven hours, Cameron? As cold as a thousand knives stabbing you all over your body?'

'Kerry, I don't know. It was in the Arctic. I assume it was very cold, yes.'

'And what if there are big bad-assed fishes?' she said dangerously, digging her nails into his arms.

'Well, you'd either be in a lifeboat or on the rescue ship,' Cameron said, trying to pull his flesh away from her talons. 'I doubt you'd know what fish were near you.'

'But what if, in my panic, I'm running around on the deck crying so hard that I accidentally run off the side of the ship and there's a big m'a-fucka'a of an octopus waiting down there for me? Or! What if someone pushes me?' she said, shooting daggers across the table accusingly at Meredith and Imogen.

'Why would an octopus be waiting for you?' asked a baffled Cameron.

'Because they are the snakes of the sea,' Kerry whined, 'and you know how I feel about snakes. If I even see a snake on TV, I can't breathe and I feel sick. So what happens if I plummet into the Atlantic Ocean, land next to an octopus and have a panic attack? I will definitely drown.'

'Alright!' said Meredith, loudly. 'Let's just forget the idea of a cruise.'

A tearful Kerry nodded gratefully and returned to her drink, breaking the silence ten seconds later by muttering, 'Scary, eight-legged m'a-fucka'as.'

The morning after Kerry's nautical meltdown, Imogen lay stretched out on a sun lounger outside the group's villa in the hotel grounds. In front of her, glittering tourmaline in the sunlight, was their infinity pool and beyond that, the Sea of Cortez. The mid-morning air was warm, but not too hot – yet. In her sequined Union Jack bikini, with red Dior sunglasses perched on her face and a large glass of iced mineral water on the table next to her, Imogen checked the screen of her beloved phone. No messages, apart from an e-mail from her mother, informing her that she and Imogen's three younger brothers had decided to fly over to London tomorrow for a long weekend visiting Imogen's maternal grandparents in Knightsbridge. Daddy would be at home in Belfast, in case there were any emergencies.

From the villa behind her, Imogen heard the doors sliding open and shut and the sound of dainty feet pattered slowly towards her. Imogen didn't bother to look up from her basking, since she knew instinctively who it was by the rhythm of their walk. Wearing a white Rosa Chá bikini and a pair of Chanel sunglasses, Meredith slipped gracefully on to the sun lounger next to Imogen's, with a large hat underneath her left arm to guard against excessive tanning, melanoma and, worst of all, premature aging. Depositing an enormous biography of the late Queen Mother on the table, Meredith negligently trailed her freshly-washed hair over her shoulders and settled back on the lounger, crossing her legs as she did so.

'Have you had breakfast?' she asked.

'Just a little grapefruit and some OJ,' Imogen answered, deciding to omit the five slices of smoked bacon she had stuffed into a buttered bagel. 'Is everyone else still sleeping?'

'No. Kerry's watching a re-run of *Keeping up with the Kardashians* and Cameron's in the shower.'

Imogen nodded, ignoring the fact that Meredith had blithely failed to include Catherine in her summary of people who mattered. 'What are our plans for today?'

Meredith shrugged. 'I have no idea. Nothing really, I suppose. Same as yesterday. I had a missed call from Anastasia last night, but when I tried to call her back there was no answer.'

'Doesn't she know we're in Mexico?'

'She does.'

'That's an expensive phone call.'

Meredith shrugged again, conveying that such mundane monetary matters were not something which Anastasia Montmorency, the queen bee in the year above, would ever deign to concern herself with.

'Is she back in Belfast?' Imogen asked.

'No. She's in Austria with Mariella and Lavinia.'

'Oh, that's nice. Not as nice as here, though.'

Meredith sighed appreciatively and picked up the biography, opening it at the spot near the beginning where she had left off the night before. Meredith loved biographies, provided they were about someone rich, beautiful, charming, powerful or clever. Imogen, who had spent the flight to Mexico reading and annotating *Eat, Drink & Succeed: Climb Your Way to the Top Using the Networking Power of Social Events*, did not understand Meredith's particular enthusiasm for historical biographies – the longer, the better. Then again, Meredith did not understand the strange emotional rollercoaster Imogen went on every time someone so much as mentioned a Charlaine Harris novel.

'By the way, can we just talk about how annoying Catherine was at dinner last night?'

Meredith closed the book and nodded in agreement. 'I know. I don't even know why she bothered coming out of her room.'

'Neither do I! She didn't open her great big fat stupid mouth once to actually contribute to the conversation and she sat there the whole time looking like she was about to burst into tears! Stupid moo-cow. It's not our fault that her idiot boyfriend dumped her because he realized he prefers man candy.'

'Idiot *ex*-boyfriend,' Meredith reminded her.

'Oh, that's right,' cackled Imogen. 'Mutant. I mean, okay, she got dumped. That doesn't mean she has to be such a blubbering little piglet about the whole thing. Maybe we should tell her that?'

'I'm sure she'd appreciate the advice,' smirked Meredith.

'By the way, did Blake actually tell her that was why he was dumping her?'

'Pardon?'

'Did he tell her that after four months of dating her he realized he'd rather kill himself than go near a woman again?'

Meredith laughed. 'No, I don't think so. It doesn't really matter now, does it? He's gone; we won.'

'I'd love to know what he said to her though.'

'Don't,' advised Meredith. 'We don't want her to start crying again.'

Imogen had to concede that Meredith had a point. During the eleven-hour flight from London to Mexico, a distraught Catherine had spent at least five hours wailing on Kerry's shoulder before the eyes of an increasingly bored Cameron, Meredith and Imogen. From what they could gather between her sobs and hiccups of grief, Blake had unceremoniously dumped her the morning after the end of year ball; then, the next day, she had received an e-mail from him in which he apologized for having treated her so badly and informed her that he was leaving Belfast for the summer, possibly forever. Eventually exhausted by the theatrics of her own misery, Catherine had lapsed into an unhappy slumber somewhere over the Atlantic – although Cameron could have sworn that this event was speeded along by Imogen crushing a Tylenol into Catherine's in-flight meal. The last thing she said before slipping into unconsciousness was that she would never again find anyone as hot as Blake to be her boyfriend, which, like most objectionably shallow points, was undeniably true.

'Hello, ladies.'

'Morning, Cameron!'

Sauntering out of the villa in his swimming shorts, with his dark hair still tousled from the shower and his skin smelling of shower gel and suntan lotion, Cameron was carrying a bottle of water and an apple, which he proceeded to bite into as he sat on the edge of Imogen's sun lounger.

'Imogen, can you put some of this on my back, please?' he asked, gesturing to the suntan lotion next to her.

'Sure, sweetie. Don't want to risk cancer, do we?' she trilled, nudging her packet of cigarettes out of the way as she scooted over towards Cameron and squirted lotion on to her hands.

'What are our plans today?' he asked, taking another bite of the apple.

'Nothing really,' Meredith answered. 'I think just lazing around here and then maybe go down to the hotel for dinner again this evening.'

'That sounds nice,' said Cameron. 'I think I'll go for a swim. Imogen?'

'No, you know I don't really like moving.' She gave his back a light slap before nestling back and lighting a cigarette. 'I just want to focus on basking in my own radiance for a few hours.'

Cameron nodded and dived into the pool. A few drops of water splashed up and landed on Meredith's ankles. She tutted irritably and grabbed one of the towels that housekeeping had left nearby to wipe it away. Having checked that no drop of water had dared besmirch a photograph of the Royal Family, she returned to her book. For a few moments, the only sounds were those coming from the pool as Cameron swam his lengths and the occasional turning of a page in Meredith's book.

Glancing at her watch, Imogen saw that it would only be half an hour before housekeeping arrived to clear away breakfast, tidy the villa and replenish the fridge with supplies for the afternoon. The sun had risen higher and a baking heat was now floating down over their luxurious private villa, their designer clothes, their pool and their fabulous, glamorous, dramatic, superior lives.

'Imagine living life as someone other than us,' Imogen said out loud. 'Super-unlucky.'

3
ON THE OTHER SIDE OF THE WORLD

Stewart Lawrence, Imogen's ex-boyfriend and the boy whose heart she had broken last Christmas, finally wandered out of his tent at one o'clock in the afternoon on Day Three of a music festival that he was now definitely beginning to regret attending. Sitting down on the circle of chairs nearby, he noticed that two of those they had schlepped with them from Belfast had been stolen over the course of the previous evening and there were seven empty cans of beer lying right outside their tent door. Whether they were his or not, there was now no earthly way of telling. Pulling a toothbrush out of his back pocket and dipping it in a bottle of water, Stewart reflected that he seemed to have paid an exorbitant sum of money for the pleasure of hiking his stuff one and a half miles from a bus stop to the festival entrance, before getting to roll around in the stinking dirt and sleep on the ground for five days. Every single part of him hurt and, in that moment, Stewart Lawrence would have given his right arm for a paracetamol and a hot shower.

After three days, he was also forced to concede that he could no longer carry on wearing the blue t-shirt he had arrived in and he began rifling around in his backpack for a substitute. Pulling his sweat-stained top off and spraying all around him with deodorant, before putting on a crumpled but clean red t-shirt, Stewart mentally shook himself and decided to push through this funk. So what if he and everyone around him were suffering from the first signs of exhaustion, post traumatic stress disorder and alcohol poisoning? He had been waiting for this festival since March, there were still two days left of it to go and so help him God, nothing was going to dampen his spirits.

'Our food cost me €20. I don't even want to know what that is in our money,' came an irritated voice, followed by a rather limp-looking cheese and ham sandwich and bottle of Coke being hurled aggressively in Stewart's direction. Looking at his friend Mark, who was currently grousing about the in-camp extortion, Stewart got an unpleasant snapshot of what they all must look like. Mark's hair was caked with a combination of three-day-old gel and festival mud, his face was ruddy from sleep deprivation and three days' worth of drinking, his voice was hoarse from shouting and his facial hair had gone from designer stubble into full-on bristle in the course of the last twelve hours. There were beer stains, mud splatters and some mysterious paint marks all over his blue hoodie and denim jeans. Even the man-bracelets that Mark had decided to don in the spirit of festival-going somehow seemed tired and lifeless.

'I had to pay €2 for hot water to put in my fucking Pot Noodle!' he growled. 'That's a joke, right? €2 for water!'

'Mate, do you have a spare pair of boxers?' Stewart asked, as Mark sat down on one of the remaining chairs and tucked into his controversial Pot Noodle.

'What for?'

'I need to change mine. It's been three days and Peter decided to use my only clean pair as a hat last night and then he threw them at a seagull for the banter.'

'Stew, I didn't even bring a change for myself.'

Stewart shrugged and pretended not to be too upset by this news, since he knew that he was sailing dangerously close to seeming too concerned about his personal hygiene. From behind came the voice of someone who had no such compulsions, as their friend Peter Sullivan burst into view with a beer keg under his arm and a cocky grin on his face. 'Boom baby!' he announced, slapping Stewart on the back. 'Stolen beer banter!'

'You stole that?' Mark asked.

'You don't miss a thing, do you, Poirot?'

Stewart laughed and sat down. 'Do you want some of this?' he said, offering Peter half his sandwich.

'No, cheers, mate. I got with a bird earlier and ate hers.'

'You got with someone?' Stewart asked incredulously. 'How?'

'Ah, Stew, I know it's been a while, but you must still remember how to do it?' jibed Peter.

'No, I mean, it's day three, Pete. She must stink.'

'No worse than me,' Peter shrugged happily, sitting on top of his requisitioned beer keg. 'Guess who's here?'

'Who?'

'Carolyn Jeffreys, Cristyn Evans and Melanie Scott,' said Peter. 'So fit. But Melanie's boyfriend was standing over her the whole time, looking like he was about to deck me. So I waited until he wasn't looking, kissed her on the lips, stole the beer from his tent and ran off.'

'Coral Andrews is here too,' said Mark, through a mouthful of pot noodle. 'I saw her and Joanne down by one of the burger vans. She's looking well, actually.'

'Coral?' asked Stewart, impolite disbelief dripping from his voice. Having been Imogen Dawson's boyfriend for over a year, it had been hard not to pick up some of her seething prejudices regarding the high priestess of the indie crowd.

'Yeah,' nodded Mark. 'Really well, actually. I told her we'd hang out with them later.'

'Wanna be careful there, mate,' laughed Peter. 'You go anywhere near her and you'll never have a chance with Meredith Harper.'

'Shut the fuck up!' Mark snapped. 'I'm not going anywhere near Coral and even if I was, I don't fancy Meredith.'

'Why not? Are you blind?' asked Peter.

'No,' Mark muttered. 'There's more to someone than just their looks, Peter.'

'Homo!' Peter chanted cheerfully.

Mark lowered his head and focussed with excessive concentration on eating his pot noodle, all the while trying to suppress his blushing.

The sounds of the festival were still blaring at one o'clock the following morning, but down by the beach that ran alongside the campsite the noise was at least partially drowned out by a combination of the sound of the waves and the numerous docking stations belonging to the different groups of revellers who had moved down to the beach. Mercifully, given that it was Ireland, there was no rain and the wind blowing in from the Atlantic was a relatively warm one.

Sitting around a bonfire with beers in their hands, Stewart and Mark were listening as Coral sang an accompaniment to her friend Eóin's guitar playing. She was swaying soulfully, with her eyes half-closed to convey how deeply she felt the emotions of her lyrics; her chestnut hair was swept up in a bandana, while a plethora of bangles jingled softly on her wrists. When she finished, Mark leaned across and touched her hand, 'That was incredible, Coral.'

Stewart continued to stare at the ground, silently wondering why he wasn't surrounded by ten rugby boys chanting cheerful musical obscenities, rather than stuck here listening to this outpouring of musical angst. Had Imogen been with him, she would calmly have walked over to where Eóin was sitting and sliced through his guitar strings with her nail file. Unlike his ex-girlfriend, however, Stewart was far too nice to say anything out loud, so instead he took a gulp of his beer and stared into the firelight, hoping that people would leave him alone with his thoughts.

Before Eóin could start playing again, another of the indie boys, whose name Stewart was not entirely sure of, passed him a beer, necessitating the setting down of the guitar. Glancing surreptitiously at the three boys sitting to Eóin's right, Stewart was fairly certain that at least one of them was called Phil and another was called Paddy, but he wasn't sure which was which and he was equally unsure if the third member of their triad even went to Mount Olivet, although he assumed he probably did.

Two girls were sitting between Coral and Mark – Joanne Sexton and Paula Flockley. They were in Coral's company as regularly as Imogen and Kerry were in Meredith's. To Stewart's eyes, Joanne, at least, was very pretty, with dyed blonde hair and edgy-chic glasses; Paula, on the other hand, was quiet, with long bushy hair and she seemed intensely shy – a trait that Stewart suspected was exacerbated by Coral's dominance of her.

'Stewart?'

Stewart looked up from his reverie at the boy who was addressing him from across the fire. It was either Paddy or Phil. 'Yeah?'

'Are you still going out with Imogen Dawson?' Paddy/Phil asked.

'No. We broke up in December,' said Stewart, brusquely.

'Oh, right. Didn't know. Sorry to hear that.'

Stewart tried not to be too offended. Just because Imogen believed that her private life was the school's equivalent of the tabloid press did not mean that he should be unduly surprised if someone in their year hadn't been following the popular set with the requisite religious mania. Still, the mention of his ex upset him and it was always slightly wounding to discover that people, even strangers, had somehow carried on with their lives regardless of the fact that your heart had been breaking.

'You going with anyone else?' the mysterious Paddy/Phil conglomerate asked.

Stewart shook his head. 'No. Imogen's pretty hard to replace.'

'Stewart, I'm sure you will find someone,' Coral said, consolingly. 'You're an incredible guy.'

Mark smiled and nodded. 'She's right, Stew.'

Seeing the confused face of the anonymous indie boy, Coral explained, 'Cormac, Stewart's ex-girlfriend, Imogen, is one of "those" girls at our school. You know – "the Plastics." She's very pretty.'

Cormac nodded his head politely and Stewart realized that this boy did not, in fact, attend Mount Olivet Grammar. He also realized that he did not like Coral's tone, or the way she had described Imogen as "Plastic." He glared at her, but she was too busy reaching across to take a sip from Mark's drink to notice.

'Do you have those girls at Immaculate Heart, Cormac?' Eóin asked, much to Stewart's annoyance.

'Yeah,' Cormac answered, ruefully. 'Aisleagh McGorian's like their leader.'

'Aisleagh McGorian?' Mark asked. 'Didn't she use to go to our school?'

'Yes,' Coral answered. 'And Meredith Harper taught her everything she knows. She used to be in their little group, until she transferred to Immaculate Heart.'

'Who's Meredith Harper?' asked Cormac, who was keen not to spend any longer than was necessary discussing the stunning Aisleagh, who only last year had asked him in front of twenty-five of their classmates if his face was ugly on purpose.

'She's the Empress of Evil,' Joanne answered quickly.

'No, she isn't,' sighed Coral, earning her a surprised glance from Stewart, Mark and at least half the campfire. The ferocious animosity between Meredith's clique and Coral's was proverbial at Mount Olivet. Back in third year, Imogen had even managed to reduce Coral to tears by telling her she was so flat chested that her body looked like a surf board with two grapes stuck on to it. 'I don't know why people go on about Meredith like that. She's not even that special. She's just not a very nice person, who happens to have a lot of money. That's all. If people actually stood up to her once in a while, she wouldn't know what to do. And they're all like that.'

'No, they're not,' said Stewart.

'Oh, I didn't mean Imogen. She's quite nice,' Coral replied disingenuously. 'But if you think about every girl who's considered like "queen bee," or whatever it is they like to be called, there's not really anything special about them is there? The only reason they get away with behaving the way they do is because other people let them.'

'And they do it all the time! There's a Meredith in every year,' moaned Joanne. 'It's like clockwork. Everyone knows that the most popular girl in Upper Sixth gets to be president of the Social Committee. Every. Single. Year. Allegra, Cecilia, Anastasia, next it'll be Meredith...'

'Okay, I don't understand why you keep saying Meredith is "popular,"' Coral said. 'Nobody likes her, so how can she be popular?'

'Because everybody wants to be friends with her,' answered Joanne.

'No, they don't,' scoffed Coral. 'Do you?'

Joanne shook her head swiftly. 'No, of course not, babes. What I mean is, I don't like the way they behave. Obviously. I think it's *beyond* gross. But the reason why everyone lets them do it is because deep down most of them hope that one day they'll get to be friends with them and behave in exactly the same way. That's why they always get what they want. That's why people keep voting for them in the Social Committee elections, every year, even though they're horrible to them or just don't speak to them, ever. After Anastasia, it will be Meredith and after her, it'll probably be Cameron Matthews' sister, Charlotte...'

'Fuck, I hate that stuck-up faggot,' muttered Eóin, cracking open another beer.

'What did you say?' barked Mark, who had spent most of the conversation awkwardly picking at the label of his beer bottle.

Eóin looked up in surprised panic. 'Eh... I thought you two fell out, mate,' he mumbled.

'Yeah, well, we patched things up and even if we hadn't, if you ever speak that way about him again I'll knock your two front teeth in, alright?'

Stewart laid a restraining hand on Mark's shoulder, 'Dude.'

'I'm serious. Don't speak that way about Cameron,' said Mark, still glaring at Eóin and ignoring Stewart's hand.

'Yeah. Sorry, mate. I didn't mean anything by it, like.'

Mark nodded, calmer now, and leaned back. Stewart patted his shoulder and removed his hand. Further awkwardness around the campfire was avoided by the boisterous arrival of Peter. He plonked himself down next to Stewart and helped himself to a beer, nudging Stewart's arm and winking cheekily.

'God, Peter. Another one?'

Peter laughed. 'What can I say? The ladies dig my sexy chat. She was a nice girl, though. Someone had stolen her wallet, so I took her and her mates to get something to eat from the kebab van. Jesus Christ and Saint Malachy, that place is expensive! Didn't like to think of them being hungry or anything, though.'

Stewart smiled. 'Good lad.'

'True lad,' corrected Peter. 'I pulled her afterwards. What'd I miss?'

'Nothing much,' muttered Stewart. 'Eh, Peter, this is Cormac. Cormac, Peter. Cormac goes to Immaculate Heart; Peter's a mate of mine from Mount Olivet.'

Peter got up and reached over the low-burning fire towards a slightly-surprised Cormac. 'Nice to meet you,' he said, with a firm handshake, before releasing him and allowing Cormac to hunch back in his seat again.

'So,' smiled Peter, 'what's the bant, lads?'

'We're just talking about Meredith Harper,' said Paula.

'Nice girl,' Peter replied mischievously. 'Cracking bod.'

'Do you think she's pretty?' Coral asked in a tone of feigned surprise as Mark glowered at his friend. 'I think she's quite cold looking.'

'Ice, ice baby,' Peter grinned.

'You don't actually *like* her though, do you?'

'She's never done anything on me,' Peter replied carelessly.

'She acts like royalty!'

Peter gave another infuriating shrug. 'If being popular and "Queen of Malone" and all that kind of crap is important to Meredith, then good for her. I think she's very good at what she does.'

Coral's piercing blue eyes gazed at him with re-affirmed dislike. He was everything she loathed in a boy – a loud, loutish lad who would forgive a girl anything as long as she was pretty. In Coral's mind, Peter Sullivan was nothing more than a galumphing Neanderthal ruled by his crotch and his peanut-sized brain and it was precisely because of boys like him that girls like Meredith Harper and Kerry Davison were able to parade around the school acting like they were better than everybody else.

Peter, who was more than aware of what Coral thought of him, had mastered the art of appearing artless in order to make his points heard more clearly and he took great pleasure in aggravating anyone who he thought took themselves too seriously. In that spirit, he decided to press on in his unlikely defence of the popular crowd. Stewart, who knew all too well this impish side of his friend, watched him in silent amusement, while Mark, who had now heard Peter refer to Meredith's good looks twice in the course of one day, clenched his jaw as the thought that Peter might have a crush on her himself began to germinate in his brain.

'*And* anytime I've gone to any of her parties or hung out with her, I've had a great time,' Peter declared guilelessly. 'So, no, I've no reason to dislike Meredith. I think she's good banter.'

'I'm sure she is,' lied Coral, 'but still, everything she does is designed to make people feel bad about themselves.'

'She's beautiful and she's rich,' said Peter. 'I don't think she can help making people feel bad about themselves. Girls can get pretty jealous, can't they, Coral?'

'I'm not jealous of Meredith,' Coral laughed. 'I have real friends who I love and who I can chill with and just be myself around. They love me for who I am,

Peter. Meredith doesn't have any of that and neither does anyone who's friends with her. Why would I be jealous?'

Peter smiled. 'Didn't say you were.'

Mark scratched the side of his face and took an enormous swig of his drink. He didn't know which part of the conversation made him more uncomfortable – the awkward truths Coral was deploying with rapid-fire precision or the fact that Peter was defending Meredith.

Coral, in the meantime, pressed on with her sermon. 'I mean, for example, I think Catherine O'Rourke's a really nice girl, but all Meredith and Kerry Davison ever do is pick on her,' she said, deliberately leaving out both Cameron and Imogen, in the hope that neither Mark nor Stewart would challenge her central point, 'and just look how happy she is now that she doesn't spend as much time round that group – having to behave a certain way all the time and do whatever they tell her. Ever since she's been dating Blake Hartman and started to become her own independent person, she's so much happier!'

'She's not dating him anymore,' interrupted Paula.

Stewart and Mark both turned to look at her. 'What?' asked Mark, more loudly than he had intended.

'Yeah. Both of their statuses on Facebook say "Single" now,' explained Paula.

'Since when?'

'A few days ago,' she stammered. 'Just after the exams ended.'

Stewart returned to gazing down at his hands, while Mark checked out of the conversation entirely and seemed lost in thought for the next two or three minutes. It was only when Coral asked Eóin to play another song that Mark mentally rejoined the group and began listening admiringly to the vocal skills of Coral Andrews again.

'Listen, I'm really sorry if what Eóin said about Cameron offended you earlier,' Coral said, as she and Mark walked along the beach together an hour later. 'I know Cameron's a friend of yours and just because Eóin thinks that Cameron's gay doesn't give him the right to say what he said.'

Mark, who was struggling with the effects of several hours of sustained drinking on top of three days of non-stop partying, nodded silently and dug his hands further into his pockets. His hands were cold, but the decision to keep them tucked away certainly wasn't helping his balance issues, so Coral kept close by, in case he stumbled. And because she quite liked being close to him. At this proximity, she could re-appreciate just how handsome Mark Kingston really was. Truth be told, she had always fancied him, just a little. Despite, or perhaps because of, his occasionally prickly behaviour, she, and many of the girls in her year, found Mark to be an attractive and intriguing puzzle. The strong, purposeful way in which he carried himself, the attractively tidy but not too-tidy brown hair and the warm, even smile also helped, as did his six feet in height and the body which was finally beginning to show signs of a year of gym attendance and regular performance on the school's soccer and cricket teams. Even the stench of the festival and the weird fusion of gel and mud in his hair had done nothing to dampen Coral's long-standing crush on him and she was delighted that they were finally alone together.

Tonight, she had also finally been able to banish from her mind the rumour that Mark had a secret crush of his own – on Meredith Harper. Although Mark had disappointingly failed to endorse her criticisms of Meredith back at the campfire, he had also conspicuously failed to defend her in the same way he had Cameron, which led Coral to conclude that the rumours about his feelings for Meredith were just another set of ludicrous lies spun by bored and stupid popular girls who had nothing better to do with their time. Coral was certain that no one as nice as Mark Kingston could possibly have romantic feelings for someone as morally repulsive as Meredith Harper.

For his part, Mark was pleasantly surprised at how pretty Coral looked out of her school uniform. She had also thankfully outgrown some of the more outlandish fashion mistakes she had been prone to make ever since first embracing indie chic two years ago. Tonight, she cut a striking, even a mildly exotic, figure. No doubt Kerry Davison would still have been staring at Coral's outfit in bemused wonderment and Meredith, Imogen and Cameron would either have been making catty comments or dry-heaving at the sight of her, but Mark found it – and her – refreshing.

After a few moments of companionable quiet, something Coral had just said penetrated Mark's brain. 'Does Eóin really think Cameron's gay?'

Coral shrugged. 'Well, yeah,' she said, quietly. 'Everyone does.'

'Everyone?'

Coral nodded. 'Yes. I'm sorry, Mark; I know he's your friend.'

'Don't be sorry for me,' he replied tersely. 'Cameron hasn't done anything wrong.'

'No, I know. People don't dislike him for it.'

'Eóin obviously does.'

'To be fair to Eóin, the reasons he doesn't like Cameron have nothing to do with him being gay, they're more to do with Cameron's personality. With the gay thing, most people generally think that Cameron is gay, but he's too afraid to admit it.'

'Well, that's bollocks,' Mark snapped.

'Babe, I don't dislike Cameron and I'm definitely not judging him. I'm sure deep, deep, deep down, he's a really nice guy and I know you've been an amazing friend to him, but even you have to admit it's pretty obvious that he's hiding who he really is.'

'That's not Cameron's fault!'

'No, I know it isn't, but if you're saying there's nothing wrong with being gay, then don't you think Cameron should just admit it?'

'Cameron's not some ball-less weakling, Coral. He hasn't done anything wrong!'

'Well why won't he just admit it, then?'

'He has admitted it!'

Coral stopped walking and stood staring at Mark. A gust of wind caught a loose strand of her hair, making it twirl across her face. She pushed it back and nodded, slowly. 'Oh,' she said quietly. 'I didn't know. When?'

'Fuck. I shouldn't have said anything,' Mark groaned. 'Fuck. Coral, don't... you can't say anything to anyone. It's not my news to tell. Coral, please don't tell anyone I said anything. Please. Cameron would...'

'Mark, don't worry!' she soothed, taking his hand in hers. 'I would never tell anyone anything you told me in private. Honestly. You can trust me completely.'

◇◇◇

Peter and Stewart were meandering away from the fire in the opposite direction of Mark and Coral, with Peter carrying a case of beer in a vice grip under his arms. Having stolen no less than six cases himself over the last few days, he knew better than anyone what acts of petty thievery could be lurking around the corner at any given moment.

'Jesus. Could Coral hate Meredith any more if she tried?' he asked, passing a warm can of beer over to Stewart.

'No,' Stewart said, shaking his head and opening the can. 'And it's not just Meredith...'

'What do you mean?'

'Coral laid into Kerry a couple of times, she insulted Imogen, although she was pretending to be all nicey-nicey about it, which is even more annoying, and then Eóin McEveritt really went after Cameron.'

'Frig.'

'Yeah. Mark told him that if he did it again he'd punch him in the mouth.'

'What'd he say?' asked Peter.

Stewart puffed out his cheeks, to give the appearance that what he was about to say next was a matter of supreme unimportance. 'He called him a faggot.'

Peter nodded and cleared his throat meaningfully, when Stewart cut him off before he could start. 'Pete, do not ask me the question you are about to ask, because I can't answer it. You get me? I can't.'

'Okay... but just so you know, if anyone ever gives him trouble about anything like that again, you let me know, because I won't be giving them a warning to stop like Mark did. I'll just hit them.'

Stewart threw his arm around Peter's shoulder. 'You're a good friend, Pete.'

'Eóin deserved a smack for that, Stew.'

'I shouldn't have stopped Mark going for it, but I honestly just couldn't be bothered with any of it and I kept thinking that if he actually hit him, people would be talking about it forever. Even with the way Mark reacted tonight, people are going to wonder if the only reason he got so angry was because what Eóin said was true.'

'So what if it is?'

'Maybe you don't care, but plenty of other people might, Pete. I just have a really bad feeling that Mark might have said too much tonight. No good can come from hanging out with that crowd when you're friends with anyone like Meredith or Cameron or Imogen. It's just a bad idea. They really, really, really hate each other.'

4
The Mayans in Manolos

'Are you still crying?'

Catherine looked up to see Kerry standing in her bedroom doorway, wearing a bikini and a pink t-shirt with the words *KEEP CALM AND KERRY ON* printed on it. 'No,' she answered. 'I'm just really upset.'

'About your hair?'

'No. Why?'

'Oh... No reason. So,' sighed Kerry sympathetically, leaping up on to the bed to take Catherine's hand, 'are you devastated about Blake?'

'Yes. I thought he loved me.'

'But he didn't, did he?'

Catherine shook her head and felt her eyes fill with tears again. 'No, he didn't.'

'Did he say why he was dumping you and leaving you heartbroken?'

'No,' Catherine lied. 'He just said it wasn't working out and he didn't want to be my boyfriend anymore. Then the next morning, he sent me an e-mail saying he was leaving and he was sorry.'

'Sorry for what?'

'Just stuff.'

Kerry nodded, although she was clearly disappointed by Catherine's failure to elaborate. Catherine was crying again and Kerry began stroking her hair. 'You need to wash this, by the way. I don't mind. You're upset. But greasy hair is not fabulous.'

Catherine sniffed and nodded. 'Kerry, what am I going to do without him? We were perfect together and he was so, *so* beau.'

'I know, princess, I know. It's hard, but you just weren't the right type of person for him.'

Catherine's head shot up at the use of the gender-neutral noun "person." But her panic vanished when she was confronted by the sight of Kerry's empathetic face smiling down beatifically at her.

'There, there, princess,' she cooed. 'It's going to be alright. We'll find you somebody else soon. Someone utterly delightful.'

'But Kerry I'm never going to find anyone as hot as Blake ever again. Like, he was literally the best I'm ever going to be able to do for myself. Ever!'

'I know. But still.'

'I miss being his girlfriend.'

'I know, I know,' soothed Kerry, as she lulled Catherine back on the bed and extricated herself from her. 'Why don't you have a little nap to restore your fabulousness and we'll talk about it later?'

Catherine gulped and nodded. 'Thanks and I'm sorry for being so annoying and stuff. I just feel so sad and so, like, gross. Are the others pissed off at me?'

'No!' gasped Kerry. 'Not at all, principessa. Everyone's just worried about you. Have a power nap and we'll chat about it all again later, 'k?'

'Thanks, Kerry. You're so nice to me.'

'That's because I'm very spiritual. Sleep well.'

'Thanks, Kerry.'

Kerry opened the door and waved back. 'Love you lots, m'a-fucka'a.'

'Love you, babes,' answered Catherine.

Kerry stepped out into the corridor, where Cameron was waiting for her. He looked at her, with an eyebrow raised as a silent question.

Kerry nodded. 'The bitch definitely knows.'

◇◇◇

Later that evening, Imogen tottered out of her bedroom in a pair of four-inch-high Manolo Blahniks and an Alex Perry cocktail dress she had stolen from her mother's wardrobe moments before leaving on holiday. Cameron was lounging against the pillar next to the front door, gazing down at the watch his father had given him for his sixteenth birthday.

'Where are the others?' Imogen asked, as she fastened her other earring into place.

'They're already up at the hotel. Kerry wanted a drink and Meredith got tired of waiting.'

Imogen tutted. 'I'm like five minutes late.'

'Thirty-six,' corrected Cameron, as he opened the door for her and bowed with a melodramatic flourish.

'Where's Catherine?'

'She's not coming tonight,' Cameron replied. 'She told Kerry she's not feeling well.'

'Such a shame,' smiled Imogen, as she twirled happily out the door.

◇◇◇

Left alone at the villa, Catherine wandered out to the pool area in a pair of hot pants and a cream top. Her hair was scraped back into a messy ponytail and she wasn't wearing any make up as she sat down and dipped her feet into the pool's warm water. She thought how nice it would be to take a swim at this time of night, but if the others came back and saw her swimming, they would know she had been lying about not feeling well enough to go to dinner with them.

'Excuse me?'

Catherine screamed at the unexpected sound of a man's voice. Turning to look up at the voice which she assumed must belong to a thief, a rapist or a bandit, she was surprised to see a tall, elegant boy with sandy-coloured hair and hazel eyes, holding out his hand to her in a gesture of calming apology. Next to him, standing a few inches taller, was his olive-skinned Italian friend of about the same age, with perfectly maintained black stubble and warm brown eyes.

'Gosh, I'm so sorry,' said the sandy-haired boy, in a smooth English drawl that reminded Catherine of someone she knew but couldn't place. 'I didn't mean to frighten you. I'm terribly sorry. Kerry, isn't it?'

Catherine shook her head. 'No,' she replied, after a second-too-long delay. 'I'm Catherine. Kerry's at dinner.'

'Oh, I beg your pardon,' he smiled, with devastating charm. 'I'm terrible with names. I'm Sasha Montmorency.'

Catherine took his outstretched hand and he helped her to her feet. 'Anastasia's brother?' she asked.

'That's right. And this is my friend, Francesco. Francesco, this is Catherine. She's a friend of my sister.'

'I think we have met before,' Francesco answered politely. 'At the ball in Belfast, last October?'

'Oh, that's right. I forgot,' Sasha smiled. 'I'm so sorry again for startling you, Catherine. We've been travelling around Mexico for a few weeks and my sister told me you were all in Cabo, so we thought we should pop down and say hello. We tried to call, but we haven't had much luck with our phones while we've been here, I'm afraid.'

'Oh, no, that's totally fine,' smiled Catherine who, having recovered from the shock of the boys' arrival, was enthusiastically embracing her usual social tactic of being far too loud, too entertained and too bubbly in their presence. It would be a moment before she remembered with crashing horror that she wasn't wearing any make up.

'Did you say they were having dinner at the moment?' Sasha asked.

'Yes. They're up in the hotel right now, but I wasn't feeling very well earlier, so I stayed here.'

'And how are you feeling now?' Sasha enquired politely. 'Better, I hope?'

'Oh yeah. Yeah, like, much better and stuff!'

'Wonderful. If you don't mind some company, we'd be happy to wait here with you until they get back. Or, if you would prefer to be left alone, we can go up to the hotel and find them?'

'No! No. You're totally welcome to stay,' gushed Catherine. 'That'd be so beau.'

'Is Meredith with them?' Francesco asked.

'Yeah. Yeah, she's there. Here. She'll be so pleased to see you,' said Catherine. 'Can I get you guys a drink or anything?'

'A water would be fantastic, thank you,' nodded Sasha. 'If it's not too much trouble?'

'Oh, no, not at all. Em... can I get you anything?'

'Nothing for me, thank you,' replied Francesco, sitting down on the edge of a sun lounger. Catherine didn't think she had ever seen a man move with such perfect grace; as she retreated into the villa to fetch the water, however, it was Sasha, not Francesco, who she was most aware of and she felt a pleasant fluttering of butterflies in her stomach, something which she hadn't felt since the day Blake Hartman had asked her to be his girlfriend nearly four and a half months earlier. And so help her God by the time she re-emerged with Sasha's bottle of water, she would have coated her face in a flawless sheen of make up.

◆◇◆

'Shuddup!'

Catherine, Sasha and Francesco turned at the sound of Imogen's voice eighty-seven minutes later. Catherine was perched on one of the sofas in the lounge, right next to Sasha, who gave no sign of being perturbed by Catherine's nervous proximity to him. Francesco had reclined in one of the armchairs and was sporting a facial expression that was neither bored nor interested, having left Sasha to undertake the arduous task of conversation with an ebullient Catherine.

'I will not shut up!' barked Kerry in the hallway. 'You were mean to me.'

'I didn't say your right boob *always* looks weird,' Imogen shot back. 'I said it looks weird in *that* dress. And it does. I'm sorry, but I don't see why I'm being punished for being the only friend who cares about you enough to point out the fact that your right badoopidoop looks like a squashed hippo in that outfit.'

'A squashed hippo?' screeched Kerry.

'Yes, Kerry. A squashed hippo. Can you not hear me? Has so much boob fat being squished up by whatever freakishly deforming bra you're wearing that it's clogging your ears? A. Squashed. Hippo. And, look, I'm not saying this to be mean, okay? I don't need to put you down because, right now, my lady lumps like two rising orbs of sunlight and yours...'

Imogen's tirade came to an abrupt halt as she rounded the corner into the lounge. Kerry, storming after her, gave a little squeak as she crashed into Imogen's back and stared fearfully at the two strange but very well-dressed men who were now inexplicably ensconced in her villa. A few seconds later, a slightly weary Cameron and Meredith appeared into view, quickly taking stock of their visitors.

'Oh, hello,' said Imogen with a radiant, if inebriated, smile. 'What are you two doing here?'

Both Francesco and Sasha had risen from their chairs to greet the girls. Sasha kissed Imogen and Kerry on both cheeks before giving Cameron a friendly hug, as he launched into an explanation of why they were here. Francesco, on the other hand, had walked over to Meredith and kissed her on each cheek.

'Francesco Modonesi,' he said, with a smile. 'We met last October at the ball for the pilgrimage to Lourdes?'

'Yes, of course,' Meredith answered. 'I remember.'

'I hope you don't think this is too forward of us? I thought – that is, I hoped – that Sasha's sister would call ahead to tell you that we were coming. It just seemed like too much of a coincidence for us all to be so near one another...'

'No, I agree,' smiled Meredith. 'It would have been silly for you not to visit. Do you both need to stay here?'

'No, no,' demurred Francesco, with a slight wave of his hand. 'We wouldn't want to impose. This is your holiday, as friends. We've taken a room up at the hotel. But I should very much like to take you to breakfast tomorrow, providing you don't already have plans?'

'Brunch might be better,' Meredith answered. 'Just to be on the safe side.'

Francesco nodded. 'Meravigliosa. Non vedo l'ora di farlo.'

◇◇◇

Imogen padded into the kitchen late the next morning, cursing the sunlight and its cruel attempts to aggravate her hangover. Sitting on a high chair by the island was an obnoxiously fresh Meredith, lazily tapping her embroidered silk shoes off the chair leg and sipping Earl Grey. She was wearing her hair down today and she was dressed in the embroidered white silk chiffon dress she had worn to Catherine's birthday back in April. It was Cavalli, if Imogen remembered correctly. The bodice was tight, but the skirt flowed loosely, floating down over Meredith's long legs.

'You look dreadful,' said Meredith, glancing over at her between sips.

'Thanks,' muttered Imogen, regretting the Arsenal football top she usually slept in. If she had known that Meredith would be in the kitchen looking she was posing for a spread in *House and Garden*, she would have changed into something more sensuous. 'Where are you going?'

'I'm having brunch with Francesco at the hotel,' Meredith replied.

'Oh, yes,' remembered Imogen. 'He's here with Sasha, isn't he? I didn't dream it?'

'Yes, they're here. That must have been what Anastasia was trying to call about a couple of days ago. I should go. I'm already late. I'll see you later.'

'Have fun at brunch.'

'I will,' said Meredith, pirouetting on her way out.

'He fancies you, you know,' Imogen declared, as the chiffon swirled around Meredith's legs.

'See you later,' Meredith repeated. She walked out the front door of the villa and left Imogen alone with her hangover.

◇◇◇

Fortunately for Meredith, Francesco Modonesi never expected a lady to be on time. Wearing a pair of sunglasses and a white linen shirt, he stood leaning over the hotel veranda's balcony, listening to the sounds of the other guests at brunch and the nearby ocean. Most people about to embark upon an informal date with Meredith Harper would have been paralyzed with terror, but Francesco was a picture of nonchalant ease as he waited for her to arrive. A small, confident smile even tugged at the corners of his mouth. This was going to go well.

Ordinarily, Francesco would never have considered dating a British girl, since (with the exception of his mother and grandmother) he held such a generally low opinion of them. His years of schooling in England had left him with nothing but repugnance towards the trend of leaving the house in ugg boots and sweats, with uncombed hair and chipped nail polish. To Francesco, this social fad went beyond disgusting – it was practically immoral. In his mind, the British were promiscuous, alcoholic, unkempt, caked in fake tan, unhygienic and quite possibly the worst-dressed nation in Europe.

Meredith Harper, on the other hand, possessed a kind of chic cosmopolitan grace that Francesco found wonderfully invigorating. There was something quintessentially Italian about her fashion sense, he thought patriotically. Not only was she beautiful, but she was always immaculately coiffed and perfumed. Her attitude belonged to a time from long ago, when people cared about how they looked and placed a proper value on their outward appearance – a time Francesco looked back on with infinite nostalgia.

From the stairs leading up to the veranda, Meredith finally arrived. With a parasol perched over her head, her shoes, the fetching dress and fresh-faced appearance, she looked like someone who had just stepped out of a Nancy Mitford novel. Francesco noticed the creamy smoothness of her skin, the light scent she wore and the smell of freshly-washed hair. Everything about Meredith Harper worked; everything about her was mutually complimentary. She was the kind of girl any boy should want as his girlfriend.

As he pulled her seat out for her, his eyes swept appraisingly over her dress. Up close, it was not only apparent that she had an almost flawless sense of style, but that she also had the money to back it up. Francesco could tell instantly that the dress she was wearing was a Roberto Cavalli, which would have retailed for an awful lot of money. Sitting down opposite her, he ordered two coffees and water from the waiter, before turning his attention back to Meredith.

'This resort is very beautiful,' he said politely in English, in case her Italian was strong enough to carry out greetings, but not strong enough to sustain an actual conversation. 'Sasha tells me it belongs to your family?'

'Thank you,' she answered in English, to show that she appreciated his manners, before continuing in Italian. 'Yes. It's my uncle's, technically, but my cousins Veronica and Madeleine run it for him.'

'It's lovely,' he re-iterated. 'Do your friends enjoy it?'

'Yes. Imogen has been once before, years ago, with her family, and the others seem to like it.'

'How could they not?'

Meredith smiled and decided to move the conversation on. 'How long have you and Sasha been in Mexico?'

'Three weeks. We wanted to travel together a little, before I go to university and he goes on his gap year.'

Despite loathing on principle everything about even the concept of a gap year, Meredith managed to keep her face politely indifferent. 'Where are you going to university?' she asked, lest she hear the dreaded word "Thailand" in any follow-up explanation of Sasha's plans.

'Oxford. If I get the grades.'

The hesitation between the destination and the caveat suggested that Francesco did not really believe his grades would let him down. 'Which college?' Meredith asked.'Corpus Christi – to study History with Politics,' he answered, pre-empting her next question. 'What about you? What are your plans for next year?'

'Well, if I live past results day, I'll be back to school for the next two years.'

'Do you know what you want to study yet?'

'For A-Level? Well, I would like to keep on History and Italian...'

'It would be a waste if you gave it up. You speak it perfectly.'

'Thank you. And I'm not sure about the others. Maybe French, maybe Religion or possibly English. I don't know. It all depends what I get in August.'

'Tell me about your family?' he asked, as the waiter deposited their drinks.

'Well, my mother's family are American; my father's are Northern Irish. My parents separated when I was eleven and they divorced when I was thirteen. My father hasn't re-married, but my mother has. She's a Protestant, so that kind of thing is much easier for her.'

Francesco nodded. He knew all this already, having grilled Sasha for hours during yesterday's train ride. 'And your stepfather, he is American as well?'

'Yes. He is. My mother moved back to Manhattan. We actually lived there for most of the year for a few years after I was born, which meant that there was a house in New York for her to go to when she left us. I don't think Mummy really liked the UK very much and once the divorce happened, there was no reason for her to stay in Belfast, so... she went back to America,' explained Meredith, in a matter-of-fact tone which glossed over how a child might have been considered an adequate reason for Diana to stay in Belfast. 'Then, a few years later, she married Chester. They have two children together – Sillerton, who's three, I think, and Dallas, who's two.'

'You have a brother and sister?'

'Well, half ones. Yes.'

An edge had crept into Meredith's voice at the mention of her infant siblings, so Francesco tactfully changed the subject. 'And you live with your father in Belfast?'

'Yes, he's wonderful. What about you?'

'Well, my parents are still married and my mother is English, which is why I was sent to school there. I have a sister and three brothers – Yolanda, Umberto, Cesare and Nico.'

'Are they at school in England too?'

'Yolanda isn't, but Umberto and Cesare have both started at Winchester. And I'm sure Mama will want to send Nico there too, when the time comes. Do you like your school?'

'I do,' Meredith smiled proprietarily. 'I love it.'

Francesco nodded and paused, before leaning in across the table. 'Meredith, I have a question for you.'

'Perhaps I'll have the answer.'

He smiled. 'How appropriate do you think it would be for me to ask you to dinner this evening?'

'You've already asked me to brunch,' she answered, with faux naïveté. 'Why should dinner be such a leap of appropriateness?'

'Because dinner would be a date. A proper one.'

'Ah.'

'Ah,' he repeated, still smiling.

'Well... I think you would have to ask the question directly.'

'Miss Meredith Harper, would you do me the honour of joining me for dinner this evening?'

She paused for a moment. 'Yes. I will.'

Francesco sat back in his seat as they were rejoined by the waiter. 'Perfect. Shall we order?' he said, flicking open his menu. 'And, by the way, you look beautiful.'

◇◇◇

Sweat was pouring off Cameron as he lunged to return Sasha's serve on the tennis court. It was one set all, with a third set to decide the match and Sasha was leading by five games to four. The current score was 40 – 30, in Sasha's favour, and despite Cameron's sneaking suspicion that he was going to lose, he was determined to go out fighting.

From the edge of the court, Kerry gazed on dispassionately at their exertions, still irritated by the fact that Cameron had sternly forbidden her from using olive oil instead of suntan lotion. Not entirely sure of the rules of tennis – or the point of it, either – Kerry had fleetingly been amused by how often both boys had stared down in apparent confusion at their rackets when a serve went awry, as if it was the racket's fault, rather than the player's. Kerry was reminded of her mother's saying that a poor workman always blames his tools, but then her mother had also told her that happiness didn't lie at the end of a credit card and that was clearly untrue, so it was hard to know which of Mummy's sayings she could take seriously.

The ball slammed into the net and Cameron threw back his head in defeated frustration. 'Good game, Cameron,' said Sasha, as their hands met in a shake across the net.

'Thanks. You too.'

They stood for a moment by the net, catching their breath. They had started just after breakfast, expecting to finish long before the midday heat, but both of them had played such a strong game that they had remained on court much longer than anticipated. Having been part of each other's extended social circle since childhood, this was not the first time that Cameron and Sasha had played against each another and whilst Cameron was probably the more skilled player, he certainly did not have Sasha's speed.

'So Cameron, I was wondering if you were dating anyone special at the moment?'

'No, not really,' he answered, hesitantly.

'Fantastic. Francesco and I have a friend at Winchester who we think you'd really hit it off with.'

Cameron felt a churning in his stomach. Of course Anastasia would have informed her brother of Cameron's coming out. How could he have expected otherwise?

'Oh, really?'

'His name's Alexander Weir. Alex, really. He was in Cooks – our boarding house at school – and he's a great guy. Very good looking, very funny and really bright. He's on his gap year at the moment, but he'll be coming to visit me at Easter. I told him about you – I hope you don't mind – and he had a look at your Facebook profile. He's very keen to meet you.'

Realizing that he could avoid making a decision until Easter, Cameron relaxed and forced a smile. 'Cool. Let's talk about it at Easter?'

'Marvellous,' beamed Sasha. 'You'll like him. You really will. He's wonderful.'

Cameron glanced over to the courtside, where Kerry was glowering at him from behind her sunglasses, evidently infuriated that a conversation was happening within her eyesight but out of her earshot. As Sasha threw his arm around Cameron's shoulder and began teasing him about losing at tennis, Cameron relaxed and joined in the banter. Kerry, watching the two boys as they approached her, was certain of only three things – firstly, thanks to Cameron's olive oil embargo she had acquired absolutely no tan whatsoever. Secondly, that no one looked as good in daisy dukes as she did and thirdly, that Sasha Montmorency and Cameron Matthews would make the world's most delightfully attractive couple.

◇◇◇

'I think I've just found Cameron's first proper boyfriend.'

Twenty minutes after the tennis match between Sasha and Cameron had ended, Kerry was standing by the villa's pool with a triumphant expression on her face. Imogen was sprawled out on her sun lounger, wearing a swimsuit with the words *COOL BRITANNIA* emblazoned across it. Catherine was lying on the sun lounger next to her and both girls sat up in their seats at Kerry's announcement.

'What?' asked Imogen.

Kerry's voice was rippling with self-satisfied excitement as she sat down on the edge of Imogen's lounger. 'Sasha Montmorency,' she said, breathlessly. 'They look delightful together. Like Ralph Lauren and Tom Ford got together and had a baby. A gay baby.'

'That makes no sense, Kerry, but it's a super-beau metaphor. Well done.'

'Thanks.'

Catherine was staring at Kerry with a wounded look on her face. 'Really? Sasha and Cameron? Are you sure?'

'Very,' said Kerry. 'I think they should get married. Imagine how well-dressed their children would be.'

'This is sensationally delicious, Kerry,' enthused Imogen, linking her hands into Kerry's. 'One problem.'

'What?'

'I don't think Sasha's gay.'

Kerry sighed slightly, as if she found Imogen's temporary stupidity endearing. 'Imogen, think about it.'

A look of euphoric contentment shot across Imogen's face a split second later as realization dawned. 'The Age of the Bisexual!' she gasped.

'Exactly.'

'I told you it was real!'

'I know! And now it's finally here. It's here, it's queer and I am *totally* used to it!'

Imogen shook her head in happy disbelief. 'Cameron Matthews-Montmorency. How completely fabulous. It would be the society wedding of the year.'

Kerry threw back her head in ecstasy. 'We'll be gridesmaids or broomsmen!'

'Now Kerry, we don't want to get carried away here, do we?'

'No, no,' she agreed, suddenly becoming very serious. 'Love takes time.'

'Still.'

'Still,' smiled Kerry. 'I saw them together on the tennis courts and it's lucky I wasn't wearing olive oil at the time because the sparks flying from those two would definitely have set me on fire.'

'Is olive oil flammable?' asked Imogen.

'Must be,' shrugged Kerry. 'It's oil, babes.'

'Right, of course,' nodded Imogen. 'Gosh. Sasha and Cameron. Cammy and Sash-Sash. Sexy Age of Bisexual times, Kerry. Sexy AOB times.'

'What's going on?' asked Meredith, stepping from the villa out to the poolside.

'Cameron's getting married,' trilled Kerry. 'He and Sasha Montmorency were definitely hitting it off down on the tennis courts. It's delightful and it's delicious and...'

'It's the Age of the Bisexual,' interrupted Imogen. 'Obviously, I am unsurprised by this development. It was only a matter of time before we felt the AOB's impact. And, oh my god, how was *your* date?'

'It was actually really nice,' said Meredith, resting her hand on the top of Imogen's sun lounger. 'He's very confident and very charming – just the way I remember him. He asked me to have dinner with him this evening.'

'Like another date?' asked Kerry, excitedly.

'Yes.'

Imogen and Kerry squealed and clapped their hands. 'Oh my god, Meredith. This is *so* exciting. Isn't it, Kerry?'

'It's delightful. Utterly delightful. This is clearly a great day for new love. Stay here, I need to get a drink from the kitchen. Anyone want anything?'

'Can I have a bottle of water, please?' asked Catherine, who still looked upset by Kerry's theory about Sasha.

'Sure,' answered Kerry, as she shimmied inside the villa.

'You know, I've never actually been on a real date before,' said Meredith, managing to keep any signs of nerves out of her voice.

'I know!' beamed Imogen. 'That's why I'm excited for you and not vomiting with jealousy. He is beautiful, Mer-Mer.'

'He is very handsome.'

'Angels crafted him from hand,' Imogen ruled. 'Tonight is going to be perfect. You'll be the most attractive couple in the restaurant. Without doubt.'

'Is that thing about Cameron and Sasha true?'

Imogen shrugged again. 'No idea. Doesn't mean we can't get excited about it though, does it?'

'That's true,' reasoned Meredith.

'Totally different subject, but I've been thinking about our birthdays and I've come up with a fantastic idea for them.'

'Which is?'

'This year, you and I have a joint birthday party.'

Catherine gasped at what she had just heard come out of Imogen's mouth and even Meredith was staring at her in uncharacteristic shock. Sharing attention in any way, shape or form was Imogen's *bête noire*. This, after all, was the girl who, at the age of four, had pretended to faint at the altar in order to draw attention away from her baby brother's christening and place it back where it properly belonged – on her.

'Think about it, Meredith. Our birthdays are only four days apart – it makes perfect sense. Just imagine how amazing the party would be if we combined both of our b'days into one. It would be like the High Holy Day of Fabulousness!'

Mulling over Imogen's idea in her head, Meredith had to concede that it certainly did have possibilities. It was hard to imagine an event which would cause a greater buzz than the news that two of the most popular girls in school were having a joint birthday party. It would definitely blow anybody else's out of the water and the two of them did have competition looming in September from Kerry's, which year after year somehow managed to trump everybody else's.

'It's fabulous,' Meredith declared after a few seconds' thought. 'Fabulous.'

'Isn't it? I can't *wait* to start telling people!' exclaimed Imogen.

'It's such a beau idea,' beamed Catherine. 'People will like die when they hear about it. Will it be themed or...'

'We don't know,' snapped Meredith. 'I'm going inside.'

◇◇◇

Sasha Montmorency was tying a towel around his waist as he emerged from the shower into the main part of the hotel room he and Francesco had booked in the resort. Francesco was on the balcony, smoking a cigarette and gazing out over the ocean. Sasha said a silent prayer of thanks for whoever had invented air conditioning as he stepped out to join his friend and was suddenly confronted by the stultifying heat of the Mexican afternoon.

'How was brunch?' he asked.

'Perfect,' Francesco answered. 'Everything about her is just... perfect. She's incredible.'

Sasha grinned and nudged his friend on the shoulder. 'Look at you all smiley-smiley,' he teased. 'She is very beautiful and my sister really likes her.'

'I know. I think Anastasia has been trying to set the two of us up together for a while.'

'Yes. Anastasia likes to be involved,' Sasha laughed. 'She'll be really pleased to hear you two have hit it off.'

'How was tennis?'

'Great. I won. Cameron plays a really good game though, which is wonderful, because it's a little annoying having to win too easily all the time, you know?'

Francesco nodded. 'You like Cameron a lot, don't you?'

'Absolutely. We'll have to make sure we all get time for a drink together before we leave.'

'I'd like that,' Francesco said, neutrally. 'Did you mention Alex to him?'

'Yes. They'll get along brilliantly when they meet. As soon as Anastasia told me he'd come out, I immediately thought of setting the two of them up together. You're still thinking about Meredith, aren't you?'

'I'd forgotten what it was like to be around her,' Francesco admitted, as he stubbed out his cigarette. 'She's perfect, Sasha. Absolutely perfect.'

◇◇◇

Picking up the telephone in her bedroom, Meredith placed an international call to the mobile of Sasha's sister, Anastasia, the current president-in-waiting of Mount Olivet's Social Committee and queen bee of the outgoing Lower Sixth. After a few rings, the call was answered in the aristocratic tones that everyone in Belfast intrinsically associated with the Montmorencys.

'Hello?'

'Anastasia? Hi. It's Meredith.'

'Meredith! How is Mexico?'

'Fabulous. It's so beautiful here. How's Austria?'

'V. v. fun. I hear you have some visitors?'

'Yes. Sasha and Francesco arrived last night.'

'I told them you were all in Mexico at the same time. You don't mind?'

'No, not at all. It's lovely to see them.'

'Especially Francesco?'

Meredith smiled. 'Yes. He's very charming.'

'He's Italian. Of course he is.'

'We had brunch together this morning.'

'And?'

'It was actually a lot of fun. Francesco's very easy to get along with and it's such a relief to be able to have a proper conversation with a boy who isn't Cameron.'

'I'm sure. When are you seeing him again?'

'This evening. He asked me to go for dinner with him at the hotel.'

'As in a date?'

'Yes.'

Anastasia tended to eschew visible signs of excitement as something vulgar, but her voice took on a distinctly pleased lilt. 'You'll have a fantastic time.'

'Well, yes. I was wondering – what do you know about him?'

The satisfaction vanished from Anastasia's voice and it became brisk and business-like. 'Well you've seen what he looks like, so that needs no explanation. Very, *very* well-off – his parents own a railway company or something like that... possibly more than one. I think they're the only ones to run on time since Mussolini. It might be politically incorrect to say that... I heard that his father's family have a title, but I don't think the father's in line to inherit it. His mother's English, which is why they sent him to school at Winchester, where apparently he was very popular, which is always re-assuring – even if Wykehamists can be a bit tweedy. I probably shouldn't say that considering my brother and all my cousins go there, but, whatever. Sasha says the family have homes in London, Genoa, Venice and a place in Switzerland for skiing. Francesco's had one long-term girlfriend; she was Quebecois, very pretty, quite well-off and went to Cheltenham – Ladies, not Grammar. I never met her, but apparently all the boys hated her. It lasted eighteen months – the relationship, not Cheltenham. They broke up in March because she met somebody else – although who could compete with Francesco Modonesi? She must have been mad. He speaks fluent English, French and Italian, obviously. The boys say he has a fairly good sense of humour, excellent dress sense, drives a moped – which only Italians can really get away with, I think. He enjoys the theatre and he's apparently quite interested in politics – Sasha says he's a libertarian, but as long as he's not a socialist, who cares? He's an *excellent* polo player. He goes running and he likes tennis. And I *think* that's about it. Oh, and he's a Sagittarius.'

'You knew I was going to ask about him, didn't you?'

'I like to be prepared.'

Meredith laughed. 'Thank you.'

'You've got to tell me everything afterwards. Even by your standards, Meredith, Francesco's a winner. Now – have you ever tried Kaiserschmarrn? They serve it everywhere here and it's delicious. But Mariella keeps offering it to me, which makes me think that it's probably highly fattening. Just because she's gained five pounds doesn't mean the rest of us have to swell up like some tubby zeppelin. Oh, hi Mariella! I didn't see you there! I'm just on the phone to Meredith. She's in Mexico!'

◇◇◇

Cameron was standing in his bedroom trying to pick out a shirt for dinner, which they had ordered to the villa so as not to intrude on Meredith's date in the restaurant, when Kerry skipped in excitedly and bounced on to his enormous bed.

'Hello, princess,' he murmured absent-mindedly. 'I don't know what to wear for tonight.'

'Guess what I did to Catherine today?' Kerry whispered excitedly.

'Taught her how to read?'

'Better. At lunch time, she was out by the pool with Imogen and I told them that I thought you and Sasha would make an utterly delightful couple of proud gay men and she looked like she was going to cry!'

'Sasha isn't gay,' said Cameron.

'That's what we thought about Blake, my love.'

Cameron rolled his eyes and turned back to his shirt collection.

'Don't you see what this means?' Kerry asked. 'She definitely has a crush on Sasha!'

Cameron stopped rifling. 'Really?'

'Oh, yes,' giggled Kerry. 'You know she gets very obvious about guys she likes and when she heard that you and Sasha are in love, she looked sick, angry and very, very sad.'

'Sasha and I are not in love.'

'That doesn't matter! Catherine basically looked like she couldn't believe it was happening all over again. Oh, Cameron, my beautiful homosexual darling, it was hilarious!'

'I'm glad she has a crush on Sasha,' Cameron said brutally, 'and I'm glad she thinks he has one on me. She deserves to know what that feels like.'

'She does,' said Kerry with a devout nod. 'She does.'

'I know she knows Blake's gay. I just don't know how long she's known for. Not that I care anymore. I just... I just hate her, Kerry. She's so pathetic.'

'Did I hear fighting?' asked a happy-looking Imogen, popping her head round the doorway.

'No,' said Cameron, now calm again. 'No fighting.'

Imogen looked disappointed but stepped into the room nonetheless, running her eyes over Cameron's topless form. 'Oh, Cameron, look at your sexy bod! Better not let Catherine see you like that! You know how she gets around attractive gay guys.'

'Thanks, Imogen. That wasn't inappropriate at all,' muttered Cameron sarcastically.

'So, huge news!' she announced, clapping her hands together. 'Okay. You know the way Mer-Mer's birthday is on the twenty-seventh of July and mine is on the first of August, but every year we throw two separate b'diddy bashes? Well, this year we've decided that it would be super-fabulous to merge them together and just throw one, big, massive, über-beau party for the two of us. How fun is that? Am I right?'

Cameron leaned back against the armoire in fear as Kerry rose slowly from her position on the bed, glaring at Imogen like one of the Furies. 'What?'

◇◇◇

Dinner had finished and a warm breeze was blowing in off the Sea of Cortez as Francesco slowly walked Meredith back to her villa. Dressed in a linen shirt and a pair of Ralph Lauren trousers, Francesco cast his eyes appreciatively over Meredith and her Lanvin cocktail dress. Her hair once again trailed attractively down her back, although tonight it was slightly feathered (a cunning plan to make it look deliberate if the heat accidentally wreaked havoc with her ordinarily sleek locks); a diamond bracelet glistened around her dainty wrist in the moonlight and a solitaire diamond twinkled from the fourth finger of her right hand. Noticing the cobbles, Francesco gallantly offered her his arm. Standing next to one another, they looked even better as a prospective couple than Francesco had hoped. They looked perfect.

'How long are you planning to stay in Cabo for?' she asked.

'That rather depends.'

'On?'

'On you.'

'Oh.'

'I think Sasha would like to move on in the next four or five days, though.'

'Where to?'

'Guadálupe,' Francesco answered. 'He wants to see the basilica.'

'Please don't tell Imogen. Pilgrimages are like crack to her,' Meredith half-joked. 'She'll insist on coming with you. She once punched a twelve-year-old to buy the last *MARY IS MY HOME GIRL* t-shirt from a stall at the Christmas market.'

Francesco stopped, unlinked his arm from Meredith's and turned to face her.

'I have a question for you.'

'Another one?' she teased.

'Another one, yes – the most important one, actually. I want you to understand that I don't usually move this quickly when it comes to things like this, but I like you, Meredith. I like you very much and I like us together. Ever since we first met, I haven't been able to put you out of my mind. If I hadn't been dating Sabine at the time, I think I would have asked you there and then if you would have dinner with me. I think you are remarkable – you are beautiful and you are clever and you are charming. I think you're wonderful.'

Meredith's throat had gone slightly dry. Taking her hand in his, Francesco finally popped the question that a million girls would have killed to receive from him. 'What I want to know is – will you consider being my girlfriend?'

5
Dancing Queens

From: "Meredith Harper" <sizezerois4heifers@msn.ni>
To: "Imogen Dawson"   <eurovision_queen@msn.ni>

Imogen,

How many people haven't responded? I literally hate it when it people think it's OK to leave an RSVP to the last minute. It probably seems OK when the most stressful thing they have to organise for one of *their* fugly parties are a few packets of crisps and some lukewarm bottles of WKD, but when you're organising something like *our* birthday party, it takes a lot more notice to get everything just right.

New York was great. I'm at my mother's house in East Hampton right now and it's v nice to get up here for a few days, because the city really is far, *far* too hot this time of year. I went to visit my aunt and uncle in D.C. for a few days and the heat there was actually unbearable until the evening, plus I'm sure going in and out of air conditioning that often and that quickly must make you ill.

Apart from that, no major gossip. I'm really looking forward to getting home next week. Make sure that you get the caterers sorted – it's probably better that we do that bit at my house, rather than yours.

Love,
Meredith xx

PS – You're right. Catherine definitely has lost weight. She's probably cried away like three pounds. Buy her those cupcakes she likes so much and make sure she eats them like a pig at its trough.

The news that Meredith Harper and Imogen Dawson were co-hosting a joint seventeenth birthday party had shot through the teenage gossip network of Belfast and County Down faster than the scandal of Imogen's adultery had last year. The party had already earned a cryptic mention in *Ulster Tatler*'s gossip column, much to Imogen's delight and Kerry's smouldering resentment.

Even the boys in Meredith and Imogen's extended social circle seemed to be fairly excited at the prospect of the girls' co-party, reckoning that it would 'definitely be good banter'. Their excitement, however, was as nothing compared to the rapture sweeping the girls of Mount Olivet, most of who seemed to regard the impending soirée as a cross between the MTV Music Awards and the Second Coming of Christ.

Walking through the streets of Belfast, on an afternoon two weeks after the music festival, Mark Kingston still had no idea whether he should respond with a yes to his invitation. He knew that it must have come from Imogen, since Meredith had gone straight from Mexico to visiting her relatives in America and she had not yet returned. Even if she had, Mark was not entirely sure that she would have gone so far as to invite him to her birthday, despite the uneasy truce the two of them had entered into at the end of last year. Imogen, who had never quite forgiven Mark for yelling at her on the night she had broken up with Stewart, had probably only issued the invite under pressure from Cameron and so it was difficult for Mark to feel entirely comfortable with the idea of attending the "party of the summer."

As he entered Victoria Square for lunch, walking quickly down the steps into the shopping mall, he saw Catherine O'Rourke and her eighteen-year-old sister, Orla, coming towards him. Like Catherine, Orla O'Rourke was a very pretty girl. However, with slightly more height and long ginger hair, she was probably the more physically striking of the two sisters. Mark did not know Orla particularly well, since they had never really spoken to each other beyond a few polite exchanges at some of Catherine's parties. Unlike Catherine, Orla had gone to a faith school, attending Stella Maris College in Cultra, and Mark was acutely aware that given he had once turned down Catherine's less-than-subtle romantic advances, Orla might not be his biggest fan. Orla, however, was always perfectly polite when she met him and as he approached the two sisters, she beamed a welcoming smile.

'Hi, Mark!'

'Hey. Have you guys been shopping?' It was a stupid question, considering that they both had shopping bags slung over their shoulders, but at least it would get the conversation going.

'Yeah!' gushed Catherine. 'It's like so dark and stuff in Hollister, but the people who work there are so hot. Like, so beau.'

Mark nodded, noticing that Catherine didn't look too bad herself, having kept much of the tan she had acquired in Mexico. 'How's your summer been?' he asked.

'It's been great! I just got back from Mexico with the girlies – and Cameron – and it was amazing. And me and Orla are going to Florida with the family, after Imogen and Mer-Mer's b'day, but before results, because I don't think our parents will want to speak to me *après*.'

'God, I am not looking forward to results day,' Orla moaned. 'I'm a dead woman.'

'Are you off to uni next year, then?' asked Mark.

'Well, if I get the grades, yeah. I've got a conditional offer from Saint Mary's for teaching.'

'That's cool. What do you need?'

'Two As and a B.'

Mark offered a platitude about how he was sure she would get them, even though he had absolutely no idea about Orla O'Rourke's academic capabilities. 'Was there any banter in Mexico?' he asked.

'Not really. It was just like really good fun and stuff. The resort was *so* beau! And we were treated really well, because Mer-Mer's family, like, own it and stuff. And then, when we were there, I was out by the pool helping Meredith and Imogen come up with the idea of having a joint birthday this year, because it's just like so random having two separate parties every year when their birthdays are only like four days apart from each other... and, OMG, I totally forgot! So, you know Anastasia Montmorency's brother?'

'Kind of,' answered Mark, who had met the guy once and thought he was the single most rah human being he had ever encountered. 'Sasha, right?'

'Right! Well, he came to stay with us for a few days and he brought his friend from Italy, Francesco, with him. They went to school together. And he's like the most handsome man *ever*...'

'Yeah, I've met Francesco,' Mark interrupted, a trifle harshly.

'Have you?'

'Yes, at that Lourdes party last year.'

'Remember, Mark bought my ticket when I was sick?' prompted Orla.

'Oh, that's right!' exclaimed Catherine. 'I forgot! Sozzles. Anyway, so, Sasha and Francesco came to stay for a few days and like, mostly Sasha and I hung out together, but, guess what?'

'What?'

'Francesco and Meredith are now boyfriend and girlfriend! How beau is that?'

A leaden feeling attacked Mark's gut. 'Really?'

'Yeah. They're so cute together. Like, he'll be over to visit her loads and she can go see him in Oxford...'

'He's going to Oxford?'

'Yeah, to do History, I think. Or Politics. Why?'

'Just wondering. I'm really sorry to hear about you and Blake, by the way.'

'Oh,' said Catherine, her face falling. 'Yeah. It's okay. It just wasn't really working out and he's away for the whole summer, so...'

'I didn't know that. Where to?'

'I'm not really sure, actually,' Catherine stammered, glancing in panic at Orla. 'I think maybe away with his family. The Americans. He made the plans after we broke up.'

'Ah, okay. Well, here, it was nice seeing you both, but I'm meeting a friend for lunch...'

'No problem,' smiled Orla. 'We need to go meet Mummy at City Hall, anyway. Have a nice lunch.'

'Thanks. Good luck with the results.'

'Thanks! You too.'

'See you later, Catherine.'

'Bye, Mark. Have fun at lunch!'

Mark waved as the two sisters walked away and, glancing at his watch, hurried towards his lunch date.

◇◆◇

'This is exhausting!' Imogen groaned, hurling her party planning portfolio on to her vast, King-size bed. 'Kerry, why won't you do this for me?'

'Because I have to conserve all my energy for my own party, which I am hosting *alone*,' Kerry replied pointedly from the place where she had ensconced herself on Imogen's mountainous pillows.

'It's all completely pointless anyway, because once Meredith gets back she's just going to change everything!'

'That's what you get for organizing a joint birthday party with her,' Kerry declared smugly. 'Personally, I can understand why Meredith thought it was such a good idea to include you. It's definitely better to factor you into the plans rather than have you turn up and try and steal all the attention for yourself, like you did at mine last year.'

'Yes, well, God got me back for that one, didn't He?'

'Yes, He did. That's because He loves me. I'm delightful.'

'I wouldn't worry about it too much,' comforted Cameron, leaning on the doorway between Imogen's bedroom and her bathroom. 'It's not as if you don't know how to organize a party, Imogen.'

'This is obviously stressing you out, princess,' cooed Kerry. 'Why don't you just cancel the whole thing and have one on your own?'

'Cunning, Kerry,' said Cameron. 'You could leave the planning for one evening, Imogen, and we'll go out to take your mind off it?'

'Out?'

'Out-out,' Cameron answered. '*Out*-out.'

'As in a rampage?' asked Imogen. 'A hardcore, dirty, no-holds-barred *rampagia*?'

'Yes,' said Cameron excitedly.

'How delightful,' Kerry whispered.

◇◇◇

Coral had been waiting for Mark for about three or four minutes when he entered one of the chain restaurants in Victoria Square, moments after saying goodbye to the O'Rourke sisters. She smiled as she saw him walk towards the table and she kissed him on the cheek when he reached her.

'Hey babe,' she smiled. 'You smell great.'

'Thanks. You too. Sorry I'm late; I ran into Catherine on the way here.'

'O'Rourke?'

'Yeah, with her sister Orla,' said Mark, shucking off his jacket and sitting down opposite her. He noticed that she looked very pretty today, again.

'How is she?'

'Fine. Good, actually. I think.'

'Did she say anything about her and Blake breaking up?'

'She just said it wasn't working out and that Blake was leaving for the whole summer.'

'And she seems okay with that?' Coral asked.

Mark shifted uncomfortably in his seat. 'Eh, yeah. I think so. She seemed to think it was a pretty normal break up. She wasn't devastated or anything, which isn't like her.'

'She can be very high maintenance, but I suppose if you've lived in that group for five years, your nerves are bound to be ruined, aren't they?'

'Yeah,' Mark agreed. 'That's very true.'

'Are you okay?'

'I'm fine. Why wouldn't I be?'

'I don't know. I was just asking.'

Mark ran his hands though his hair and half-looked down for a moment. 'Sorry,' he said. 'I didn't mean to snap at you. Will you go out with me?'

Coral's face in that moment was distinctly unlovely. Her mouth dropped open and she stared at Mark in bewilderment at his dramatic non-sequitur. Mark smiled at her, his eyes sparkling with instant new-found amusement at Coral's sudden inability to say or do anything.

'Ehm... what? Pardon? I mean, did you just ask me... to be... like, really... as in, really?'

'Really,' he answered, still grinning. 'I really like you, Coral, and I think we'd be great together. I'd really, really like to be your boyfriend, if you'll let me. But if you think it's a bit random or too soon...'

'No! No! Not at all,' Coral replied, adjusting her volume mid-way through the sentence.

'No to the question or no to it being too soon?'

'I would like you to be my boyfriend,' she said, with a happy smile spreading across her face. 'I really like you too, Mark.'

Mark reached out across the table and took Coral's hand in his. 'Great. So, what can I buy my new girlfriend for lunch then?'

◇◇◇

The next morning, Cameron woke up to a scene of utter devastation in his bedroom. Lying next to him, still in her cerise party dress, was a comatose Kerry Davison, with one of her curls stuck to her lip gloss, the half-eaten remains of a Snickers bar in one hand and a tiny plastic windmill in the other. One shoe was hanging limply from Kerry's toes, whilst the other – inexplicably – had been set with great care on top of Cameron's wardrobe. How or why, he had no idea.

On the floor, on a distinctly deflated inflatable mattress, Imogen Dawson was snoring, with her head on the edge of the bin and rosary beads wrapped around her left hand. Gingerly stepping over her, Cameron looked down at his abs to see that at some point in the course of the evening someone had written *PROPERTY OF KERRY DAVISON* on them in eyeliner. On his bathroom mirror, another person had scrawled *SEXY BIATCH* in lipstick. What had they done last night?

Pulling closed the balcony window curtains, he tried to ignore the thumping in his head and swirling sickness in his stomach. Standing still for a moment to steady himself, his lower leg was grabbed by Imogen. 'Cameron,' she whispered. 'Help me.'

Looking down at her, he saw that at some point in her drunken haze of the night before, she had evidently remembered that it was a bad idea to go to sleep with one's make up on and had thus tried to remove it. She hadn't quite succeeded, however, and had consequently created enormous panda eyes, lipstick smeared up to her right ear lobe and the words *PROPERTY OF KERRY DAVISON* were smudged in eyeliner on her forehead.

'Am I still beautiful?' she implored.

'Yes,' nodded Cameron. 'Of course you are.'

'That's good,' she muttered, before flopping back into the bin. 'That's nice.'

From downstairs, to his anger and paradoxical amusement, Cameron caught the smell of soda bread frying in the kitchen, along with bacon, sausages and egg. They were his father's foolproof way of torturing his son after a night of drinking, knowing that Cameron could not remonstrate, nor turn down the food, without admitting why. Shuffling into the bathroom, ignoring the *SEXY BIATCH* lipstick graffiti, Cameron tried dimly to piece together the tattered fragments of what had gone on the night before. In the midst of his recollections, he realized that he must have left some of the curtains open, because he heard Kerry growl, 'Oh, someone turn the Sun off, please!' Hurrying back to close the drapes nearest his bed, Cameron sat down, cradling his head. 'What did we do last night?'

'It was delightful,' slurred Kerry, rolling over in the bed, as Imogen quietly vomited into the wastepaper bin.

◇◇◇

Cameron, Imogen and Kerry were never able to entirely stitch together the fabric of their evening together, but several moments were, eventually, to come back to them in fulsomely embarrassing detail.

Their night had begun with a collective shimmy to AM:PM on Upper Arthur Street, the same venue where Cameron had hosted his sixteenth birthday dinner. The food had been delicious and without Meredith around to act as the group's communal gastric band, they had ordered all three courses and round upon round of cocktails. The first member of the group to be torpedoed by this strategy was Kerry, who had the bad luck to order her second cosmopolitan at exactly the same moment as the bartenders changed shifts for the evening. Whoever was now in charge had concocted a cosmopolitan so lethal that, when it arrived at their table, it was practically translucent. Apparently, the added cranberry juice had been nothing more than a token gesture in this particular concoction and by the time Kerry had ploughed her way through it, her eyes were very slowly beginning to glaze over. Exhibiting the kind of compassion that had made their group famous throughout the school, Cameron and Imogen noticed their friend's difficulties and responded by ordering her two more cosmopolitans and a shot of Goldschläger. When she had shown herself reluctant to keep drinking at the fevered pace they were demanding of her, they retaliated by proposing toasts to Marie-Antoinette, Oscar de la Renta, Carrie Bradshaw and every single member of the Kardashian family. Feeling obliged to honour such beacons of fabulousness, Kerry had drunk on cue.

Mid-way through their main course, Imogen was tapped on the shoulder. Turning round with her brightest smile and most exaggerated hair toss, just in case it was someone attractive, she saw her ex- and first boyfriend, Freddie Carrowdale, dressed in a red and white striped shirt, with four buttons open, and a pair of distressed Abercrombie jeans. Tall, toned and with slightly long chestnut hair, Freddie was unthreateningly and unremarkably handsome, except for his green eyes, which Imogen considered the most beautiful orbs of ocular splendour she had ever seen. Whereas Stewart had excelled in sport, Freddie, whose sole sporting pursuit was surfing at his family's home in Helen's Bay, excelled in academia and he had unsurprisingly been elected as Mount Olivet's Head Boy for the forthcoming year – his last year at his beloved school before attempting to gain a place at either Cambridge or Harvard.

'Freddie!' Imogen gasped, as if she hadn't seen him in years. 'How are you?'

'I'm well, Gini. How are you? How was your holiday?' he smiled, returning the kiss on the cheek which she had leapt up to bestow on him.

'Super-fantastic. What have you been up to?'

'Nothing much, really. I'm just back from a few weeks in Portugal with the family. You should come up to the house some day, when the weather's good. All of you are welcome, of course,' Freddie finished politely.

'Gosh, I'd love that,' Imogen smiled. 'That would so beau. How's the family?'

'Really well. Yours?'

'They're great,' replied Imogen, ignoring the fact that only three hours earlier she had punched her eldest brother Christopher in the face because she thought he smelled funny.

'Well, I was just leaving and spotted you, so thought I would come over and say hello. Have a good night.'

'You too. Oh, Freddie, wait! You're coming to my birthday, aren't you?'

'Of course. I wouldn't miss it.'

'Fabulous. Have a great night!'

As Freddie disappeared out of view, Imogen settled back on her seat with a contented shuffle. 'I always forget how good looking he is.'

'You're not seriously thinking of dating him again, are you?' asked Cameron, witheringly.

'I didn't say that. And anyway, why not? What's wrong with him?'

'He's boring!' declared Kerry. 'Dull, dull, dull. Pretty box with no present inside.'

'He's very sweet and very ambitious, Kerry. He's going places, you know.'

'Freddie's alright,' said Cameron, whose family had been socializing with Freddie's for years. 'I don't think he's *that* boring. I'm more worried about the fact that you've been out with him before Imogen and it didn't work.'

'Cameron, that was ages ago!'

'It was two years, Imogen.'

'Practically a lifetime,' she sniffed. 'And I never would have broken up with him if Jesús hadn't started stalking me in Argentina.'

'Jesús didn't stalk you!' corrected Kerry. 'You went after him like Catherine after a gay guy! Sorry, Cameron. Don't look at me like that. I said I was sorry.'

'If you ever compare me to Catherine again, I'll stab you in the eye,' Imogen said, taking a sip of her drink. 'All I was saying was that Freddie is a really nice, attractive guy and it's a shame that we don't see more of him.'

'Imogen, you can't get a boyfriend just because Meredith has one,' said Cameron.

'No. You. Can't,' declared Kerry.

'No, no, that's not what I was thinking at all,' Imogen murmured airily. 'Isn't this food scrummy?'

With thoughts of Freddie and the pleasing contrast of his emerald eyes and his Portuguese-bestowed tan dancing in her mind, Imogen was already beginning to forget the stress of the birthday organization and even the issue of settling their dinner bill didn't seem to dampen her spirits. To be fair, settling a bill was probably the easiest thing the group ever did as a unit, since their tactic was to throw money at any of life's problems until they went away.

Leaving AM:PM with a huge tip in their wake and crab-dancing across to a nearby nightclub, where their trusty fake IDs once again saw them through, Imogen proceed to blow all her money on expensive shots with amusing names in the first fifteen minutes. Never one to let bankruptcy stand in the way of a party, she carried on ordering two more bottles of champagne at the bar and a round of Screaming Orgasms, before breezily declaring, 'Cameron, pay the man!' as she sashayed over to their table to rejoin Kerry, who was so drunk by this stage that she hardly seemed to have noticed Cameron or Imogen's temporary absence from her side.

At midnight, Imogen decided that the evening needed to be kicked up a notch. Why she thought this was anybody's guess. Cameron had apparently already completely forgotten that back in Belfast he was supposed to be temporarily keeping his homosexuality on the down-low and had thrown a massive strop when the DJ refused to play *It's Raining Men*; furious on his behalf, Kerry had last been seen trying to clamber over the DJ's booth, jabbing her finger in the poor musician's face and screeching something that sounded suspiciously like 'hate crime'.

'We need to drink more!' Imogen shouted, as her friends rejoined her at the bar.

'Imogen, I can't afford any more,' Cameron said, forlornly shaking his head. 'My Dad is going to kill me!'

Imogen slammed her hand on the bar and screamed, 'Tequila! I want tequila!'

'Tequi*laaaa*,' sang Kerry, providing a tuneless descant over Imogen's chant. 'Tequila*lalalala*,' before throwing her hands up in the air and squealing, 'Jazz hands!'

Recognizing defeat, Cameron stood next to the bar with a triumphant Imogen, whilst Kerry continued singing her new tequila song in the background, merrily unaware that the conversation had moved on.

'Can I have a Southern Comfort and lemonade and three shots of tequila, please?' Cameron ordered.

A dark look crossed Imogen's face. When inebriated, she was even more tyrannical than usual and the fact that Cameron had dared order himself a drink that she had not approved of seemed to have riled her. She said nothing, however, until Cameron had paid for everything and they had all imbibed their shots, with Kerry momentarily flailing her hands around her hair as if she was trying to swat away a fly. Gazing at the SoCo and lemonade that Cameron had so rebelliously bought for himself without her permission, Imogen calmly lifted up the salt shaker, removed the lid and tipped the entire contents into his glass.

Turning to gaze at her in confused fury at this totally unnecessary act of vicious sabotage, Cameron picked up his sucked out lemon and lobbed it down Imogen's top, before throwing three ice cubes down there for good measure. As Cameron looked at the frothing remains of his butchered drink and Imogen skipped around shouting, 'Ice nipple! Ice nipple!' Kerry returned to the dance floor, burling around and singing, 'Tequila! It makes me happy!'

Two hours later, their taxi arrived outside the club and, with great difficulty, Cameron and Imogen managed to persuade Kerry to leave rather than pursue her newfound vendetta against the DJ. Their driver, a ruddy-faced man in his early fifties, was standing by the car waiting for them, holding the door open to the back seat; Kerry and Imogen slid in and Cameron took his seat in the front.

'Thanks, Trevor!' Imogen trilled, despite the fact that the taxi man's name was definitely not Trevor, nor had she any reason to think that it would be.

'Eh... alright...' he muttered, having seen much worse in twenty years as a taxi driver. 'Where to?'

'Malone Park, please,' Cameron asked, in an accent which seemed to have become perceptibly more "Malone" now that he wanted people to know he definitely came from there.

'BT9 where everything is fine!' giggled a happy Kerry from the back seat.

'I want to stop at the garage,' Imogen announced, as the taxi sailed past the Grand Opera House.

'Is the one on the Malone Road okay?' the man Imogen had christened "Trevor" asked.

'Oh, it's better than okay,' Imogen snobbishly declared. 'It's the best.'

'No. Imogen, I am not buying you anything else tonight,' Cameron said, having just enough sense left to realize that she had all-but bled him dry. 'Please, do *not* stop at the garage. Thanks.'

Regarding Cameron beadily through her champagne goggles, Imogen leaned into the front and placed her mouth right next to the taxi driver's ear. 'Trevor,' she whispered, 'Trevor? Trevor, you better stop at the garage. I want snicky-snacks.'

'Well, if this young man is paying, Miss, I'm afraid I have to do what he says.'

'Oh, I am *very* disappointed in you, Trevor,' Imogen hissed menacingly. 'Very disappointed.'

'My name's not Trevor.'

'*Very* disappointed.'

For a few minutes, Imogen remained silent, plotting her next move and it was only when the taxi passed Eglantine Avenue that she realized that if she didn't come up with an idea quickly, she was going to be denied her snacks by the obviously-miserly Cameron. Then, she hit upon the brilliant idea of exploiting the weak link in the chain.

'Kerry,' she whispered. 'Kerry!'

'Tequi*laaaa*,' Kerry sang back softly, as if unaware why she was being bothered.

'Do you want a snack?'

Kerry shook her head. Imogen pinched her, but she kept shaking it nonetheless.

'Do you want a treat?' Imogen asked, changing tack.

'Oh, yes!' exclaimed Kerry. 'I love treats.'

'Cameron, Kerry wants to stop at the garage on the Malone Road, please. She would like a treat. Now.'

'No, she wouldn't,' snapped Cameron, who was beginning to think that stopping in order to get some fresh air mightn't be a bad idea, but could not quite bring himself to give in to Imogen on yet another point this evening.

'I want a treat!' Kerry roared, before immediately changing her tone into a baby-like whine. 'Please. Oh, please, Cameron. Please, princess, please?'

'Fine. Can we stop at the garage, please?' asked Cameron, reluctantly.

"Trevor" smiled, with the air of a man who had seen it all before. 'No bother.'

Stumbling out of the taxi, Imogen made a mad dash to the twenty-four-hour service window to place an enormous order before Cameron could check her spending. A box of chocolates, a family-sized packet of crisps, two chocolate bars, four packets of sweets and three bottles of Diet Coke were being carried across by the cashier; meanwhile, Kerry stood in front of a bizarre collection of potted plants with tiny coloured windmills in them. She was staring in enraptured wonderment.

'I would like one of these, please!' she announced, triumphantly hoisting one up under her arm and waddling up behind Imogen, whereupon the plant sailed through the loop in her arm, crashed to the ground and spilled over the forecourt.

Scrambling down to her knees, Kerry scooped the dirt back in with her bare hands, before the eyes of an impatient Cameron, who was trying to steady himself against Petrol Pump Number 4, and a disbelieving cashier, who could quite clearly see what Kerry was doing. Having retrieved about three-quarters of the soil, she crawled along to the display area and switched the damaged pot with a fresh one, hoisted it into her arms and lumbered back to the window, where Imogen had cunningly spent the last three minutes smiling brightly to the cashier, as if nothing was wrong.

'There we are! No harm done,' said Kerry, plonking the new plant down in front of the cashier, with soil smeared over her hands.

'Right,' sighed the exhausted cashier, who was far too tired to care what these idiots were doing so long as they left and left soon. 'That'll be £21.27.'

'Cameron, pay the man!' Imogen barked, before spinning round on her leopard print Louboutin heel and returning to the taxi, with Kerry shuffling behind her, carefully carrying the plant like it was a caber.

Re-entering the taxi, Cameron turned on Imogen in a rage. '£21.27? What did you buy? You said you only wanted a snack!'

'Kerry was the one who bought a plant!'

'I love it,' Kerry cooed. 'It's a present.'

'Who for?' snapped Cameron.

'Jesus,' Kerry answered, with an air of great mystery.

'What?'

'I dunno.'

'Did you at least get me Maltesers?' Cameron asked Imogen.

'Yes,' Imogen answered truculently, livid that Cameron had dared question her shopping.

'Good. At least you did something right. Pass them over.'

In response, Imogen fished them out of her bag, set them on her palm and slammed down on the packet with her fist. 'They're a bit squashed,' she said calmly, passing them over to a near-apoplectic Cameron.

◇◇◇

The next morning, subsequent enquiries eventually established that the proprietary eyeliner scratched across Cameron's abdomen had been placed there by Kerry when they returned to the house, because she wanted to share the bed with Cameron, rather than the air mattress. Even through a distillery's worth of alcohol, Kerry had not forgotten that despite any row embarked upon during the course of the evening, Cameron and Imogen could be counted upon to ally with each other again the moment they got back inside, to ensure that they scored the best sleeping places at the expense of everybody else. At what point and for what reason she had decided to write the same thing on Imogen's forehead were two mysteries that were never convincingly solved.

Emerging on to the landing outside his bedroom, Cameron stepped over a box of chocolates that Imogen had fought so hard to be able to buy, eaten one and then thrown contemptuously on the floor. On the opposite side of the house, at the end of a brown road of spilt dirt, the little potted plant had been left outside his parents' bedroom door, apparently as a thank you gift from Kerry for having them to stay. It was nice to know that, on the verge of liver failure, Kerry Davison still hadn't quite forgotten her manners.

◇◇◇

Although he would rather have died than admit it to Meredith or Imogen, Cameron really did love visiting Mark and Stewart in Saintfield. The village lay eleven miles outside Belfast and about half an hour on the bus routes, so technically speaking it wasn't too far away from Malone, but there was something reassuringly relaxing for Cameron about coming here. He could even wear a hoodie here. A Jack Wills one, yes, but it still felt daringly relaxed.

'Is this the first time you'll be seeing the new house?' Mark asked, as they meandered up the Main Street, passing the eighteenth-century Presbyterian church on their right. Cameron, a loyal Anglican, thought it was quite pretty – for a Presbyterian church.

'Well, yeah,' Cameron replied awkwardly, since his failure to visit Mark's new home before now implicitly raised the spectre of the boys' five-month feud last year. 'Saintfield is nice, though. Handy to Stew's.'

'Yeah, definitely.'

'How was the festival, by the way?' Cameron asked teasingly as they crossed the road. 'Did you commune with the great indie goddess of funk?'

'It was really good. Guess who we ended up hanging out with?' Mark said, trying to hide the nerves in his voice.

'Who?

'Coral Andrews.'

'Oh,' said Cameron, his eyes dancing with amusement. 'So you actually did commune with the great indie goddess of funk?'

'Ha ha. Very funny.'

'God, poor you. That must have been as much fun as having your nipples twisted off backwards. What did Coral have to say for herself? Let me guess – flowers are great, love is amazing, everybody's equal, 9/11 was a conspiracy and it's what's inside that counts. Or did she just spend five days happily lecturing you on what a big, bad, evil, capitalist clique we are?'

'She's my girlfriend.'

Mark bit the inside of his bottom lip and tried to stare at Cameron defiantly, daring him to criticize his decision. But even he could feel the uncertainty seeping into his gaze, so God only knew how obvious it must be to Cameron, who remained frozen, as if Mark had just told him that Catherine had been nominated to go on *University Challenge*.

'She's your what?'

'Girlfriend,' Mark replied, his eyes darting away from Cameron's face as he said it.

'Since when?'

'Two days ago. I asked her at lunch.'

'End it.'

'What?'

'End it now.'

'No!'

Cameron placed both of his hands at the top of Mark's arms. 'Mark, listen to me: I know you have a great desire to help the weirdos and freaks of life and I think that's great. You're like the brother I never had and if you accidentally killed someone and needed help burying the body at night, I would gladly help. But this – *this* – is too far. Coral Andrews does Satan's work. She thinks she's special because she's decided to make herself "different" to everybody else. But it doesn't make you special, Mark; it makes you retarded.'

Mark shrugged Cameron's hands off him and started walking again. 'Cameron, seriously, you can't talk that way about my girlfriend. It's not cool.'

'Mark, you have never even mentioned having a crush on Coral *Man*drews and now you're acting like she's your love lobster!' Cameron exclaimed, inwardly congratulating himself on having invented such a clever play on the word "Andrews" in the middle of such a hideous trauma.

'Yeah, well, you never mentioned Meredith being in love with that greasy Italian bloke, either, did you? So I guess people change.'

'Is that what this is about? Meredith and Francesco? How did you even find out about that?'

'Catherine. I saw her and Orla in Victoria Square and she told me.'

'That fat-lipped troll! Why can't she keep her big mouth shut for once?'

'Why should she? It's not like it's a big secret. I don't even care, Cameron.'

'Right. Of course you don't. You don't care so much that you're now dating the "girl" Meredith hates the most in the world and let me remind you, Mark, that is a *long* list to top. You clearly heard Meredith was dating Francesco and then asked Coral to be your girlfriend to make her jealous. Well, guess what, genius? That plan is going to backfire because the moment Meredith finds out you've even gone within ten square feet of Coral, it's Game Over for you ever getting together with her.'

'I don't want to get together with Meredith!' Mark retorted. 'I don't. Just because she's beautiful, it doesn't mean... Look, Coral and I will be much better together than Meredith and I ever would.'

'Has it ever occurred to you that the stupidest actions in your life almost always seem to be provoked by your feelings towards Meredith?'

'No,' Mark replied, failing even to convince himself.

'Mark, if you keep this kind of thing bottled up, you end up acting crazy. I know. I've been there. I bought the t-shirt. It was a medium. I have superb abs definition.'

'I do like Coral,' Mark said. And this time he was telling the truth. 'We have a good time together. She's different.'

Cameron flinched instinctively at the word. 'Okay. Fine. All I'm saying is, if you need to talk about Meredith, talk to me and I promise I won't ever say anything to anyone about it.'

'I know that. But I won't need to. After all, like you said, even if I did fancy Meredith, this thing with Coral's nixed it, hasn't it?'

Cameron was struggling to control competing feelings of sympathy for his best friend with equally strong sensations of revulsion at the mental image of him being with Coral. Luckily for Mark, this current dichotomy meant that the expected temper tantrum didn't get the chance to materialize.

'I think I'll have fun with Meredith,' Mark said, looking at the ground as they walked towards his house. 'I think I'll like having her as my girlfriend for a while... What?'

'You said Meredith,' said Cameron, struggling to keep a smug grin under wraps.

'What?'

'You said "Meredith." You said "I think I'll have fun with *Meredith*. I think I'll like having her as my girlfriend for a while."'

'Crap. Shut up. That didn't mean anything, okay? It doesn't mean... Slip of the tongue... Whatever. Balls.

And, okay… I know you won't tell anyone what we've just talked about, but please, *please* don't let that Mandrews nickname catch on either, Cameron. She is technically my girlfriend, even if you don't like her.'

'I can't promise anything about the Mandrews name,' he said. 'It might slip out.'

◇◇◇

'Coral *Man*drews?' cackled Imogen. 'Oh, lover, that is genius. You are truly witty!'

'Thank you, lover,' Cameron replied from the other end of the phone line. 'I definitely nearly chundered on myself when he told me and I remembered we'd shared a can of Coke earlier in the day. Now that I know where his lips have been, I actually feel ill. I'm not even joking.'

'I'm not surprised, sweetie. Everybody knows that she has pauper cooties.'

'She really does.'

'Did he say why he had decided to seppukku his own popularity by dating her? I mean, what on earth prompted him to do something so disgusting?'

'I have no idea,' Cameron lied smoothly. 'He said he liked spending time with her and he thinks she's pretty.'

'Maybe he's gay?' Imogen opined.

'Mark is not gay,' Cameron replied wearily.

'Oh come on, Cameron! You'd have to be at least bi-curious to find those mannish shoulders of hers attractive, and,' she added pointedly, 'he's always been *very* possessive of you.'

'Imogen, that doesn't mean anything. It's just a bromance.'

'Oh God, Cameron, don't be so naïve. You know that we're living through the Age of the Bisexual.'

'Oh, not this again…'

'I'm not making this up,' Imogen declared. 'It's science, Cameron! I read about it in a magazine.'

'When does Meredith get back?'

'Tomorrow morning. She should be back at the house just after eleven.'

'Okay. And we're all having lunch together afterwards, right?'

Imogen yawned down the line. 'Yes, I think so. All of us. Kerry accidentally ended up inviting Catherine.'

'Seriously?' groaned Cameron. 'Like we didn't have enough of her idiocy in Mexico?'

'I know. Alright, sweetie, I've g-2-g. I need to tell everyone I know the news about Coral and Mark, laugh at them behind their backs, vomit in disgust and then send Mark a congratulations message on Facebook.'

'That's nice of you,' Cameron said.

'I know. I'm delightfully fake.'

6
The Return of the Queen

Meredith Harper returned to Malone two days later, just after eleven o'clock in the morning. Catherine, Cameron and Imogen were waiting to greet her, as the Harpers' chauffeur-driven Mercedes pulled into the driveway of her home. For a moment, it struck Cameron as faintly absurd that they had all lined up to meet Meredith upon arrival, as if they were waiting to welcome the Queen home from a triumphant tour of the Commonwealth. He wondered if Kerry had planned to meet them at the restaurant so she could avoid participating in this deferential tableau.

As Billy, the Harpers' long-serving driver, held the door open for her, Meredith's pair of thigh high Stella McCartney boots touched down on to the driveway. She stepped elegantly from the car, with her phone clutched in her right hand. Her hair was slightly more limp than usual and she was using her Chanel sunglasses to hide the signs of fatigue around her eyes, but apart from that Meredith had emerged remarkably fresh from a seven and a half-hour overnight flight from Newark. Along with the McCartneys and the shades, she was wearing a short grey skirt and a black cashmere sweater; a new Mulberry handbag hung over the same arm carrying the phone. She smelled, as she always did, like a mixture of vanilla and bergamot body butter and her favourite Theo Fennell perfume.

'Billy, don't worry about bringing the bags in anytime soon,' she said to her driver. 'There's no rush.'

After going through the ritual of hugging her three friends, Meredith inserted her key in the front door and let herself in to the cavernous entrance hall. Everything about the Harpers' home spoke of quiet but immense wealth and impeccable taste. There was a faintly stale smell at the moment, reflecting the fact that for the last two weeks neither of the Harpers had been in residence. With Meredith in Mexico, New York, Washington and then the Hamptons, her father had taken the opportunity to go on holiday to Morocco for a few weeks, on what sounded to Cameron suspiciously like a romantic getaway. If so, he prayed Anthony ended things before Meredith discovered it and unleashed the fury of a thousand winters on her prospective stepmother.

'Where's your father?' Imogen asked, as they followed her into the entrance hall.

'He's in Marrakech,' Meredith answered, as they moved up the staircase to her rooms. 'He'll be back this evening. How's the party planning going, Imogen?'

'Fabulously. More or less everyone's RSVP'd.'

'Cameron, I love those jeans on you. Who hasn't responded yet?'

'Victoria Stephenson, Peter Sullivan, Sasha Montmorency, Olivia-Grace Wallace, Tangela Henton-Worley, Mark Kingston, Titus Pitt and your dashing new bf,' Imogen responded, reading from the party planning notepad that she now kept permanently near the top of her handbag. 'That's eight altogether.'

Meredith bit back the urge to remind Imogen that she could count. 'Sasha's not going to be home for the party. I thought he might be, but he's decided to travel on to Peru or Uruguay or somewhere like that...'

'Sasha's not coming?' Catherine cried out, unexpectedly and very loudly.

'That's what I just said,' Meredith replied, coldly.

'Did you think he could be your plus one?' Cameron smirked at her.

'I... eh... I just thought he was nice,' she answered, lamely.

'Oh, yeah, he is,' Cameron agreed. 'He's so nice. He'll be back in time for my birthday in December, so I'll make sure he says hi to you then, Catherine.'

Meredith smiled at Cameron's cruel and deceptive implication that he was in regular contact with Sasha and at the confused misery on Catherine's face. Clearly, Cameron was still enjoying inflicting psychological revenge on her for her relationship with Blake.

'Like I was saying before Catherine decided to trample all over the rules of volume, Sasha's a no. Victoria's boring and if she hasn't bothered replying by now, I don't see why we should go to any special effort to track her down. Apparently Olivia-Grace is still on holiday in Tunisia, but she'll be back two days before the party, so I'll e-mail her this evening just to check; I'm sure she'll be coming. Tangela's an idiot, but she goes where Anastasia goes, so mark her down as a yes.'

'What about Titus and Peter?'

'Titus would turn up to the opening of an envelope, so he'll be there. And, Cameron?'

'Yes?'

'Peter?' Meredith asked, impatiently. 'Why hasn't he RSVP'd?'

'Oh, he's just really disorganized,' Cameron shrugged. 'He'll be there, though.'

'Not if he doesn't reply,' Meredith answered. 'And, yes, Francesco will be coming. He's flying in the day before and staying with the Montmorencys.'

'Sexy times,' Imogen enthused, as Meredith swung open the double doors to her bedroom. 'What about Monsieur Kingston?'

'What about him?' Meredith asked, setting her sunglasses down on the coffee table by the fireplace and tossing her handbag on the sofa.

'He still hasn't replied.'

'I didn't even know he was invited until you mentioned him earlier,' Meredith replied.

'Is there a problem?' Cameron asked, with just the tiniest hint of an edge creeping into his voice.

'No,' Meredith said. She sat down on the edge of her bed to remove her boots and as she sat, the luxuriously soft mattress rose up around her and the sheets crinkled slightly. 'I just didn't know you wanted to invite him, Imogen.'

'I didn't really. It was Cameron's idea and I figured since you and Mark at least don't completely hate each other anymore, why not?'

'That's fair,' Meredith said indifferently. 'What are our plans for the rest of the day?'

'We're meeting Kerry for lunch at Harlem in an hour,' Imogen answered. 'Then I said we'd meet the caterers with Mummy at four to go over the plans for Saturday.'

'Sounds perfect. After that, I'm going to take a quick look over the guest list and I said I would have dinner with my godmother this evening. Just give me a moment to get changed and then we can go.'

◇◇◇

The one thing you could always give Kerry Davison credit for was that no matter how much she might disapprove of what her friends were doing, the moment anyone outside the group caused them even the tiniest twinge of irritation, she pounced, and so despite her resentment over Meredith and Imogen's joint birthday party, she reacted with characteristic outrage at the news that people had failed to RSVP so close to an event.

'Not okay!' she declared, staring fiercely at her four lunch companions. 'I don't see why you should be bothering to host them, if they can't be bothered to reply.'

'To be fair, Olivia-Grace is still on holiday,' Cameron reasoned.

'And what about the others?' Kerry snapped. 'It's just sheer, inexcusable bad manners not to let people know.'

Meredith flicked her hair behind her shoulders. 'Kerry's right.'

'Yes, I am. I don't care how stupid or lazy people are – it takes five seconds to reply to an invite.'

'And Sasha's definitely not coming?' Catherine asked, despite Meredith's earlier confirmation that Sasha would still be in South America.

Cameron answered with a light laugh. 'Not unless he's planning on flying in from Machu Picchu for the evening.'

Meredith picked up her glass of Diet Coke, with her customary extra slice of lemon. 'I agree with Kerry. I don't think we should allow people in if they just turn up on the night. It's not fair on the caterers and it's not fair on us.'

'You absolutely *cannot* let them in if they haven't RSVP'd,' declared the Empress of Party Planning. 'Why should you?'

Cameron took a forkful of his chicken, hoping that he wasn't about to be blamed for Peter's tardiness. It was so rare to find Meredith and Kerry completely in agreement on a topic of conversation that you forgot what a potentially terrifying and unstoppable unit they could be when united.

'Does anyone want to split a toffee pudding with me?' Imogen asked.

'Oh, me please!' smiled Catherine, who didn't especially like toffee.

'Did I tell you Freddie's coming?' Imogen said to Meredith, ignoring Catherine's offer.

'Carrowdale?'

'Yes.'

'No, but he's on the list, so I assumed he would be.'

'Imogen fancies him again,' Kerry whispered conspiratorially, again reminding Cameron just how unsettling he found it when Kerry and Meredith were on the same page.

'I do not! I just think he's very attractive.'

'He is very attractive,' Meredith conceded. 'Which is lucky, because it's not as if he's going to set the world alight with his personality.'

'That's what I said,' Kerry said. 'Pretty box, no package.'

'Oh, he has a package,' Imogen smirked. 'I've seen him in his surfing gear.'

'Oh God, Imogen,' sighed Cameron.

'Anyway, Freddie's lots of fun and he's invited us to his house at some point this summer, when the weather's good. Maybe he and Titus can have a pool party, like they did last year?'

'As long as we don't have to end up on the beach,' Meredith ruled. 'I hate sand.'

'I like the beach,' Kerry said.

'Sand is disgusting, Kerry, and it gets everywhere.'

Cameron smiled at the subtle but immediate change in the atmosphere around the table, as Kerry silently bristled at Meredith's dismissive imperiousness. Taking advantage of the hiatus in conversation, Imogen bit her lip and smiled across the table at Meredith: 'So, Meredith, tell us – how are things with Francesco?'

'Well, he came to see me in New York,' she said, taking a sip of her drink.

'And?' breathed Imogen, excitedly. 'Did he meet your mother?'

'No. She was in the Hamptons with Chester and I didn't particularly want to drag him all the way up there just to meet them. Chester can be so... *much*. We stayed in the city and he met my grandmother instead. She seemed to quite like him.'

'How long did he stay for?'

'Three days. He really was only calling in after he said goodbye to Sasha in Guadálupe.'

'They went to Guadálupe! Why did no one tell me? I love pilgrimages.'

'I know. I didn't know that's where they were going until after they had been there,' Meredith lied. 'After New York, he went home to Genoa for a week to see his family and then he's coming here.'

'That's very sweet of him.'

'He's *so* beau,' Catherine smiled.

Cameron was playing with his unused dessert spoon, shifting it between the second and fourth fingers of his right hand. 'What do you like about Francesco, Meredith? You never really told us.'

'I'm not the kind of person who goes on and on about their boyfriends, Cameron.'

'But you do really like him?' Cameron asked.

'Of course I do. He's perfect.'

'Yes, he is! He's delicious. I take it he's going to be your plus one to the party?' Imogen asked, innocently.

'Well, it's not officially a "plus one" kind of thing, but since he's coming all the way from Italy, yes, I suppose he is.'

'Well, in that case I better ask Freddie to be mine! Oh well. Does anyone want to split a toffee pudding with me?'

'Mucho couples around these days,' Kerry mused, as she sprinkled some salt over her lunch. 'You and Francesco, Imogen and Freddie, Mark and Coral...'

'What?' Meredith asked, her head snapping in Kerry's direction.

'Yeah,' said Kerry mischievously, still displeased about Meredith's beach comment earlier. 'They've been dating for like a week. She posts on his Facebook all the time. Did you not know?'

Cameron threw an unimpressed stare at Kerry and Imogen tried unsuccessfully to keep an excited grin from spreading across her face. The two of them had been trying to predict all week how Meredith would react to the news.

'No, Kerry, I did not know,' Meredith replied. 'Shockingly, the dating antics of Mark Kingston and some buck-toothed hippie didn't exactly make headlines in the Hamptons.'

Kerry began innocently humming a little tune to herself, as she re-focussed on eating her lunch. Meredith knew that she had just been socially upended by a vengeful Kerry, who had chosen to torpedo her in front of the entire group for disagreeing with her beach statement earlier. A feeling of unhappiness tinged with sea-sickness was sweeping across her body and it was a full seven seconds later before Meredith realized that nobody had actually spoken yet and everyone was still looking at her, waiting for her to continue.

'That's hideous,' she replied, with a mirthless laugh. 'Even Mark could do better than that.'

Cameron nodded slowly, noticing that Meredith had gone from looking pale to positively ashen. 'I'll go halfzies on that toffee pudding, Imogen, if you still want it,' he said.

◇◇◇

On the night of Imogen and Meredith's joint birthday, Catherine stormed into her family's kitchen in a light blue cocktail dress. Her youngest sister, Caoimhe, was sitting at the table reading, while their mother Mary stood next to the nearby AGA.

'Where are my hair straighteners?' Catherine asked, glaring accusingly at Caoimhe.

'I don't know.'

'Caoimhe, don't lie! I just found them in your room.'

'Why are you asking me where they are then?'

'Caoimhe, stop taking me stuff without asking. You always do this and then I can't find anything when I need it! I'm seriously already late and I spent like fifteen minutes looking for those stupid hair straighteners and they were in your room the whole time!'

Caoimhe shrugged. 'Sorry, I forgot.'

'You shouldn't have taken them without asking me in the first place. You're too young even to be using them. Mum!'

'Catherine, calm down. It's only a pair of hair straighteners and you've still got plenty of time to get ready before your daddy leaves you over to Meredith's.'

'Mum, you always take her side,' Catherine exclaimed. 'It's so unfair! She always steals my stuff.'

'Well, when you were her age you used to take Orla's things all the time.'

'Yeah and you told me off for it!'

'And Orla complained that I always took your side, too,' Mary smiled. 'Caoimhe, don't take your sister's things without asking her.'

'She never gives them to me when I ask,' Caoimhe replied.

'That is such a lie!' Catherine shot back, with a look of pious outrage. 'I lend you stuff all the time.'

'Like when?'

'Girls, that's enough,' Mary ruled. 'Catherine, go and finish getting ready. Caoimhe, would you tell your daddy his dinner's ready?'

Furious that Caoimhe had not been more sharply reprimanded, Catherine flounced out of the kitchen and back upstairs to her bedroom. This was exactly the kind of thing she didn't need right before Imogen and Meredith's party. She was very aware that after the humiliating disaster of her relationship with Blake, her position in the group was weaker than ever. Nor had she helped matters by being such anti-banter in Mexico. Tonight, therefore, Catherine was determined to regain her friends' approval. She had nearly bankrupted herself in purchasing presents for them and she had spent the best part of two days arranging them in glittery boxes, like home-made gift sets, before using her art skills to stencil Meredith and Imogen's names on to their respective presents and decorate the boxes with photographs that she knew would mean something to each girl personally. A portrait of Anne Boleyn clutching a red rose stared out haughtily from the top of Meredith's present, circled with a hand-designed silver frame, stencilled personally by Catherine. Cluttered around it were pictures of Clarke Gable and Vivien Leigh kissing in *Gone with the Wind*, the Chanel logo, an Aquascutum model, the *Vogue Italia* title, photographs of Anna Wintour and Bette Davis, a portrait of Gabrielle de Polignac and a cut-out of Meredith from last year's *Bright Young Bling* spread in *Ulster Tatler*. On Imogen's, Evita Perón and Our Lady of Lourdes jostled for places with Henry Cavill, Alexander Skårsgard, James Dean, a road map of Knightsbridge and a photo of a windswept Kimora Lee Simmons. They were going to love these.

Plugging her straighteners into the wall, Catherine stared at herself in her dressing table mirror and breathed in deeply. Tonight, she was going to be funny and confident and energetic. She was going to make them like her all over again. After all, they were her best friends.

◇◇◇

Catherine's father deposited her at the gates of Meredith's house, before deftly trying to navigate his way through the cars clogging up Malone Park, as dozens of youngsters were left off by their parents. Moving her way nimbly up the driveway and around the fountain which stood in its centre, Catherine noted that lots of other people were already here. She was only ten minutes late, but the party was well underway. That could mean only one thing – this year, she hadn't been invited to come along earlier than everybody else to help with the preparations. It was not a good omen for the security of her position within the clique. Fighting to control her panic and to balance both Imogen and Meredith's presents, especially difficult in a party dress and heels, Catherine rang the doorbell and was greeted by a smiling butler, who she didn't recognize. He must have been hired for the night.

'Can I take your coat, miss?' he asked.

'Oh, thank you!' said Catherine.

'Guests can leave their presents on the dining room table,' he explained, as he helped Catherine out of her coat.

'Oh that's okay, thanks,' smiled Catherine, who was determined not to relinquish her presents until she placed them directly into Meredith and Imogen's hands. She wanted to personally witness their reactions.

'Champagne, miss?' asked one of the hired waiters, proffering a tray.

'Yes, please!' trilled Catherine. 'Thank you so much.'

With the two boxes tucked under her arm, Catherine awkwardly took a sip of her drink and smiled nervously at some of the boys from the school's First XV rugby squad. Tonight, they had all made an effort to look nice and were smartly dressed in jackets, fresh shirts and a variety of discreetly coloured trousers. There were a few flashes of Burberry and Hermès from the squad's wealthier members, but even those not boasting designer labels had made an impressive nod towards respectability. Catherine was terribly intimidated by the squad's rowdy lad banter and even when they were on their best behaviour, like tonight, she still found herself paralyzed when confronted by their muscles, height and confidence.

The squad consisted of twenty-three members, but only twelve had been invited. Meredith had absolutely refused to extend invitations to those boys she considered inappropriate for a gathering in Malone – namely those who did not know when to switch-off the raucousness. Imogen's relationship with the First XVs, once golden, was still on shaky grounds ever since she had cheated on Stewart and so she too had insisted that only the squad's more polite members be invited, lest she be heckled at her own party.

Three of the Lower Sixth rugby boys – Matthew Kilbride, Oran Cahill and the team's captain, Quentin Smith – were standing drinking champagne together and they smiled at Catherine as she approached. Quentin even said hello to her, eliciting nothing but a semi-incoherent squeak from Catherine, who would much rather have said something urbane and sophisticated. Not least because she thought Quentin was absolutely gorgeous.

Shuffling past the lads and gingerly setting her champagne flute down on one of the tables, Catherine entered the dining room. The table was indeed groaning with presents, just as the butler had said, and groups of people were clustered around the room, sipping cocktails mixed for them by a hired bartender working from behind a wet bar in the corner.

Some of the Lower Sixth popular crowd – or, rather, the new Upper Sixth popular crowd – were grouped together, all looking aloof and well-groomed. With her free hand, Catherine waved to the group's leader, Anastasia, a beautiful socialite with a strong upper-class accent that reminded Catherine very much of her brother, Sasha. Anastasia smiled back at Catherine's greeting, although there wasn't much warmth in that smile, and Catherine felt the eyes of Anastasia's right-hand woman, Lavinia Barrington, trail up and down her body. Since Lavinia didn't smile, Catherine could only assume that, mercifully, there mustn't be anything wrong with what she was wearing.

'Hey guys!' she grinned. 'How are you?'

'We're really good,' sighed Anastasia. 'How was Mexico?'

'So much fun! I met your brother.'

'Yes, he said.'

'Did he?'

'Well, he mentioned that he spent a few days in Cabo,' Anastasia replied, leaving Catherine unsure if the dreamy Sasha had said anything about her specifically. Spotting the disappointed look on Catherine's face, Lavinia exchanged a knowing look with Natasha and Mariella. They smirked.

'So many hotties here tonight,' Mariella said, in her languid Malone drawl. 'Hotties abú.'

'Yeah, I know,' beamed Catherine. 'I was just talking to Quentin Smith. He's so hot.'

'What were you guys talking about?' asked Lavinia.

'Oh, just like, y'know...'

'Right.'

'Yeah.'

'You can leave your presents on the table, by the way,' Anastasia said, apparently irritated by the effort of having to look at Catherine in such an awkward pose.

'Oh, no, that's okay, thanks. I want to give them to Mer-Mer and Imogen myself. Have you seen them?'

'I think they're outside,' said Anastasia. 'Imogen was talking to Freddie Carrowdale last time I saw her.'

'Yeah, I think she fancies him again,' said Catherine.

'Are you serious?' gasped Mariella, scenting gossip. 'Didn't they date like back in first year or something?'

'Third year, but yeah,' Catherine answered. 'They were like the first people to like properly start actually dating that we knew, apart from Peter Sullivan, but he's like had a girlfriend ever since he was seven or something. Hey, Anastasia, can I ask you a question? It might seem a bit weird – but, uhm, did Sasha date anyone in high school?'

Anastasia looked at Catherine like she was the single stupidest human being she had ever had the bad luck to encounter in conversation. 'How on earth would that even be possible? Sasha went to an all-boys boarding school.'

Catherine's relief was almost palpable. 'Oh, no reason! I mean, right, yeah, I totally forgot about it being only for boys. Thanks! Oh, and btw, don't tell anyone I told you about Imogen fancying Freddie again. I don't think people are supposed to know yet. See you guys later. Kisses!'

Lumbering out of the dining room with the gift boxes still under her arm, Catherine wondered for a moment if she would get in trouble for saying that thing about Freddie and Imogen. Of all the people she didn't want to annoy tonight, Imogen was definitely top of the list. Meredith was meaner, but her barbs and insults were often so clever that half of them sailed right over Catherine's head. There was nothing subtle or avoidable when Imogen decided to take you down. Still, it had been worth it to have the unexpected opportunity to find out that Sasha Montmorency definitely was not gay. Kerry was wrong about him and Cameron was probably going to make a fool of himself, yet again, by crushing on a boy he'd never get.

Happy images of how she would look as Sasha's girlfriend danced across Catherine's mind as she passed back through the entrance hall towards the lounge, shaking her head politely at the waiters passing out canapés and keeping her eyes peeled for any sign of Kerry, Imogen, Meredith or even, as a last resort, Cameron. Half-way through the lounge, she was accosted by an equally confused Tangela Henton-Worley, a member of the group of girls Catherine had just left in the dining room.

'Have you seen Anastasia?' she asked. 'I've been looking for her for ages!'

'Oh yeah, she's in the dining room,' Catherine answered.

'Who's with her?'

'Mariella, Lavinia and Natasha. Why?'

'Are they all in there? That's so annoying. I've been texting Mariella for like the last half an hour and she hasn't replied.'

'Has she read them?'

'Yes! It came up on my phone that she had.'

'Oh... maybe she just has bad signal then? Meredith says she gets bad signal here all the time. It takes her ages to reply to my text messages because of it.'

'Oh right, maybe,' nodded Tangela, slightly mollified.

'Have you seen Meredith or Imogen? Or Kerry?'

'Yeah – Kerry's outside,' Tangela said disinterestedly. 'I think Imogen's out there, too. See you later.'

'Bye.'

As she stepped out through the double doors on to the patio, Catherine gazed in wonder at the lights woven around the patio pillars. An ice sculpture stood amidst a table of frosted drinks; hired waiters and waitresses moved unobtrusively between the guests, replenishing drinks, taking orders and handing out hors d'oeuvres. Further out in the garden, Catherine could dimly see some of the workers setting up for the fireworks display at the end of the evening.

Most of the people out on the patio seemed super-old. Lots of men in suits, who must be business associates of either Meredith or Imogen's parents, were milling around near well-dressed Malone mummies ranging from mid-thirties to early fifties. Ensconced in one of the patio armchairs, surrounded by a gaggle of admirers enthralled by her latest anecdote, was Meredith's ninety-year-old godmother, Lady Portlester, with a gin and Dubonnet in her right hand. A magnificent diamond brooch glistened from her evening gown and Catherine had to admit that for a woman just short of her ninety-first birthday, Lady Portlester had a delightful face of make up on.

'There you are,' sighed Kerry, bearing down on her with a cosmopolitan clamped in her right hand. 'Where have you been?'

'Caoimhe stole my hair straighteners and then when I got here I started talking to Quentin Smith and...'

'You were talking to Quentin Smith?' Kerry asked.

'Yeah. He was super-nice and stuff.'

Kerry nodded her head disbelievingly, before turning her attention to the presents. 'What are those?'

'They're my presents for Imogen and Mer-Mer.'

'You're supposed to leave them on the dining room table.'

'I wanted to give them to them myself,' Catherine explained, already feeling less confident.

'Well, they're hardly going to want to carry them around all night, are they? What do you think of my dress?'

'It's so nice,' complimented Catherine. 'Like, so beau.'

'Thanks,' Kerry smiled. 'I didn't really know what to wear, because I didn't know how over-the-top the party was going to be, but this kind of style is always in fashion – even at a party where Imogen has definitely decided on way too many lights. It looks a colourless Disneyland, doesn't it?'

'Eh, yeah,' agreed Catherine. 'Yeah, it does.'

'You're right. It's too much. Sad. What did you get them?'

'Just like loads of little things and stuff,' Catherine said. 'I made some of them myself.'

'Nothing special then?'

'No,' she mumbled. 'Not really.'

'Yeah, that's probably best,' Kerry answered, staring out over the garden. 'They can't expect amazing presents if they have both their birthdays on the same day.'

'Yeah, that's true.'

'Why haven't you got a drink yet?' Kerry asked, finishing off her cosmopolitan.

'Well, I can't really drink very well with the boxes. I don't want to spill on myself.'

'Eugh! Right, let's get rid of the stupid boxes then,' said Kerry, wrapping her hand around Catherine's spare wrist. 'Come on! Let's go find the little birthday beasts.'

◇◇◇

Mark Kingston trailed his hand down Coral's side as they made out on his sofa. A completely forgettable Angelina Jolie movie was playing on the television screen behind them and a half-eaten pizza sat on the lounge table, still in its delivery box. Coral's phone beeped for the sixth or seventh time and she disengaged herself from Mark with a smile to reach over and get it.

'It's Paula,' she announced. 'She says she's been for her driving lesson down the Malone Road and she was stuck behind five Mercedes and a Jaguar trying to turn into Malone Park.'

Coral snorted with derision at this image and set the phone back on the table. Just like that, thoughts of the party were once again dominating Mark's brain. Part of the reason for turning down Imogen's invitation had been that it was the only proper thing to do. Now that he was Coral's boyfriend he could not legitimately go to a party where she was not welcome and there were few places on Earth where Coral Andrews would be less welcome than Meredith Harper's birthday party. However, Mark also knew that part of the reason he hadn't gone was because he had a lurking suspicion that Francesco was going to make an appearance. When he had first voiced the idea of not going, the scorn and ridicule he had expected from Cameron never materialized. Instead, Cameron had been nothing but supportive of the idea, leaving Mark wondering if this was because Francesco would be there and Cameron didn't want any awkwardness. Not that he cared, of course, but he could remember Francesco from the party last October and he seemed smarmy and irritating.

'Did you get invited?' Coral asked, interrupting his self-analysis.

'Yeah.'

'Why didn't you go?'

'It'd be boring. Plus, I'd rather spend the evening with you,' he smiled, as he pulled her back in towards him.

◇◇◇

Meredith sat at the dressing table in her closet, staring at her own reflection, with an inscrutable expression on her face. Her right hand was placed delicately under her chin, with the elbow resting on the table. She had come up to change her necklace; the clasp was loose and she was afraid of losing it. It sat on the table in front of her, shimmering seductively in the soft glow of the closet's half-dimmed lights.

There was a soft knock on the closet door and Meredith jumped, before turning to see Francesco leaning in the doorway, smiling. His beard had grown slightly fuller, although it was still perfectly maintained and his brown eyes were twinkling as they looked at her.

'Is everything alright?' he asked.

'Yes,' she smiled. 'I just came up to change my necklace.'

'Is something wrong?'

'The clasp is loose. I didn't want it to fall off and get trampled on.'

'Let me take a look at it,' he said, walking over to her. 'Perhaps I can help?'

'Oh, don't worry about it. Daddy can send it off to the jewellers tomorrow.'

'But it's such a beautiful necklace and you look wonderful in it. It would be a pity to have to change it for the rest of the party.'

Francesco picked up the necklace and began to inspect the clasp. He spent a moment or two fiddling with it, before smiling in satisfaction. 'There! Sometimes these things just need tapped a little. May I?'

Meredith turned back to face the mirror, as Francesco trailed her hair over her left shoulder, leaving her neck free. He brought the necklace up to her neck and clasped it closed. It snapped shut with a definitive "click" and Meredith smiled as Francesco brought his head down to rest next to hers. Gazing into the mirror, he smiled again and kissed her on the cheek.

'There. Perfect.'

◇◇◇

Standing at the bottom of the stairs, Cameron had nearly finished another glass of champagne when he was approached by the beaming figure of Peter Sullivan, in an Abercrombie & Fitch shirt and pair of grey trousers.

'Dude!' he smiled, wrapping Cameron in a bear hug. 'How are you?'

'I'm good,' Cameron replied, patting Peter on the back as they broke the hug. 'What about you?'

'Can't complain, can't complain. What did you think of the news about Mark and Coral?'

'I wasn't exactly thrilled.'

'She's a fucking head-melt,' Peter said ruefully. 'Should've heard her at the festival, mate. Jesus, Mary and Holy Saint Patrick. It was the definition of shanter. I felt like I was having a pint with Betty No-Bant.'

'Is that when they got together?' Cameron asked, making a mental note that now he was with Peter he would need to swear more in order to reach the acceptable quota of expletives per conversation. After all, he was in lad territory now.

'I don't think so. I think maybe they pulled then. I dunno. I know he asked her out when we got back to Belfast,' Peter answered, shaking his head again. 'I really don't know if I can handle having her around all the time. Or those fucking munters she's friends with.'

Cameron laughed. 'Did you have a good time apart from that?'

'At the festival? Yeah, yeah. *So* much talent, mate. So much. What about you and Mexico?'

'Yeah, it was good banter,' Cameron answered, deftly avoiding making any specific comment on holiday hotties. 'Sasha Montmorency and Francesco stopped by for a couple of days, but mostly it was just me and the girls. It was good fun.'

'Sasha and Francesco? So you did have some talent around then?'

'Pardon?'

'C'mon! Those two are better-looking than half the girls in school. Am I right?'

'I don't know.'

'Mate, are you gay?'

At that second, Kerry careered into view, clutching an apple martini. 'Have you seen Imogen and Meredith?' she asked, impatiently. 'I've been looking for them for like an hour... Okay, fine, that was lie. I'm sorry. I've been looking for them for like five minutes, but each one of those minutes has been *very* tiring. Catherine needs to give them these stupid presents, so we're finding them, getting rid of them and then taking Catherine to get a drink.'

'Where is Catherine?'

'What?'

Cameron repeated his question, prompting Kerry to glance around her in the sudden realization that somewhere between her trip to the bathroom and a second trip to the bar, she had inexplicably managed to misplace Catherine. 'Oops... Hold on,' she sighed. 'I'll be right back. And if you see Imogen, text me.'

Cameron nodded and tried to smile, as Kerry swept back into the crowds in search for her present-toting friend. Peter just continued to stare at Cameron with a look of enquiry on his face.

'Well?'

'Well, what?'

'Well, are you?'

'Am I...?'

'Gay?'

'Eh... why do you ask?'

'Ah, Cameron, for fuck's sake, strap on a pair.'

'Well... yes, I think so. I mean, yes. I am.'

Peter nodded and clapped him on the shoulder. 'See! That wasn't so hard now, was it, big lad?'

Cameron looked both grateful and confused. 'It really doesn't bother you?'

'Any hole's a goal,' Peter said cheerfully.

'Okay, that was probably profoundly unnecessary,' Cameron laughed. 'How did you find out?'

'It wasn't too hard to figure out. I've kind of always thought you were and that you'd "come out" or whatever it's called, eventually.'

'Why did you ask me now, though?'

'Every time your name was mentioned at the festival, Stewart and Mark would look at each other and they got very protective... I dunno. I just had a hunch that there'd been a development.'

'Yeah.'

'Someone said about Catherine and Blake breaking up and Mark and Stewart both looked like they'd shit themselves, so...' Peter shrugged and took another drink, noticing that Cameron had begun to blush at the mention of Blake's name. 'Dude, did you and Blake buck?'

It was possible that Cameron was even more surprised by this second question than he had been by the first one. His voice dropped to a whisper and he looked at Peter in scandalized panic. 'Pardon?'

'Did you?'

'Well, no, we didn't.'

'Why not? He's a good looking guy; you're a good looking guy...'

'How do you even know Blake is gay?' asked Cameron.

'Are you joking? Did you see the way he looked at you? He practically had a semi every time you came into the room, Cameron. *No one* can be straight and look at someone the way he used to look at you. I thought everybody could see it, but they didn't seem to. Ah well, it's not their fault. I'm uncommonly wise in the ways of love.'

'Peter, you can't tell anyone.'

'Cameron, don't be fucking stupid – you know I wouldn't. I've got your back. Maybe not in the way you like, but I've got it.'

'Fuck up.'

Peter laughed and threw his arm around Cameron's shoulders. 'Well, good for you,' he said, before ruffling his hand affectionately through Cameron's hair and laughing. 'That's my wee mate.'

◇◇◇

'Imogen, there is no such thing as the "Age of the Bisexual,"' Freddie said, with a strained laugh.

'Freddie, there are scientists working on this. Sexual scientists.' Imogen replied, emphatically. 'You can Google it.'

'Well, I'm not bisexual.'

'Oh, Freddie. Everybody is. Except me. And God knows I've tried. You see, the thing is, I have massive trust issues when it comes to women...'

'There you are!' announced Kerry, who had appeared at Imogen's side, towing Catherine behind her. 'I've been looking for you all night. Better organized present depositing scheduling might have helped, Imogen.'

'Well, you can sort that out for your party in September, babes. You can do anything you like then, because it'll all be up to you and nobody else.'

'Happy birthday!' cried Catherine, cutting Kerry off before she could make her riposte. 'I made you a present.'

'Oh gosh, Catherine, thanks,' smiled Imogen, hugging her. 'Oh, Henry Cavill – yummy! Just put it over on the dining room table with the others and I'll open it later.'

'Oh. Okay,' Catherine said, with a wounded smile, before turning round and disappearing into the crowd again.

'That was sweet of her.'

'She said she couldn't really afford proper presents this year because both birthdays are on the same day,' Kerry said. 'That's probably why it's homemade.'

'Is it cheap?' Imogen asked, in a swift alteration in mood. 'Is it seriously cheap after the amount of money I spent on her stupid birthday?'

'It's in a cardboard box,' replied Kerry vindictively. 'What do you think?'

Freddie smiled an awkward half-smile at both of them and took a sip of his drink. 'Nice of her to make the effort though.'

Imogen instantly turned to Freddie with a luminous smile, while Kerry stared at him in irritated contempt. 'Yes,' Imogen agreed, linking her arm through Freddie's. 'It was super-nice of her, wasn't it?'

Kerry rolled her eyes and took a sip of her drink. It was at times like this that she remembered just how unbearable she found Imogen when she was around prospective new boyfriends. She missed Cameron.

◇◇◇

At ten o'clock, Imogen's parents stood alongside Meredith's father in the entrance hall to commence the speeches. Edgar Dawson's speech about Imogen was certainly the more comedic of the two. He regaled the crowd with stories of Imogen's more outrageous childhood moments – like when Imogen, aged seven, had punched her brother Christopher in the mouth and then accused him of biting her fist. Or how she had once interrupted her parents' date night by kicking down the dining room door, dressed in her duvet as the Queen of the Night and attempting to sing an aria from *The Magic Flute*.

'Imogen, my darling, you have brought love and light and an incredible amount of fun into my life and Mummy's for the last seventeen years. And despite my best efforts to make you learn a lesson, there's part of me that can't help but hope you never will. Long may it continue. To Imogen!'

'To Imogen,' toasted the guests; they applauded Edgar's speech as he ceded the floor to Anthony Harper.

'Many of you will not believe this,' he began, 'but when Meredith was born she was an unusually quiet baby. I remember almost no tears, apart from the moment when her mother attempted to put a family heirloom on her head for her christening. It was a boy's bonnet and Meredith was not pleased.'

Polite laughter filled the room. Meredith, standing next to Francesco, smiled and kept her eyes cast decorously downwards. Doing so allowed her to look beautifully modest, but it also enabled her to hide how much she disliked hearing about her mother.

'When Meredith was a child, she excelled at everything she did. Her mother arranged for her to attend homework club, after-school tuition, language lessons, tennis lessons, piano, singing, Holy Communion classes, ice skating, ballet, drama, horse riding and others that I'm sure I've probably forgotten. In every activity and from every teacher, the same report came back – perfect. Well, "perfect" if she liked the activity, that is; sadly, "perfect" is not exactly a word I've heard coming from her more recent Science teachers, but you can't ask for everything! Anyway, "a perfect pupil" was how most of her tutors described her. As a father, that makes you very proud. But it was not just in language lessons or tennis or piano or ponies where Meredith was "perfect." You see, to me, she was not just the perfect pupil, she was also the perfect daughter. For the last six years, it has been just you and I, Meredith. Without you, I don't want to imagine what my life here would be like. You always smile when I come home, you make me laugh with stories of your school day and, sometimes, you make me despair of them too. You have brought your friends into our home and introduced them to me – all of them lovely, all of them welcome and, as Edgar rightly said, all of them endlessly entertaining. Meredith, tonight it is hard not to feel a nostalgic for the little girl in the ballet shoes, but it is also hard not to feel happy about the young lady you have grown into. As always, I am very, very proud of you. To Meredith.'

'To Meredith,' toasted the crowd, as emotional tears streamed down Kerry's face. Confronted with Anthony's love for his daughter, Kerry had decided to forget her current irritation with Meredith and had instead merrily embraced the sentimentality of the occasion. Meredith walked forward and kissed her father on the cheek. He whispered something in her ear and she laughed. Anthony reached forward and hugged Cameron too, before shaking Francesco's hand, as Meredith embraced her aged godmother.

'Isn't it a lovely party?' Kerry wept happily.

7
JUDGEMENT DAY

The two weeks immediately after Imogen and Meredith's joint seventeenth birthday party passed quietly enough, but with the looming presence of results day darkening the horizon like a gathering thunderstorm. The only scandal, if you could call it that, was that three days after the party, Imogen's Facebook profile gleefully announced that she and Freddie Carrowdale were once again officially an item. Apart from that, the summer continued much like the one before. Freddie, with Imogen now acting as self-appointed co-hostess, began organizing summer barbecues at his parents' house in Helen's Bay. When the weather was bad, his best friend Titus arranged parties in his indoor pool and with Imogen now firmly established as Freddie's girlfriend, it meant that she and her clique could vet the guest list. Drunk with power, Kerry had her old rival, Lisa Flaherty, banished into the social wilderness.

A day after Freddie and Imogen announced their big news, Catherine jetted off for a twelve-day holiday in Florida with her parents and sisters, and Kerry's dad later returned to spend the month in Northern Ireland, having lived for half the year in Argentina ever since his divorce from Kerry's mother eight years earlier. With Catherine in America and Kerry necessarily spending quite a lot of quality time with her father, Imogen, Meredith and Cameron clicked along in a pleasing and fairly unremarkable series of soirées, pool parties, mixers, club nights, fundraisers and social evenings at various golf, cricket and yacht clubs.

Meredith found herself relaxing more than she had at any point since dispatching her duplicitous e-mail to Blake at the start of July. Given his lack of response, Meredith felt reasonably hopeful that he had taken the decision to stay in America permanently. She had also managed to avoid fixating too much on the nasty business of Mark and Coral. It had been disconcerting, even mildly annoying, when Mark had not turned up to her birthday party, because a small part of her was looking forward to appearing on the arm of Francesco, when Mark was stuck dating a bandana-wearing rhinoceros who worshipped Eva Cassidy more than Imogen did the Virgin Mary. However, having heard close to nothing about the Kingston-*Man*drews (Cameron could be so witty) love affair in over half a month she had been able to repress thoughts of Mark, almost completely, and give herself over to the pleasurable task of enjoying the rest of the summer.

The signs that the summer idyll was coming to an end first began to show themselves on the fifteenth day of August, when the Feast of the Assumption rolled by and Imogen kept casting entreating glances to the statue of Mary during Mass, begging her to save Imogen from the disaster looming in the shape of the GCSE results. Imogen had a pathological revulsion towards punishment and she feared more than anything that her socializing schedule would be interrupted if her grades proved disastrous. When the congregation responded to the prayer that the Virgin should 'pray for us sinners, now and at the hour of our death,' Imogen crossed herself with the fervour of a sinner who seemed quite certain that death, or something much worse, was imminent.

◇◇◇

The morning of the results dawned one week later, with Imogen tapping her foot nervously on the floor of Meredith's closet as Meredith knelt round the corner praying in her own little corner of treasured religious *objéts*. There were no shrill, hysterical prayers like the ones which had been battering Heaven intermittently ever since Imogen had first been gripped by the fear of academic rustication; instead, Meredith simply prayed that the Queen of Heaven would not let the Queen of Malone fail her exams. Because that would be anti-beau.

Unlike Imogen, who degenerated into a kind of medieval mania of retrospective piety at the first sign of trouble, Cameron went into total emotional shutdown, to the point where he actually seemed to become more relaxed. At the same moment as Meredith and Imogen were leaving Malone Park to make their way down to school to collect their results, Cameron had gone off to play a game of morning tennis, serenely acting as if there was no earthly reason why he should be rushing towards school as soon as the gates opened.

It was therefore well after eleven-thirty when Cameron finally showed up at Mount Olivet Grammar, freshly showered and wearing a navy blue Austin Reed sweater and his favourite pair of jeans. A pale and nervous Kerry was sitting with Catherine on the low brick wall outside the front entrance of the school. Catherine was clutching her results slips in one hand and had another wrapped around Kerry, who was mumbling distractedly to herself.

'Hello, ladies.'

'*Emergencia*!' squeaked Kerry, grasping at his hand from where she sat.

'What's wrong?'

'I can't go in there!' she muttered. 'I told my Dad I'd been predicted all As and Bs. And I definitely wasn't.'

'Kerry, why would you do that? It's only going to make him angrier when you... well, when you really don't get all As and Bs.'

'I know that! I know that now, Cameron. But, well, at the time it was just so much easier to tell him that. It made him buy me presents. Like this delightful ring from Swarovski. *J'adore.*'

'It's very pretty,' comforted Cameron, sitting down next to her.

'I bet if you go in you'll do so much better than you think, baby cakes,' said Catherine, rubbing Kerry's shoulder.

Even in the depths of her terror, Kerry could not possibly let Catherine get away with trying to make the hideous nickname of "baby cakes" catch on. She shrugged her shoulders aggressively, throwing off Catherine's hand. 'No, I won't!' she barked. 'And there's no point trying to lie to me about it now. I'm dead.'

'What did you get, Catherine?'

'Two As, four Bs and four Cs,' she beamed. 'I'm so surprised.'

'That's really good,' Cameron said. 'Congratulations and stuff.'

'Thanks! I was like literally three points off failing in English Lit, but I got As in Art and Home Ec, so I'm really pleased. Orla did really well with her results, so I was really hoping I wouldn't be, like, the retard in the family.'

Kerry swivelled to fix Catherine with a poisonous stare. 'Retard? Retard! That is a *very* offensive word, Catherine. No wonder you practically failed English.'

'I got a B in English Language and I didn't mean it that way.'

'You are so racist.'

Cameron stood up. 'Right, come on, princess, we'll go in together.'

Two tears instantly trickled down Kerry's face. 'Cameron, I have never felt fear like this. Not even when I thought my proud gay colourist Patrick had accidentally dyed my hair ginger.'

'Let's go. See you later, Catherine. And congratulations again.'

Kerry linked arms with Cameron and hobbled fearfully into school, staring as some of her classmates sped past seeking out abandoned corners of the school corridors to open their envelopes in private. Two of the Christian Union girls ran by, holding hands and breathing in a sort of faux-panicked way that only people who are secretly pretty sure that they are going to get all As can produce.

Imogen was standing by the results board, texting Freddie and looking considerably cheerier than she had in Meredith's closet earlier that morning.

'Well?' asked Cameron.

'Not too bad,' she shrugged. 'I failed Physics, but I'm not ugly so I don't really want to be good at science.'

'You passed everything else?' Kerry said, blanching.

'Yeah. Two A stars, two As, two Bs, three Cs and the Physics failure, obvi.'

'What did you get A stars in?' asked Kerry, in a voice so incredulous it bordered on rude.

'English Lit and Italian. Cameron, go in and check what you got in Latin. I'm dying to see how somebody else did.'

'Why didn't you just ask Daniel? I saw him standing back there by the vending machines.'

'I can't ask Fat Daniel a question! You know he smells like cheese,' exclaimed Imogen.

'Fairzies. Right, I'm going to go to the cloaks and then I'll see you in the foyer.'

Imogen looped her arms through Kerry's and began frog marching her in the direction of the school office. 'Come on, Kerry. We'll get yours together! I want to see what you got in Physics.'

As a weakened Kerry was hauled into the office by Imogen's forceful nosiness, Cameron began walking towards the boys' cloakroom. He passed the school academic notice board and checked under the Hs: -

>HARPER, Meredith Elisabeth Anne
>HARRIS, Patricia Jayne
>HARRISON, Kyle Ryan James
>HARTMAN, Blake Joshua Elijah

Cameron felt a tightness in his chest at the thought that Blake might be back in school today and maybe explain where he had been all summer. His eyes ran quickly across the board, doing a swift grade count and hoping that Meredith or Imogen didn't arrive to catch him pathetically checking on Blake's scores. Three A stars, five As and two Bs. Not too bad at all. In fact, quite impressive.

'Hey, Cameron.'

Cameron spun round at the unexpected sound of a female voice behind him. His shock did not dissipate when he discovered himself standing face to face with Coral Andrews. She looked confident and happy today – even pretty, he conceded reluctantly. And she was smiling at him with a honey-sweet grin that made Cameron want to vomit directly on her – sweet Jesus – were those flip flops?

'Hello, Coral.'

'Cameron, could we talk really quickly? I know you're really busy, but it'll only take a minute.'

'I can't think of a single reason why not.'

'We haven't really had a chance to talk properly since Mark and I started dating and I know you and him are really close and that you and I haven't always gotten on the best.' She was still smiling at him as Cameron wondered where this disgusting little speech was going. 'But I just want you to know that, from my side of things, I never had a problem with you and I think the whole thing was just a misunderstanding, by both of us. Mark thinks you're great and so I'd really like for us to be able to get along.'

Cameron's face seemed interested in everything Coral said, but inside he was regarding her with a new level of detestation. He had to give her kudos for her strategy, because now if he didn't agree with her she would be able to go crying to Mark about how mean and unreasonable Cameron had been. Alright then. If that's how she wanted to play it, Cameron would play along. And win. He knew ways of being fake that this gag reflex inducing hipster hadn't even dreamed of.

'I'd really like that too, Coral. And thank you so much for making the first move. I'm terrible at things like that.'

Coral beamed and wrapped Cameron in a hug that he would shudder at the memory of until the end of his days, but for now he kept smiling and returned her embrace. Just in time to hear Mark's delighted voice from down the corridor.

'Hello, you two!'

Coral and Cameron ended their hug and turned to face Mark, with false smiles painted on to both their faces. Mark looked both perplexed and ecstatic at what he was seeing. He put his arm around Coral's waist, pulling her in towards him, and grinned at Cameron as if he was Santa Claus, Jesus and Willy Wonka all rolled into one. Peter and Stewart walked up after him, with Peter casting a disapproving glance at Coral from behind her back.

'How'd you do?' asked Mark, still happier than Cameron could remember seeing him at any point in the last two years. 'Cam?'

'I haven't checked yet. I had to talk Kerry off a ledge and then I was on my way to the bathroom.'

'Oh, I'm sorry,' gasped Coral. 'I didn't mean to interrupt! I didn't know you still hadn't gotten your results yet. I just wanted us to have a chat for a bit, you know, just the two of us.'

Mark kissed her on the forehead and Cameron reached out his hand to wrap it affectionately around Coral's wrist. 'No!' he enthused. 'Don't apologize. I wasn't in any rush, Coral, and it was so good bumping into you.'

'Awh, thanks, Cameron.'

Meredith appeared next to this unlikely group, with her Birkin slung over her arm. She did not speak initially, but glanced down at Cameron's hand on Coral's wrist quizzically. Cameron smiled blandly and removed his hand. Meredith's eyes moved up and down over Coral's form, still pressed against Mark's. She spotted the flip flops and her lips curved maliciously. Peter was struggling to keep a powerfully amused grin under wraps and in their shared hatred for Coral, he appreciated anew just how completely Meredith Harper could dominate a group, even by saying absolutely nothing at all.

'Have you got your results yet?' she asked Cameron, ignoring the others.

'No, not yet,' he said with a shrug. 'You?'

'Yes. Four A stars, two As, three Bs and a C.'

'Physics?'

'Obviously.'

'Congratulations, Meredith,' Stewart said. 'That's really well done.'

'Thank you,' she smiled. 'How did you two guys do?'

'Well, I thought I'd done pretty well with four A stars, four As, two Bs and a C,' Stewart joked, before cuffing Peter round the shoulder. 'But then Pete pulled out nine A stars and two As.'

Coral and Cameron both turned to stare at Peter in undisguised shock that the Lord of Lager had done so astonishingly well. Meredith, however, seemed unfazed and laughed. 'Congratulations, Peter. You are a dark horse.'

Peter winked at her. 'You know me, Meredith.'

Mark felt a stab of jealousy deep in his gut, as he remembered Peter's defence of Meredith back at the start of summer. Now she was being as close to flirtatious as he had ever seen her with anyone who wasn't Cameron. He tightened his grip around Coral's waist, possessively drawing her closer towards him. Meredith and Peter's little moment was broken by the dramatic arrival of Kerry into the circle, barging past Meredith and hurling herself into Cameron's arms.

'*Emergencia*,' she sobbed. '*Emergencia*!'

'What's wrong?' he asked, patting her hair gently.

'Things didn't quite go as well as her lie to her father may have implied,' explained Imogen, sauntering up behind Meredith. 'Still, I don't know why she's crying so hard, she only failed one subject and it was Physics.'

'That doesn't even count, Kerry,' said Meredith.

'I got five Cs!' Kerry cried into Cameron's shoulder. 'What am I going to tell my father?'

'Tell him you passed nine subjects,' advised Imogen. 'That's how I'm going to spin it to Edgar.'

'Ten!' snapped Kerry. 'I passed ten.'

'But you failed one.'

'Yes! I was taking eleven. I was taking Ad Maths.'

Imogen and Meredith both did a double take. 'You were taking *what*?'

'Ad Maths. I got an A star in Maths when I took it a year early,' Kerry explained tearfully, as Cameron hoped she didn't cry too hard into his Austin Reed.

'You're good at Maths?' Imogen asked in disgust.

'Very!'

'That's embarrassing.'

'Kerry, I think your results are great,' said Coral. 'Congratulations.'

Mark nodded. 'Yeah, Kerry, well done.'

Kerry turned round from her place on Cameron's shoulder, belatedly realizing that she was standing in a circle with Coral Andrews. Her face was all at once a fusion of self-pity, confusion, impatience and loathing. She opened her mouth to say something, before changing her mind and burying herself once again in Cameron's chest.

'Why!'

'There, there, princess.'

'Sweetie, you really don't need to worry. You passed ten GCSEs and took Maths a year early. I'm sure Paul will be pleased.'

Cameron gingerly passed Kerry over into Imogen's arms. 'I really need to go to the bathroom. I'll meet you guys in like ten minutes.'

'I'll come with you,' Mark said, kissing Coral goodbye on the lips and waving to the others.

The moment he was out of earshot, Meredith stared pointedly at Coral's feet. 'Nice sandals, Coral. When's Moses coming to lead you to Israel?'

'Say all you want, Meredith. Your poison just washes right over me.'

'I'm surprised to hear you even know what washing is, Coral, but okay.'

Stewart cleared his throat. 'Ladies.'

'You're right we should go,' announced Meredith. 'See you boys tonight and, Coral, best of luck with crossing the Red Sea later.'

As Meredith, Imogen and a still-shaking Kerry sailed off in the opposite direction, Coral turned to Stewart and Peter in disgust. 'Can you believe that?'

'Aw, don't worry, Coral,' Peter smiled. 'I think your Jesus sandals are dead nice.'

◇◇◇

'Cam, thank you so much for making the effort with Coral,' Mark said, as he washed his hand in the boys' bathroom. 'I really appreciate it.'

'No problem.'

'Honestly, I didn't realize what a pain it must have been for you all that time Meredith and I hated each other until I started going out with Coral and kept worrying that you two wouldn't get along.'

'Well, I don't exactly love the way she behaves, but I know that she's in your life and since she's important to you, it just makes more sense that we get on,' Cameron said, whilst gleefully imagining how much fun it would be to kidnap Coral and leave her on a deserted island. Bet the filthy little Bolshevik wouldn't love nature so much then, would she?

'Right. I get that. That's exactly how I feel about Meredith.'

'I don't feel about Coral the way you feel about Meredith,' Cameron teased. 'I have no self-loathing desire to get inside her, uhm, I'm guessing... lady boxers?'

'Cameron, stop that. C'mon. I hate when you do this. There's no point in me even denying that I fancy Meredith anymore, since you don't believe me when I do.'

'No, I don't.'

'And Coral doesn't wear lady boxers.'

Please dear God don't let me vomit right here and now, Cameron prayed silently. *If he tells me what kind of underwear she actually squeezes her tree-hugging thighs into, I just want to be allowed to instantly die before I get the mental image.*

'Cool,' Cameron shrugged. 'Right, I can't put this off any longer. I need to go get these results.'

The two boys walked out of the bathroom and made their way towards the school office, passing a devastated looking girl who neither of them knew well enough to talk to. Mark smiled in what he hoped was a comforting manner; Cameron, discomfited by public displays of intense feeling from anybody who wasn't Kerry, looked through her as if he couldn't see or hear her snivelling.

'Good luck,' Mark said. 'Do you want me to come in with you?'

'No, I'll be fine. Thanks, though.'

Cameron edged his way into the results office, receiving a loathe-filled glare from Callum Quigley, an aesthetically-challenged boy in Cameron's school house who had been best friends with Coral Andrews in junior school and had loyally nurtured a cantankerous hatred of Cameron ever since.

'Cameron Matthews, Stormont, please,' he said to one of the office ladies, giving his name and house.

'Here we are, dear. Good luck.'

'Hope you didn't fail too many,' Callum said, as he walked by.

'You mean like you did at life?' Cameron shot back, before turning his attention to his results slip.

MATTHEWS, Cameron Robert (12S)

School House: Stormont
Form Teacher: S. Vaughn

History	A*
Religious Studies	A*
Drama	A*
Latin	A*
English Literature	A
English Language	A
French	A
Biology	C
Mathematics	C
Physics	C

'What did you get?' whispered a tear-stained Kerry, now standing in front of him with Imogen and Meredith at her side.

'I didn't fail any!' Cameron said disbelievingly. 'I was one mark off a D in Physics, though.'

'Oh how nice for you!' Kerry hissed.

'Oh my god, there was coursework for Maths,' Cameron realized, reading the section of the results sheet where he saw a "0" marked for submitted coursework.

'I know,' Imogen nodded. 'Surprise-o-rama.'

'I can't believe we didn't know you sat Maths a year early, Kerry,' Meredith said.

'And I can't believe Cameron didn't fail *any*! You must have been a secret reviser. You secretly revised, you evil little witch. Do you not remember the rules? If the ship is sinking, we all drown together.'

'Kerry, I really didn't revise,' he answered truthfully. 'I did a little bit of work for the subjects I like, but that's about it.'

'What did you get overall?' Imogen asked. 'What did you get in Latin?'

'Four A stars, three As and three Cs,' he counted. 'A star in Latin.'

Kerry reached up, snatched the results slip out of Cameron's hands, hurled it on to the floor and then burst into tears on Imogen's shoulders.

'There, there,' Imogen soothed. 'At least you're pretty.'

'I know!' sobbed Kerry. 'I know!'

◇◇◇

'Oh, darling, I'm sure Daddy's bound to be thrilled with the A stars eventually. And it's not as if you were ever going to really use Physics, is it? I'm sure once he's calmed down, he'll realize just how unreasonable he's being.'

'Mummy, he needs to understand that a C is a pass! I didn't "fail" Maths, Latin and Biology. I *passed* them.'

Clarissa Dawson nodded. 'I know, darling, I know. And Daddy will too, at some point. It's just that he puts such a lot of stock in things like grades and results and books.'

'I got good grades!'

'Oh absolutely, darling. Of course you did. I mean, two A stars. Gosh, it's just tremendous! And what were they in again, angel?'

'English Lit and Italian.'

'You see! All those summers on Lake Como when you were a baby really *did* pay off!'

Imogen stared stonily out the passenger window, still fuming at her father's decision to focus solely on the lower end of her results. Clarissa glanced over nervously at her only daughter and sighed. Sometimes Edgar really did take his zeal for academic excellence too far. Considering that she had been using some of her textbooks to stabilize the leg of her dressing table for the last six months, Imogen really had done very well –

apart from the blip in Physics and less-than-impressive pass grades in Mathematics, Biology and Latin, but it wasn't as if everybody was going to be able to replicate Edgar's own uniformly excellent school-era grades, was it? Imogen had a very busy social life; she wasn't going to be able to spend her whole life locked up in a library studying, like an unattractive child could. Clarissa Dawson had always lived with a terrible fear that one day she would birth a geek and so she was profoundly grateful that Imogen was as far from geek-chic as it was humanly possible to be. Edgar just didn't understand that there was more than one type of education and Imogen was excelling in the all-important arena of life skills. Or rather, social skills, which in Clarissa Dawson's mind amounted to the same thing. She felt a sudden surge of indulgent affection for her only daughter and reached out to squeeze her hand.

'Oh, darling, don't worry about it. Daddy can be so silly when he wants to be. Why don't we leave the clothes for Africa off at Saint Ignatius's and then go and buy you a special little treat for doing so well today? Won't that be fun?'

Imogen softened at the news that the first of her post-exams treats would be coming her way and without her father around to check their spending, she was fairly certain that this would mean a new pair of Louboutins or Jimmy Choos. 'Thank you, Mummy!'

Clarissa smiled and flipped the car indicator. 'I just want to nip in and deposit this cheque, darling, before I forget, alright?'

'Yes, Mummy.'

Clarissa and Imogen drove into a small shopping area in the town of Carryduff, six miles outside Belfast. There was a bank, a few shops and restaurants.

'Mummy, can I please run and grab a Diet Coke while you're in the bank?'

'Of course, sweetie,' Clarissa said, handing her a £10 note. 'Grab me an elderflower cordial or something, if they have it.'

Imogen sprung out of the car and walked over to the nearby shop. A few people of about the same age as her were standing inside, talking about their plans for the night and how everyone had fared in their GCSEs. Every club in Northern Ireland was going to be packed to the gills with students and Imogen was therefore relieved to be going to Cecilia Molyneux's house party instead – Cecilia's very last as an official Mount Olivet girl (MOG). As of next month, the former president of the school's Social Committee would be a student of Manchester Metropolitan University. Imogen mentally shuddered at the thought of her own graduation from Mount Olivet, almost exactly two years away and a terrifying prospect when dwelt upon. She lifted a small bottle of Diet Coke from the drinks refrigerator and looked around for anything with elderflower in it for her mother.

'Imogen?'

'Blake?'

Blake Hartman was standing next to her with a nervous smile on his face and a can of Sprite in his left hand. 'How have you been?'

'Fine,' Imogen answered, still in the grip of shock. 'Fine. You're back.'

'Yeah. Yeah. I got back yesterday.'

Imogen nodded, but she kept staring at him in bewilderment. 'Where have you been?'

'I went back to America for a bit to see my Mom. I hadn't really seen her since last summer and she needed help with moving house. Plus, I wanted to clear my head after breaking up with Catherine. I don't know if you heard about that?'

'Oh, I heard. She cried all the way to Mexico.'

Blake looked uncomfortable. 'Really? I'm sorry to hear that. It was just the right thing to do at the time. Is she okay now? '

'Yes, yes.'

'Good... Hey, uhm, how's Cameron?'

At that question, years of clique etiquette belatedly kicked in and Imogen remembered what she was supposed to do in such situations. She had to make sure that everyone outside the group knew that everything inside it was fabulous in every conceivable way. 'He's great,' she enthused. 'Absolutely fantastic, actually. So jealous of how well he tanned when we were out in Mexico and now he's just done so super-well with his results, too. Also, don't tell anyone I told you, but I think he's fallen in love.'

'Oh?'

'Yes! I really can't tell you who, but it's someone we met out in Mexico.'

Blake's jaw clenched. 'What's his name?'

Imogen pretended to look surprised and lowered her voice to a whisper. 'Oh my gosh, you know that Cameron's gay? Seriously, Blake, right now, that is *so* hush-hush. But, okay, since you already know, I can tell you. His name's Sasha Montmorency, Anastasia's brother. He's just graduated from Winchester, which is like this super-expensive private school in England and he lives up at Helen's Bay. You know, in that big mansion by the waterfront? I think you came there a few times with us when you were dating Catherine? Anyway, you *can't* tell anyone I told you that, because not a lot of people know, but honestly if you could have seen the two of them in Mexico... Seriously, Blake, they're so hot together, it's unreal. Like, I think Cameron may have found *the* most perfect guy in the world. And they're just so sexy together, you know?'

'Right. Okay. That's cool. It was nice seeing you again, Imogen.'

'You too, Blake. See you in September?'

Blake nodded and turned away. 'Sure. Have a great summer.'

◇◇◇

One hour and eight minutes later, Imogen burst into Meredith's bedroom with a bag containing her new Alexander McQueen clutch dangling from her right arm. Meredith was sitting on her sofa, flicking idly through the pages of *Vogue* and wondering what to wear to Cecilia's party.

'What?'

'Blake Hartman is back. I ran into him in the Spar in Carryduff and he's back. I mean, he's back-back. Back-to-school-with-us-in-September-back.'

'You're positive?'

'Yes. As he was leaving, I said "See you in September?" And he said, "Sure."'

Meredith stood up and began pacing. 'Why is he back?'

'I have no idea. He gave me some bullshit story about being in America to help his mother move house and to get away from Catherine...'

'Well, that bit might be true.'

'And then he asked how Cameron was.'

Meredith stopped and spun towards Imogen, with a very dangerous look on her face. 'And what did you say?'

'I told him that Cameron was thin, tanned, happy and that he might be about to start dating Sasha Montmorency. Blake looked like he was about to punch the display area.'

'Imogen! Sasha is definitely not gay. When are you going to realize that Kerry's gaydar is almost as bad as Catherine's?'

'Okay, first of all, nobody as pretty as Sasha can be completely straight and secondly, even if he is, who cares? Blake's never going to know that! All I wanted to do was to make sure that he knows Cameron is doing fine without him. Better than fine. Although weirdly Blake was the one that brought up the subject of Cameron being gay and I never thought he'd do that – due to him himself being the single most embarrassing closet case in history.'

'He brought it up?'

'I said Cameron was seeing someone and Blake asked "What's *his* name?"'

Meredith swallowed. 'That's interesting.'

'What are we going to do?'

Meredith walked around the room slowly for a minute, trying to take stock of the situation. This news was potentially much worse for her than it was for Imogen; Imogen, after all, knew nothing about Blake's letter to Cameron or Meredith's decision to withhold it from him. The only way she could ever have gotten away with it completely was if Blake had stayed in America and obeyed her in never contacting Cameron again. Now, he was back and the only ray of hope was that Imogen's lie about Cameron and Sasha might finally have finished off any hope Blake still had for initiating a reconciliation. The last thing Cameron needed was to be sucked back into the unique vortex of emotional dysfunction created by Blake Hartman.

'I don't know,' Meredith admitted. 'I need a moment to think.'

'You know what we have to do, don't you?' Imogen asked.

'What?'

'I need to get slightly emotional in order to explain this...'

'Gross.'

'No, I know, but listen. Last year, when the whole Cameron-Blake-Catherine thing was in full-swing, I started thinking about how all of our lives had ended up in such a complete mess and it's basically because we got too clever for our own goods and in the process became too stupid.'

Meredith sat next to Imogen. 'Explain.'

'We never used to lie to each other. Everybody else, yes; each other, no. And that's what went wrong last year. We were all so busy lying to each other that when things turned to disaster, we had no idea who to talk to.'

'So you think we should just tell Cameron everything?'

'I don't know,' Imogen admitted. 'All I know is that before we decide what to do, *we* should decide what to do.'

'Pardon?'

'Kerry. You and her have basically been working against each other for the best part of a year and look where it's got us: four failed relationships, a mental breakdown, three broken hearts and somebody actually fleeing the country to get away from us. I'm worried if we don't stop now we're going to end up in prison. We need to include her again. If you want to make sure she doesn't accidentally end up discovering something that could destroy everybody's friendship then she needs to know exactly what's going on, all the time. That way she's keeping the secrets, not trying to uncover them.'

'You always overestimate her, Imogen.'

'Do I? In the space of six months, she managed to deliberately out Cameron to me, accidentally out him to Mark, nearly annihilate our friendship, accuse my ex-boyfriend of being a sex addict and she did all of that while still managing to find time to nap for two hours every afternoon, party every weekend, drink like a sailor and have one epic FIB! She is *very* dangerous when left to her own devices, Meredith. And you know I'm right.'

◇◇◇

Kerry arrived forty-five minutes later, wearing her white Max Azria party dress and carrying her pink overnight bag. Her curls were immaculate and Imogen could tell that since leaving school six hours earlier, Kerry must have spent at least four of them scrubbing, exfoliating, styling, hair spraying and waxing to achieve the "naturally pretty" look she was currently sporting for Cecilia's results night party.

'I'm not getting any presents for my exams!' she cried, by way of a greeting. 'Paul was *very* angry. He said he had a worthless workshy for a daughter and I got confused and told him it wasn't my fault I didn't have enough confidence in myself. I can't wait until he goes back to Argentina to live with his stupid old cows. I bet he never yells at them!'

It was at that point that Kerry noticed three glasses and a chilled bottle of rosé champagne on Meredith's coffee table. Sitting next to it were her favourite chocolates and a bowl of strawberries, with sugar and cream helpfully arranged on two nearby saucers. All of her favourite things conveniently lined up in a row.

'What have you two done?' she asked fearfully.

Imogen and Meredith, who had been standing on either side of the coffee table, exchanged a look. Imogen walked over to Kerry and guided her on to the sofa. Kerry's eyes were alive with paranoia and her mouth was hanging open stupidly as she was steered into her seat.

'Oh my god, you've killed someone, haven't you?' she whispered. 'Catherine?'

'We haven't killed anyone yet,' explained Imogen, 'but Meredith has something she would like to tell you.'

Hearing that Meredith was the chief culprit, Kerry seemed to become even more alarmed and turned to stare at the waif-like brunette in awestruck panic. Meredith cleared her throat. 'Yes, I do and don't interrupt me unless you absolutely cannot help yourself, okay? I am aware that you may want to say "I told you so" or "I knew it!" and we have agreed that you are allowed a *maximum* of three throughout this entire story. Agreed?'

'Fine.'

Meredith exhaled. 'Right. Well, do you remember when…'

'I'm sorry, but am I going to get any of that champagne?' Kerry asked, staring pointedly at the empty glass in front of her. Imogen groaned and reached forward to pour the drinks. 'Pass the strawberries too, please.'

'You don't really understand the point of not interrupting, do you, Kerry?' Meredith asked.

'No, not really,' she admitted, dunking a strawberry into the sugar bowl and swirling it around. 'I'll try harder next time, I promise.'

'Do you remember when you thought that it was me who had invited Michael the Immaculate Heart Molester to Cameron's birthday party and destroyed Imogen's torn-between-two-lovers dating plan?'

Kerry attempted to look innocent. 'Did I? I don't remember that.'

'Yes, you did,' replied Meredith. 'Cameron told me.'

'That treacherous he-beast!'

'I panicked because I knew you were going to tell Imogen and since we had no idea who it was who *actually* invited Michael the Immaculate Heart Pervert, I thought it would be better for all concerned if someone took the blame for it so we could all move on. Someone other than me, obviously. When we were in Dublin in December, Cameron told me about him and Blake's first kiss, so I took Catherine out to lunch, basically threatened to tell people that she was dating a closeted gay guy and then threw in the offer to include her on the group holiday to Mexico...'

'If she would tell us she invited him and not you?' Kerry finished.

'Yes,' said Meredith. 'Which she did, because she's weak and pathetic.'

'Wait!' interrupted Kerry. 'When was this?'

'February,' Meredith answered. 'The week after Saint Valentine's Day.'

'She knew since February?' Kerry gasped. 'She knew in February and she kept dating him?'

Imogen nodded. 'Tragic, we know.'

'But if she didn't invite Michael to the party, then who did?'

Meredith shrugged. 'We don't know. He might just have been making up the fact that he got an invite...'

'Or it could actually have been Catherine,' Imogen interjected. 'She might have realized that Meredith's offer was the perfect way to get herself out of ever getting properly caught. If you get what I mean?'

'Right. Anyway,' said Meredith, hastily resuming her story before anyone noticed the gaping hole in Imogen's logic, 'Catherine agreed to say that she was the one who had invited him and you two bullied her for a couple of weeks, then forgot about it. So my plan worked. I think we all seem to keep forgetting that it worked. Originally. Until I realized that Cameron was not exactly dealing with it as well as I'd hoped...'

'Nervous breakdown times, abú,' supplemented Imogen.

'Exactly. That's when Imogen and I decided to persuade Catherine to break up with him in the only way we could: secret sabotage.'

'That thing on Sports Day!' Kerry exclaimed. 'When you said Blake was weird, but you couldn't quite put your finger on what it was that made him weird. I *knew* that was something! I am always right.'

'Yes, well, again, it looked like it was working, until the morning after the ball when Blake unexpectedly dumped Catherine and fled Belfast,' finished Meredith. 'Which was fine, because at least it meant they were finished, but now he's back in Belfast. Yes, he's back! Imogen saw him in Carryduff this afternoon and he's back. As in, back permanently. Starting back to school in September. Back. And the thing is, he now knows that Catherine knew since February and…'

'You're worried he's going to tell Cameron, aren't you?' said Kerry, smugly. 'What a mess. This is not fabulous, ladies. Not fabulous.'

'That's not all,' said Meredith.

'It isn't?' asked a surprised Imogen.

'There's a letter.'

'What kind of letter?' Kerry barked. 'From who?'

'From Blake to Cameron.'

'I didn't know about this!' Imogen roared.

'Hurts, doesn't it?' taunted Kerry.

'What does this bollocking letter say?'

'Oh, the usual,' said Meredith contemptuously. '"I love you," "please forgive me," "I'm sorry."'

'How did you get it?' Imogen asked.

'I ran into Blake the day before we went to Mexico and he gave it to me and asked me to give it to Cameron for him.'

'Well, that was moronic,' said Imogen, rolling her eyes.

'Then I e-mailed Blake and told him I'd given it to Cameron and Cameron never wanted to see him again,' finished Meredith.

A stunned silence greeted Meredith's latest and final revelation. After a few seconds, Imogen spoke, 'My God, Meredith. You are on fire.'

'Fires of stupidity,' she said ruefully, sitting down in the armchair. 'I didn't think he'd come back and now I have literally no idea what to do next.'

'Well, well, well,' sighed Kerry, a supremely triumphant expression lighting up her face. 'After six long months, you've finally remembered the group's number one rule.'

'"Me no likey prison?"' Imogen prompted.

'No!' snapped Kerry. 'Safety in numbers. Our lives are far too complicated and fabulous for us to keep things to ourselves. If you're doing something bad, you have to get all your friends to do it as well. That way, everybody is everybody else's alibi and if we get caught, the blame gets evenly spread and we can make hilarious jokes about it later. Can I have some more champagne, please? We do *not* do things on our own!'

'I do feel better for having finally gotten all that off my chest,' admitted Meredith.

'Of course you do!' Kerry proclaimed.

'But what are we going to do about Blake?' Imogen asked. 'If he runs into Cameron, he's going to say something about the letter or the e-mail and then…'

Kerry's hand shot up into the air, as if she were asking a question in class. 'Can I say something, please? I would just like to say that I am bored by all this. I am bored by Blake Hartman and this whole stupid, boring mess. For the last three months, all we have done is talk and think about him, which is ridiculous. Blake

Hartman is not fabulous! He is not even out and proud. He is dull, uninteresting, closeted and I hate him. Yes, I've decided. I hate him. Look at us! It's results night and we're sitting around talking about some randomer who we haven't seen for the whole summer and who, let's face it, is basically a glorified B Lister. So what if he's written some stupid letter to Cameron? Too little, too late! It's not going to change what he did and it's not going to change the fact that he's a prick, is it? Oh ladies, what happened to us? Since when did we start caring about things like truth and feelings? We used to care about things like parties. And hair! I miss the days when the biggest thing we had to discuss was what shoes went with what outfit and what level a Fabulous Induced Breakdown had to reach before you should start stirring rescue remedy into your cereal! I vote we get rid of this Blake Hartman fiasco once.'

'How do we get rid of it?' asked Imogen. 'He's back!'

'Cameron is not going to end up with someone like Blake,' Kerry ruled. 'He's going to end up with someone like Sasha. I say that we shouldn't give him the stupid letter and if he ever does somehow find out about it, hopefully enough time will have gone by that he won't care that much and if he does still care, then we'll just tell him that Meredith didn't want to give it to him before the holiday in case it ruined Mexico for him. Then she forgot about it when we got back.'

'He won't believe that,' objected Meredith.

'He doesn't have to believe it,' retorted Kerry. 'He just has to pretend to. Let's be honest, it's not as if Cameron wouldn't do the same thing to any of us if he was in our position. If we mention this letter and everything going back to you blackmailing Catherine in February, then we're just going to have to spend another three months talking about Blake "sad face" Hartman. And I'm sick of it! I had to listen to Catherine talk about him all the way to Mexico and Cameron talk about him all the time we were *in* Mexico. All because you two didn't include me in the loop! I have to be included. If we're going to be lying bitches, we may as well do it together.'

'Cameron doesn't really like making the first move,' Meredith mused. 'It's unlikely he'll even get into a conversation with Blake, actually.'

'Exactly!' said Kerry. 'Exactly. From now on, we don't say anything and we don't do anything, unless we absolutely have to. Blake Hartman is dead to us. Do you hear me? Dead. Sometimes the best policy is the simplest. Do nothing and hope for the best. I mean, it's not as if Blake will initiate contact with Cameron. If he was going to, he'd have done it by now. We're fine. We just have to hope and pray that *if* they do ever talk again, it'll be way too far in the future for them to fix things. Blake Hartman is not a threat to us and we have to stop thinking as if he is.'

'He's not even really that good looking, is he?' Meredith asked.

'No, not at all,' Kerry lied, with great enthusiasm. 'We're saving Cameron from a relationship with an overly-tall B Lister with weird fingernails.'

'He is quite tall, isn't he?' nodded Meredith.

'Freak,' said Imogen, in disgust.

'This is a delightful plan, Kerry,' congratulated Meredith. 'Do nothing. Simple and delightful. Like a Chanel jacket.'

'Ladies, we are now re-entering an age of fabulousness,' said Kerry, caressing the air with her hands. 'Nothing and no one is getting in the way of our merriment ever again. Agreed?'

'Agreed,' nodded the other two.

Kerry clapped her hands in a delighted gesture. 'We have to start getting ready now to baptize the Age of Fabulous. We'll probably need more champagne.'

Meredith leaped up from her seat. 'The Age of Fabulous. Well done, Kerry. Cute hair by the way.'

'Thanks. It took three hours and I had to let Padre stand next to me to continue his lecture about how I have the attention span of a fruit fly and the work ethic of a benefits fraudster, but it was totally worth it. They're the perfect curls to start the Age of Fabulous with. Perfect.'

◇◇◇

Imogen left Kerry and Meredith toasting the new AOF (Age of Fabulous) an hour later to cross the road back to her own house to get prepared for the party. She had selected a gorgeous green velvet Coco Fennell backless cocktail dress and she just hoped her mother had picked it up from the dry cleaners in time for the festivities. Half-way through her preparations, when she had finished her make up but hadn't changed into the dress yet, her brother Christopher's voice hollered upstairs. 'Imogen! Imogen!'

'What?' she screamed, sticking her head out the door. 'Christopher! What is it?'

'Stewart's here to see you.'

Imogen bit her lip in confused worry. This was certainly unexpected. Why was Stewart here? Maybe he had come over to yell at her about Freddie? Either that or ask her to be his girlfriend again. Jealousy could make people do crazy things. But was it crazy? Maybe dating Stewart Lawrence for a second time wouldn't be such a bad idea? Admittedly, it would necessitate a potentially awkward break up with Freddie a mere two weeks after they had started dating, but if push came to shove, she would much rather have Stewart than Freddie. Stewart may not be as pretty-handsome as Freddie was, but he was more rugged and more manly. Also, Stewart had been the first and only man she had ever had sex with. Obviously that had to count for something – more than something, because the idea of letting just anybody do that to her made Imogen's skin crawl. She was an empress amongst women and must be treated as such.

She had been very happy with Stewart for most of the year that they had been together and he had been nothing but a gentleman considering how appallingly she had treated him in the end. Maybe, given a second chance at their love affair, Imogen could make amends for the awful thing she had done by cheating on him with Michael the Loathsome Immaculate Heart Relationship Destroyer? It would soothe her conscience and help restore her still-fragile relationship with the First XVs. Finally, she knew that it was statistically unlikely that she would ever find someone as good looking, supportive and kind as Stewart. Certainly not all in the same boy.

Yes, now that she thought about it, if Stewart had come round to try and win her back – and, let's face it, what other possible reason could there be for him to turn up unannounced on her doorstep for the first time in nine months? – then it might just be a very good idea indeed. A wonderful one, in fact. She would need to put on a necessary token show of resistance about ending things with Freddie so abruptly, but eventually, with an emotion-laden sigh and perhaps a few unshed tears brimming beguilingly in her eyes, she would say yes to Stewart's romantic pleas. And make both of them very happy.

'Hey you,' she smiled, as she entered the sitting room where Christopher had left Stewart to wait. 'This is a lush surprise.'

'Hey. I hope I'm not interrupting preparations for tonight?'

'Don't be silly. You're never interrupting,' she said, hitting him playfully on the arm. 'Congratulations on your results, btw. V. impressive.'

'Thanks. I'm pretty pleased. Congratulations to you, too. I bet Edgar and Clarissa were happy?'

A dark look passed over Imogen's face. 'Edgar was a beast, Stewart. A savage beast. Sometimes I don't think he'll be happy until he has some ICT-loving heifer for a child. Anyway! What brings you here? You smell fantastic. Is that the cologne I bought you for your birthday?'

'Yeah, it is. Good memory, Gini! Can we sit for a minute?'

'Is something wrong?'

'No. Not really,' he smiled. 'It'll just be easier if we sit.'

Rapidly losing faith in the idea that Stewart had come to try and woo her back, Imogen sat nervously on the sofa. 'Is this about me and Freddie? Because I wanted to tell you about it, Stewart, but then I thought it would look like I was calling up to gloat, which is really not what it would have been at all…'

'No, it's not Freddie,' Stewart said. 'I'm not exactly over the moon about it, but he's a nice guy and I suppose we both had to start dating other people eventually. I wanted to tell you before I told anybody else and I'm not going to tell any of the guys until after tonight, because I don't want to make a big thing out of it, but I kind of felt like you had the right to know before they did.'

'Stewart, what it is?'

'I'm leaving. I'm transferring schools.'

'Say what?'

'I've already put my application in to take my A-Levels at Imperial and I'm pretty sure they're going to offer me a place.'

'Imperial Academy? As in the one two miles away? Why? What's the point? You're going to leave Mount Olivet to go two miles down the road?'

'Yes. I am,' he said, with a slightly sad smile that Imogen knew from long experience meant Stewart regretted any upset his decision had caused, but had nonetheless made up his mind.

'But you're on the rugby team,' she said helplessly. 'You can't go and play for Imperial. They're our biggest rivals. What are you going to do during the Schools' Cup Final? You'll be lynched.'

'I want to take Economics for A-Level and Mount Olivet doesn't offer it as a subject. Imperial does.'

Imogen's eyes had filled with tears. This was not the first time economics had ruined her plans. 'Stewart, you can't leave. Mount Olivet... it's the best. You know that! You can't leave. You just can't! I'm sorry, Stewart, but this is completely ridiculous. I've never heard of anything so stupid in all my life. Who on earth would want to leave our school? People are dying to get into it and you're just going to leave! It's absurd.'

Stewart remained calm and he was speaking to her in a voice which a patient parent might use to an obstreperous toddler. 'Imperial is a great school too...'

'It's not in Malone.'

'No, it isn't,' he grinned. 'But I'm not from there either, Imogen, remember? I really want to take Economics for A-Level and plus maybe it'd be nice to get a bit of a fresh start. I think this is the right decision for me.'

'You know that if you move school, you'll lose touch with pretty much everyone at Mount Olivet, Stewart.'

'That's not true.'

'Yes, it is. Everyone always says they're going to keep in touch, but if you leave you're not going to have anything in common with the boys anymore. You won't have any of the same in-jokes, you won't know what teachers they're talking about or what parties they're going to and you're going to have to start putting most of your energy into making friends with the socially dysfunctional mutants at Imperial and before you know it, you won't have spoken to Mark or Cameron or Peter or Alistair or Colin or any of the guys from the squad in ages. You may as well kiss goodbye to all of those friendships, Stewart.'

'I don't know that that's not going to happen,' he admitted, 'but I hope it won't. I've made up my mind and I wanted to tell you first, Imogen, because despite everything that happened back in December, you have without doubt been the most important person in my life at this school and I didn't want you to find out from anybody else. Please don't tell anyone until tomorrow. I want to be able to party tonight with the guys one last time as a proper Mount Olivet boy.'

'It's your decision, I suppose.'

Stewart patted his legs with both hands and then stood up. 'I should go and let you finish getting ready.'

'For everything I did... with Michael... I really am sorry, Stewart. It was very stupid and I regret it. Very much. But I don't think...'

'Imogen, don't worry about it. It's in the past.' He pulled her up by her hand and the two of them hugged. 'You and me... we really are fine.'

◇◇◇

For seven years, Cecilia Molyneux, Louise Mahaffy, Emily Rhys, Sarah-Jane Rogan and Olivia-Grace Wallace had been fixtures of the Mount Olivet social scene. Every queen bee has her own style for keeping the troops in line and since Cecilia was not exactly the brightest of women she hadn't been able to rely on Anastasia's chic venom or Meredith's manipulative brilliance to stay in control.

Instead, she had ruled by a policy best described as glamorous terrorism. There was no telling when Cecilia might find something offensive and fly off the deep end into a tantrum of epically vindictive proportions. It was this policy, coupled with her frequent parties, which had catapulted her into the position of her year's queen bee at the age of thirteen. Tonight, five years later, Cecilia's epic, fabulous, alcohol-soaked and hairspray-scented reign was coming to an end. These girls had known the names of every bouncer at every nightclub in Belfast, they had turned the tanning mitt into a more recognizable symbol at Mount Olivet than the Red Hand of Ulster and they had flirted shamelessly with any of the attractive male teachers under the age of thirty-five. Now, they and all their back-combing splendour were about to vanish from the corridors of Mount Olivet, never to return.

Cecilia's house at the north end of Malone was therefore buzzing for her last school house party, as everyone from the cool kids of the incoming fifth year to the it-girls and rugby boys of the outgoing Upper Sixth crowded in to see her out in style. The party itself went as well as Cecilia could have hoped. She had managed to settle several old scores, mainly with her ex-boyfriend when she vividly illustrated just how over their relationship she was by making out with Quentin Smith right in front of him. Since Quentin was technically in the year below Cecilia, Cecilia's most dependable friend and *de facto* publicist, Emily Rhys, had managed to spin the story of their hook up as a delightful example of the luscious Cecilia acquiring a toy boy. Two more of their posse, Olivia-Grace and Sarah-Jane, had decided to make out with each other, before Sarah-Jane curled up unconscious in the foetal position on Cecilia's bed.

Following the bombshell from Stewart, Imogen had been much more quiet than usual and quite brusque with Freddie, whose repeated questions about what was wrong only seemed to make her more irritable. Eventually, she ditched him and swanned off to another section of the party where her spirits were lifted by Peter's impression of a horny walrus, achieved by using two tampons he had stolen from Cecilia's bathroom for tusks. Full merriment was restored when Imogen was cornered by Lavinia and Mariella, who wanted to compliment her about her new dress.

Kerry, who had already explained the point but not the inspiration for the Age of Fabulous to Cameron, had taken to toasting it at any given moment and telling everyone around her that they too could participate in its magnificence, before inexplicably pointing to some poor girl from another school and slurring, 'Not you.' Cameron, who had been drinking like a trooper all evening, giggled wildly at this before deciding to take himself off on a little walk to explore the rest of the party; at some indeterminate point during this stroll, which he himself could neither pinpoint nor remember, he had apparently managed to suffer and recover from a complete nervous breakdown, as Kerry's text records showed the next morning.

> **CAMERON** (12:05 a.m.)
> Kerry, I don't know where I am. Where are you?
>
> ---
>
> **CAMERON** (12:08 a.m.)
> Kerry, seriously. I thinck i have a probnlem. Where are you!
>
> ---
>
> **CAMERON** (12:10 a.m.)
> Emergencia! Come get. me. I'm in a room.
>
> ---
>
> **CAMERON** (12:10 a.m.)
> In a room come get
>
> ---
>
> **CAMERON** (12:13 a.m.)
> SERIOUsly

CAMERON (12:15 a.m.)
Why wont you help me? Wereh are you? Kerry.
I need help. Something's wrong wir me.
xxxxxxxxxxxxxxxxxxxxxxxxxxxxxxxxxxxxxxxx

CAMERON (12:19 a.m.)
OMG! How much fun is this party!?!

After his walrus impression, Peter started making out with Tangela Henton-Worley in the linen cupboard, only to be interrupted by Kerry. Since Kerry had taken Peter as her plus one to the leavers' ball in June, she evidently thought he should subsequently have taken up life as a monk, since no other woman could ever compete with her. Taking in the sight of Peter's tongue down Tangela's throat, Kerry had gasped in melodramatic shock, clutched her heart and loudly whispered, 'Santa Maria!' Peter had broken the kiss and decided to take a swig from his bottle of beer before explaining. Unfortunately, that was the moment when Kerry decided to fling the door closed again, which slammed the bottle into Peter's tooth and chipped it. Peter, with a bruised lip and gums, still managed to milk the story for a few laughs twenty minutes later, while Kerry glared on furiously and drunkenly wondered why no one cared about the chip on her heart.

◇◇◇

Cecilia Molyneux's final party did not end until just after half-past five in the morning and as the sun was beginning to rise over Belfast, the outgoing queen bee lurched into the daylight to bid farewell to Meredith, Imogen, Cameron and Kerry, stepping over the topless body of Stephen Dryton, the First XVs' fullback, who had decided to take a nap on the lawn.

'Seriously, like oh my god you guys, seriously,' said Cecilia, shaking her head and putting on a pair of sunglasses. 'I cannot believe this is actually over and stuff. Like, I know it sounds totally spesh but I really like never thought I'd be leaving Mount Olivet. I thought I'd be a MOG forever.'

'Once a Mount Olivet Girl, always a Mount Olivet Girl,' comforted Imogen.

'Oh my god, you're so right, babes. Like, big up to all my girlies.'

Meredith, Imogen and Kerry dutifully lifted their right arms up to their chin and pumped the air slightly, with their hands bent back at a ninety degree angle and quietly said, 'Woo-woo.'

'Oh my god, I'm going to miss that *so* much,' sighed Cecilia. 'Like, what the fuck am I going to do with my time now that there's no one left to make fun of? Do you know what I mean?'

'Totally,' nodded Meredith. 'Maybe you'll find some ugly people in Manchester?'

'Do not let the freaks take over now that I'm gone. Oh! Seriously, you guys, you don't even know it until it's over, but school is like legitimately the best years of your life. It was just the best banter ever. Seriously – next stop: death. That's it. The whims are over. OMFG, I'm totally having a meltdown, you guys, I apologize.'

'Do not apologize,' Imogen said, as Kerry shook her head in agreement behind her. 'Just let it out, sweetie.'

'I just wish I had had more time, you know? I wish I'd drunk more and I really wish I'd flirted more with Dr O'Hare. He was so hot. And do you know what? I seriously wish I'd gone to more parties.'

◇◇◇

Second only to the agony of results day is the agony caused by the parent-teacher-student conferences which happen in the days immediately after it. For some, like Cameron, they were relatively straight forward, in that he and his parents simply had to confirm the AS-Level choices he had provisionally made the term before. Getting slightly carried away with the success of his GCSE results, apart from the science and mathematics he had conveniently airbrushed out of his memory, Cameron and his mother Caroline had both toyed with the idea of him sitting five AS-Levels, instead of four, before his father stepped in to insist that they both stop being so utterly ridiculous. In the end, Cameron went for History, Religious Studies, Theatre Studies and Latin, although there had been an agonized debate over whether he should choose English instead (or as well as, if Caroline Matthews had had her way).

For others, like Meredith and Imogen, who had been waiting to see which way the wind blew with their results, it involved altering some of their previous choices and refining others. Sitting on four A stars, two As, three Bs and a C, Meredith opted to carry on with History, English, French and Italian, whilst Imogen had gone for Italian, History of Art, Religious Studies and English. Blithely ignoring her father's death stares, Imogen had waved to various friends throughout the interview, miming for them to call her later. For those who lacked Imogen's brazenness, like Kerry Davison, the morning was a much less enjoyable process, particularly since she had not been able to dissuade her father Paul from coming along for a "chat" with her teachers.

'The first thing to say is that Kerry has great natural capacity,' Mr Courcy, a twenty-something teacher in the Maths department said, 'and we would very much like her to continue on with the subject.'

'Do you really think she's capable of pursuing it to A-Level?' Paul Davison asked bluntly. Sitting next to him, Kerry's lip quivered.

'Oh absolutely,' nodded Mr Courcy. 'She has an A star in Maths and an A in Additional Mathematics.

Which is extremely impressive. I would strongly recommend Maths for one of her choices, Mr and Mrs Davison.'

'Oh, that's fantastic. Isn't it, Kerry?'

Kerry ignored her mother and glanced up at her father, who was nodding thoughtfully.

'The only thing is,' Mr Courcy said, with a chuckle, 'we've never seen someone get an A star in Maths and a D in Physics. How'd you manage that one, Kerry?'

The joke was not well-received. Kerry's lip quivered again, this time for slightly longer. 'Don't know,' she whispered tearfully. She looked up at her father, who was glowering at her. 'Don't know,' she repeated, shaking her head.

'She's very upset,' Janet Davison explained. 'She thought she would do slightly better.'

'We have that in common,' Paul declared brutally.

'Let me be clear,' Mr Courcy said, hoping to goodness that a student wouldn't burst into tears in front of him, 'Kerry has done very well in the subjects she's hoping to carry on. She has more than enough points to qualify for readmission into the sixth form and it would be a shame to forget that she only failed one subject – and that was by a very slim margin, as I understand it. There's no reason to expect that she won't do very well at AS and A-Level.'

'Well, that's good,' Janet nodded. 'Isn't it Kerry?'

Paul Davison stood. 'Thank you for your time, Mr Courcy.'

'Thank you,' Mr Courcy said nervously, standing to shake everybody's hand. 'See you next week, Kerry.'

The Davison family stood up and left Mr Courcy's table, as another family took their place. Crossing the hall, Paul Davison spotted Cameron Matthews laughing as he said goodbye to a tall, well-built rugby boy with black hair and a cut lip. As Peter Sullivan left Cameron,

Paul Davison marched over to join him, trailing Kerry and Janet in his wake. Cameron, who had last seen Kerry's father at her Marie-Antoinette-themed sweet sixteenth last autumn, straightened up as the paternal unit bore down upon him.

'Hello, Cameron. How are you?'

'Very well, thank you, Mr Davison.'

'I'm pleased to hear that. And how are your family?'

'Really well. Mum and Dad just left. They might still be out in the car park, if you want to...'

'No, no. I'll catch up with them later, thank you,' Paul said firmly. 'So Cameron, I gather you were in all of Kerry's classes last year?'

'Eh, yes,' he nodded. 'Well, most of them. Apart from Chemistry and Spanish, oh, and Maths, but apart from that, yes. Most of them... I think.'

'I see. Not a lot of work seems to have been done in most of Kerry's classes, does there, Cameron?'

'... No, sir. Well, sometimes... maybe. I don't know.'

'No, I don't think there was,' Paul said, with a polite but very decisive smile. 'And what subjects are you keeping on this year?'

'Religion, Latin, Theatre Studies and History, Mr Davison.'

'History?'

'Kerry and I aren't in the same class, though,' Cameron lied in a blind panic.

'So you two won't have any of the same classes next year?' Paul asked. Kerry and Cameron shook their heads in dishonest unison.

'Well, Cameron, I'm sure you won't be too offended if I say that's probably good news for the both of you.'

'I'm not offended at all,' Cameron murmured stupidly. 'No. Okay... yeah.'

'Please send my best to your parents.'

'Yes, I will. You too.' *Are his parents even alive?* Cameron wondered in his head. *Why did I just say that? Oh, please let them be alive!*

'I'll see you later, Cameron,' Janet smiled apologetically, as she followed Paul's exit. Kerry remained behind and bowed her head, placing her hand on her chest.

'Oh my gosh, Cameron. I'm so sorry. I had no idea.'

'What?'

'My father is a homophobe,' she said, shaking her head. 'I can't believe that display of politically incorrect discrimination.'

'Kerry, keep your voice down,' Cameron whispered. 'I don't think it had anything to do with that.'

'Of course, it did! Baby Jesus and all the orphans, what a day. First I am terribly abused by that evil beast of a maths teacher when he started making jokes about my GRD – Grades Related Disaster – and then I find out I'm the daughter of a homophobe.'

'Kerry, I don't think you are.'

'Cameron, my father is clearly some sort of prejudiced bigot. I'm like a civil rights' campaigner who's been born the daughter of a Ku Klux Klan member.'

'No, Kerry, you're not.'

'Of course I am. It's practically the same thing. I've got to go, but Cameron, I apologize for my father's insensitivity. I'll see you later. Stay strong.'

Cameron shook his head disbelievingly as Kerry walked out of the hall with the air of someone going stoically to her own martyrdom. He might have been even more amused to know that the moment Kerry cunningly tried to flip the tables from her father berating her for her grades to her berating him for his homophobia, Paul Davison would shred his daughter's accusations by reminding her that she had a gay uncle in Toronto and then by pointing out that he had assumed Cameron was gay, and possibly involved with Mark Kingston, for years. With no ammunition to retaliate, Kerry had no alternative but to make several meaningless promises about working harder in the incoming year and not going out to any more parties. A promise which lasted until fifteen minutes after her father boarded his flight back to Argentina on Tuesday.

Leaving aside his verbal dressing down by Paul Davison and Kerry's spirited attempt to cast herself as Belfast's answer to Rosa Parks, Cameron was reading a text from Stewart as he left the hall and almost literally bumped into Robert and Blake Hartman.

Pastor Hartman beamed and patted him on the shoulder. 'Cameron, hello. How are you?'

Cameron stared at the two of them for what he felt must have been two to three minutes, but which in reality was nothing more than a second before his manners kicked in. 'Pastor Hartman, hi.'

'Cameron, it's okay to call me Robert.'

'Robert, yes, sorry. I forgot. I'm very well, thank you. I'm just on my way into town now.'

'Did you get your subjects picked for next year?'

'Yes, I did. Mum and Dad came with me. They've just left.'

'What subjects did you pick?' asked Blake. Now that Blake had spoken for the first time in the conversation, Cameron had no choice but to look at him, something he had tried to avoid by hitherto focusing all his attention on the pastor.

'History, Latin, Religion and Theatre Studies.'

'Awesome. Not English?'

'No.'

'I think I'm going to go for ICT, Spanish, Technology and PE.'

'Cool.'

'Yeah. Yours too.'

'Anyway, I'm late,' Cameron announced, turning back to face Blake's father. 'It was nice seeing you both and good luck with the choices, Blake.'

Pastor Hartman patted him on the shoulder. 'Thanks, Cameron. Enjoy the rest of your summer.'

Cameron smiled and left the two men. Robert looked down at his son, who seemed downcast all of a sudden. 'What happened with you and Cameron?'

'What do you mean?'

'You two seemed to be pretty good friends at one point and then I never heard anything more about him. Did you fall out?'

'Yeah, kind of,' Blake said evasively. 'Yeah, we did. It was mostly my fault though.'

'Really? That's not like you. Did you apologize?'

'I tried, Dad, but he really didn't want to hear it.'

'If a man asks to be forgiven, Blake, he should be. That's in the Bible.'

'I know, Dad.'

'Matthew 18:21 and 22,' smiled his father, nudging him with his elbow. 'There. Aren't you impressed with your old man's powers of recall?'

'A pastor who knows the Bible,' Blake laughed. 'Shocking, Dad. Okay, the first teacher we need to speak to Mrs Vaughn, for Spanish.'

8
WAKE ME UP

Before September ends, it is a well known fact that the social dynamic of sixth year will have altered in more or less every grammar school in Northern Ireland. This change is partly brought about by the fact that as many as twenty new pupils often join the student body, provided they get good enough grades. That September, Mount Olivet's Lower Sixth was swelled by the arrival of thirteen new students – three attractive boys (one very, two quite); four kids who seemed to have been collectively struck dumb with terror at starting a new school; a very enthusiastic girl from Lecale Grammar; a quiet but intellectually brilliant emo; and the Christian Union's ranks were bulked up by four girls, three of whom sported the requisite perma-glossed lips and super-squeaky, ultra-feminine voices which they seemed to believe made them attractive to the Christian Union's boys, most of whom spent their waking hours fantasizing about girls far more like Imogen Dawson.

However, the big news that autumn was not who was arriving but who was leaving. The Science department was deeply upset to be losing Hector Colliner, a freakishly intelligent but socially awkward boy who was off to sit his A-Levels at a grammar school on the north side of the city. Heather Blount, a pretty but unremarkable girl who had once kissed Mark Kingston and stolen Imogen's hair cut, had finally persuaded her parents that she genuinely was miserable at Mount Olivet and they had sent her to Scotland to board at Gordonstoun. The real surprise was that Stewart Lawrence had left Mount Olivet to sit A-Levels in German, Maths, Chemistry and Economics at Imperial Academy, an all-boys school founded in 1832 in the city centre, from which Mount Olivet's popular boys plucked their sporting rivals and the popular girls plucked the occasional controversial boyfriend. Stewart had been sincerely liked by most of his peers. He was handsome, friendly and loyal; it was difficult not to like him. Some students muttered that the real reason for Stewart's departure was that he was still heartbroken by Imogen Dawson's treatment of him the previous year. They claimed that he had decided to transfer schools rather than face the pain of seeing her with Freddie Carrowdale, who she was dating a mere nine months after she had reached into Stewart's chest cavity and ripped his heart into teeny, tiny little shreds.

Stewart had broken the news to his First XV teammates after telling Imogen and he had begun by promising that he would give up rugby, since joining Imperial's squad could potentially mean playing against his old team during the Ulster Schools' Cup Final on Saint Patrick's Day. The Firsts were already losing six players to graduation and Stewart's departure was mourned, but their captain Quentin spoke for everyone when he urged Stewart not to give up the great game and play something reprehensibly weak like football. He was to try out for the Imperial rugby team, but expect no mercy if they ever had to play against each other – a ruling he accepted with a laugh and a hug from Quentin. Thus, on the first day of September, gazing up at the large portraits of King William IV and Queen Adelaide which hung majestically in Imperial Academy's entrance hall, in his new dark green woollen blazer, Stewart Lawrence walked over to put his name down on the try-out sheets for the Imperial rugby team. He was no longer a Mount Olivet boy; it was time to start his new life at the Academy.

◇◇◇

At exactly the same moment as Stewart was adjusting to life in a school which had no girls and no queen bees, Mount Olivet was adapting to the regime change which came with the start of each new academic year. Graduation meant that an entire clique of popular girls had suddenly vacated the school and a new set of it-girls must rise to take their place in the senior school's network of socialites. Anastasia Montmorency, elected last year to fill Cecilia's place as president of the Social Committee, had stepped seamlessly into her place as leader of Upper Sixth, whilst Meredith and her posse had assumed their places in Lower Sixth, beginning by commandeering a secluded spot in the Sixth Form Centre, far enough away from the coffee machines that they wouldn't have to hear annoying people talking but close enough to the door that they could spy on whoever came in. Finally, as predicted, the new fifth-year queen bee – occupying the place held by Meredith last year – was Cameron's younger sister, Charlotte Matthews, a tall and trim blonde who had taken the decision to replace her schoolbag with a Longchamp bag and introduced a fad of wearing Barbour jackets instead of a blazer on the way in and out of school.

Charlotte's clique, known as "the Malone princesses," consisted of her two blonde friends, Jenny Thompson and Melissa Russell. Jenny was the younger sister of Mariella Thompson and she, Charlotte and Melissa had been best friends since the age of seven, when they were given a reading at Rathkeltair Preparatory's Christmas carol service. Over the summer, the group's ranks had increased with four other girls being invited to sit with them at lunch – Alice Martin and Kirsten

Faulkner had been vetted throughout the entirety of last year by Melissa, who had eventually advised Charlotte to start asking them to parties because Alice was quite fun and Kirsten, although clingy and annoying, was far too pretty and far too rich to be excluded. Another new arrival to Charlotte's clique was Mary-Elizabeth O'Neill, who lived in a country manor house outside Belfast and carried herself with a sort of ultra-protestant detachment; she went to pony club with Charlotte and owned enough Barbour jackets to start her own saddlery. Finally, the bubbly and vivacious Celeste Fitzpatrick had been included because she knew everything about everyone and Charlotte rightly guessed that it was therefore too dangerous to leave her out.

It was, in fact, Celeste Fitzpatrick who caused Charlotte Matthews to pace down the school corridors in search of her brother, with a pursed expression as she faced the first social emergency of the term. She found him outside his form room, twenty minutes before registration. Charlotte thanked God that Cameron liked to walk to school when the weather was good, eschewing Meredith's offer of the car. Right now, she really needed to talk to him alone.

'Cameron?'

Cameron smiled at the sight of his sister approaching, but his smile faltered when he noticed how worried she seemed. 'Hey. Is everything okay?'

Charlotte grabbed his arm and pulled him away from the rest of his classmates. 'Have you told anyone else that you're gay?' she asked, quietly.

Cameron's face immediately began to drain of colour. 'No,' he whispered. 'No, not at all. Of course not! Why?'

'Because everybody knows, Cameron,' she replied. 'And I mean *everybody*. Celeste Fitzpatrick just came up and started talking to me about it. I asked Mary-

Elizabeth and she said that half the bus was talking about it on the way into school this morning.'

'But... I... I don't know... How do they know?'

'I don't know!' answered Charlotte. 'Celeste said that she heard that you and Blake had secretly been seeing each other the whole time he was dating Catherine.'

'That isn't true,' snapped Cameron. 'It isn't. What did you say?'

'Well, I couldn't deny it! You are gay, Cameron, and if you are and you deny it, then the whole thing becomes a lot worse. People make fun of you a lot more if you're closeted!'

'I'm sorry,' he groaned. 'I shouldn't have told you. I shouldn't have put you in this position.'

'Cameron, don't be so stupid. Would you rather I found out from Celeste?'

'No. But, oh my goodness, Charlotte. This is awful.'

Charlotte stroked his arm comfortingly. 'I know. It's okay.'

'It is so far from okay. This is my nightmare,' he said. 'This is actually it. It's happening.'

'Cameron, it's okay,' she repeated, grabbing his hand. 'It's fine. It's not a big deal anymore, anyway? Lots of people are gay. I just didn't think the rumour that you and Blake were... sleeping together for all of last year was very fair...'

'We never slept together!' Cameron snapped, furiously. 'That's not true! We only kissed. Twice. And once was before he even got together with *her*. He only went out with Catherine in the first place because he was afraid people would find out! He was afraid this would happen.'

'What's going on?'

Cameron and Charlotte both turned at the sound of Meredith's voice. Her Birkin hung on her arm and she was mid-way through texting Imogen, who apparently had a huge announcement to make.

'Everybody knows,' Cameron explained, struggling to keep himself from crying. 'Celeste Fitzpatrick told Charlotte this morning and Mary-Elizabeth heard it on the bus.'

'About Blake, too,' finished Charlotte.

'That's impossible,' said Meredith. 'I haven't heard anything about this. It's impossible. She's lying.'

'Mary-Elizabeth said half the Saintfield bus were talking about it,' Charlotte answered.

'Who blabbed?'

'I don't know,' Cameron replied. 'But if it was Catherine –'

'It wasn't Catherine,' Meredith ruled. 'It couldn't have been. She wouldn't want anyone to know either. Did Celeste say who she heard it from?'

'She says everyone's talking about it.'

Meredith nodded thoughtfully and then glanced over her shoulder; she caught several members of their class looking over at them. Celeste was right. Everybody knew. And Meredith had absolutely no idea how.

◇◇◇

'This is a rocky start to the first term of the Age of Fabulous,' Kerry said, as they filed in for the start of year Assembly.

'Poor Cameron,' sighed Imogen. 'You know what? I'm just going to leave my big news until later.'

'What I don't understand is how so many people knew, but none of us knew that they knew,' Meredith wondered, as she took her seat. 'I just don't understand. I usually know everything!'

'Are we sure this Celeste girl is telling the truth?' Imogen asked. 'She might just be exaggerating for effect?

Let's face it, we've all been guilty of doing that ourselves from time to time.'

'You can't be "guilty" if it's fabulous,' said Kerry. 'Anyway, Charlotte says Celeste is like the school's Perez Hilton and it's not just her that's saying it. Mary-Elizabeth O'Neill told Charlotte they were all talking about it on the bus from Saintfield and she definitely wouldn't exaggerate for the sake of it. Mary-Elizabeth has no feelings.'

'Were they talking about it on your one?' Meredith asked.

'I don't know,' admitted Kerry. 'I put my earphones in and pretend I can't hear anyone.'

'What about Blake? How's he dealing with all this?'

'That's got nothing to do with us,' Meredith declared.

'Dead to us, remember?' Kerry said.

Imogen nodded. 'Right. Right.'

'I can't believe we didn't know anything about this,' Meredith said again, after a few seconds. 'I just don't understand. We knew *nothing*. How is that even possible? God, this must be how Catherine feels all the time.'

Meredith glanced over to the boys' side of the hall, where she saw a pale Cameron sitting between Mark and Peter, with Mark sporting a bullish expression on his face, as if daring someone to say something. Cameron turned and caught Meredith's eye and she smiled encouragingly. He smiled back tightly and then stood as the school pianist began playing *Dear Lord and Father of Mankind*, which brought eleven hundred students to their feet.

When they hymn was finished, Imogen flashed a smile in the general direction of the stage as Freddie took to the podium to read the morning announcements for the first time as the new Head Boy. Freddie, obviously, did not see her since there were at least five academic years and nearly a thousand people sitting between him and her, but Imogen was determined to show the girls in her year that she was happy and confident in her new relationship and that she definitely didn't miss Stewart Lawrence.

'Good morning,' Freddie said, clearing his throat. 'A few announcements this morning: the Current Affairs Society will be meeting in the Library at three-thirty this afternoon, with the first meeting being chaired by Mr Kirk. Miss Donahue and Reverend Ferrworthy will be posting a signup sheet for auditions for this year's Senior School drama production, which will be the musical version of *Blood Brothers* and that show will be going on stage in February...'

Imogen tutted. 'God, that's a rubbish choice. Idiots.'

'I know,' whispered Meredith. 'I hate plays where poor people sing.'

'... The Social Committee will be meeting in Room U17 this afternoon at four o'clock. All committee members must attend and those who can't should notify Natasha Jenkins before the end of lunch today. Finally, Mr Cavan would like me to remind the boys in senior school that there are now seven places available on the First XV rugby squad. If anyone is interested in trying out, they should get in contact either with Mr Cavan in the PE office or with Quentin Smith, the team captain. Thank you.'

Imogen smiled. 'You can tell his father's a politician. So charismatic.'

Kerry rolled her eyes and then gasped slightly when she realized that she had forgotten her new cerise cashmere mittens. This day was turning into a complete disaster for everyone.

Blake had become aware of the rumours circulating around the school only moments after Charlotte had broken the news to Cameron. On his way into school, three boys from the year below had laughed at him and one flicked his wrist down saying, 'Ooh, have a very gay day, sir!' By the time he reached registration, he knew that it had not been a one off. A burly guy from Upper Sixth had called him a faggot outside the Geography rooms and a group of fourth-year girls had started giggling when he walked by on the stairwell. The final irrefutable confirmation came when he was rounding the corner to approach his form room and nearly collided with a very pretty girl with bouncing chestnut curls, a Mulberry bag on her arm and a disposable macchiato cup in her left hand.

'Oh my god!' she beamed, speaking quickly in the staccato rhythm of a true Maloner born and bred. 'I'm so sorry; I totally didn't see you there. Hi.'

'Hi,' he replied, politely trying to step around her, but she tilted her head and kept her smile intact. The conversation definitely wasn't over.

'Okay, so we don't really know each other, but we totally should! It's Blake, right? I'm Celeste. I'm in the year below you. Do you like my bag, by the way?'

'Eh... yes. It's very nice.'

'Thanks. It's Mulberry. It's like so heavy but totally worth it, because it looks so beau. But I'm deffers worried I'm going to get arms like one of the hockey girls if I keep carrying it around like this. Do you know what I mean?'

'Right. Sure.'

'Okay, anyway, my name's Celeste. Celeste Fitzpatrick. I'm like besties with your boyfriend's sister, so I just thought I should like totally introduce myself properly if we met. So, hi!'

'Pardon?'

'Oh my gosh, maybe it's not even official yet,' Celeste smiled, 'but you know what I mean. I'm Charlotte Matthews' best friend.'

'Cameron's not my...'

'Oh my goodness! Are you guys waiting to spare Catherine O'Rourke's feelings? That is so sweet!'

'I'm going to be late for class. Sorry.'

'Okay. Well, it was super-nice meeting you properly and, just to let you know, loads of people have already said what a totally cute couple you and Cameron make. Or will make. Whatever. See you later, babes. Let's definitely get coffee at some point. Have a great first day back!'

Like a robot, Blake carried on down the corridor, trying to process what Celeste had just said. The second he walked through his form class door, everybody stopped talking. A few smiled hesitantly at him and Blake felt his stomach clench, as for one awful second he genuinely thought he was going to be sick. He took a seat near the front of the class, next to a new girl with very light brown hair and a welcoming smile. Usually, Blake would have engaged her in conversation and offered his services as a tour guide, since he could remember the awkwardness of being the new kid at school, but today he tried not to catch the girl's eye and kept staring ahead, unseeing, as their form teacher, Reverend Ferrworthy, entered the room to begin taking the register. The new timetables were passed out, with Coral's sidekick Paula setting Blake's timetable down in front of him and looking uncomfortable before moving on. Reverend Ferrworthy launched into a speech about the importance of a work ethic for the A-Levels. Blake heard none of it.

This must have been what it was like for his parents when people found out they were getting a divorce. His father would have felt the same buzzing in his ears, the same tightness in his chest and known by the way the hairs on the back of his neck were standing up that literally everybody in the room was staring at him and judging him. Through the instincts of a religious childhood, Blake began to pray, begging God to do something – anything – to get him out of here. Nothing happened and the feeling of quiet hysteria crashed back over him as he suddenly realized that at this very moment Jack was probably sitting in another classroom in another part of the school being confronted by the rumours that his big brother was a queer.

Blake's fists began to clench into balls, as they always did when panic really took over, and in his mind's eye he saw the news somehow leaking back to his father. At least a dozen children at the school, and two of the teachers, were members of Robert Hartman's congregation and it was impossible not to fear that at least one of them wouldn't tell their parents about the pastor's big gay son. Even if they didn't say anything to Robert, what were the chances that Jack wouldn't want an explanation for the humiliation he had endured in school on Blake's behalf? In one fell swoop, Blake had undone every reason his father had for moving them three thousand miles across the ocean – to start a new life, to escape gossip, to once again be respected members of the community. He had basically destroyed his family's life in Northern Ireland and all because he couldn't keep away from Cameron Matthews.

After registration, he grabbed his schoolbag and bolted from the classroom. He didn't join the others heading towards the Assembly Hall; instead he made straight for the boys' cloakroom and swung into one of the unused disabled bathrooms. It was a large, cool room, with no windows; its only source of illumination was a harsh overhead light that Blake flicked on as he turned the lock. He heard the extractor fan begin to whir above his head. He dropped his schoolbag and crossed over to the sink, resting his hands on the two sides of the basin and staring into the mirror. He swallowed hard and tried to steady himself. He placed his right hand over his mouth, rubbed slowly and gulped again.

After two or three minutes, he turned away and walked back to the door, resting his left hand on it. In fifteen minutes, it would be time for the first class of the year. He tried to focus on Celeste's friendliness, as well as the news that many people thought he and Cameron would make a great couple. But for every one person like Celeste Fitzpatrick, there were two like the guys who had mocked him as he walked past and five like those who had stared at him awkwardly, unsure of what to do or say. It would be like this, every day, until he graduated from Mount Olivet. Or went back to America. Even then, this would probably follow him somehow. In the age of Facebook, no scandal could remain confined to one area of your life forever.

Blake pressed his head against the door and looked up into the ceiling. His eyes and throat were dry. He felt numb and he thanked God that here and now, for this one very brief moment, he felt absolutely nothing. Under the circumstances, it was the best he could hope for, but as he felt his phone begin to vibrate inside his blazer pocket, he knew it wouldn't last.

◇◇◇

Mark's fingers traced lightly along Coral's as they sat together in the cafeteria at break time. Peter sat on the other side of the table, munching his way through his second packet of crisps. Like Meredith, Mark was still desperately trying to figure out how everyone in the entire school had found out about Cameron and Blake.

'I don't know why you're so surprised, mate,' said Peter, between mouthfuls.

'You're not?' asked Mark.

'No. How long does anything stay secret in this place?'

'It must have been either Meredith or Imogen,' Coral said, tapping back on her boyfriend's fingers. 'Or Kerry. Who else could it have been?'

'Your mate Eóin apparently knew an awful lot about it on the beach back in July,' challenged Peter.

'Eóin only said about Cameron, Peter,' she shot back sweetly. 'He never said anything about Blake.'

Mark shook his head. 'Poor Cameron.'

'We should go over and say something, babe. Let him know that we're still his friends and care about him.'

'We said that to him in Assembly,' replied Peter. 'Plus, he knows we're his friends.'

Coral stood up and smiled down at him coldly. 'People need to hear that they're loved, Peter, especially in moments like this. Cameron needs to be validated and supported. Let's go over and say something, Mark. Unless you don't want to?'

'No, you're right,' he said, standing up too. 'I'll see you in Physics, Pete. Oh, here – do you have rugby practise later?'

Peter nodded. 'Yeah. After school. Why?'

'Would you ask Quentin if he minds if I try out for a place on the squad?'

Peter leaned back in his chair and smiled. 'Nah, mate, of course he wouldn't. You seriously thinking of trying out?'

'Yeah,' nodded Mark. 'I know I've always stuck more with the cricket and football, but I really enjoyed rugby back in junior school and playing with you lads at the weekends has always been pretty good craic.'

'You should definitely try out, lad. Definitely. I'll tell Quentin, but he should be sweet with it. If you get through, though, initiation's a fucker. Just warning you.'

'I'm sure I can handle it,' Mark laughed. 'I'll see you in Physics.'

'See you, buddy.'

Mark and Coral walked off, holding hands. 'You're not seriously considering auditioning for the rugby team, are you?' she asked, the moment they were out of earshot.

'Yeah, I was thinking of *trying out*. Are you okay?'

'They're the most self-obsessed bunch of lager louts in the whole school, Mark. They're objectionable in almost every single way. I thought you were more into cricket? I know it's still quite elitist, but at least it's not sexist, loud, offensive and annoying. I didn't think you were the kind of person who bought into that lairy lad culture.'

'It's just a game, Coral.'

'If you say so.'

They had arrived at the table always occupied by Imogen, Cameron, Catherine, Meredith and Kerry, who were locked deep in conversation when the couple appeared beside them. Luckily, given what they had to discuss, Catherine was off showing her eleven-year-old cousin, Niall, around on his first day of school. Kerry spotted Mark and Coral's approach before any of the others did and swiftly changed the topic of conversation, proclaiming loudly, 'Yes, well it's very difficult to find anywhere that sells platypuses!'

'Hey guys,' said Mark, with a small wave from his spare hand.

Cameron smiled back. 'Hey, you two. What's up?'

'Cameron, we just wanted to say that we think you're really brave and that whatever happens, obviously Mark and I are still completely here for you as friends. Anything you need, anytime. We love you.'

'Thanks, Coral,' said Cameron. 'I really appreciate that.'

Mark repressed a twinge of annoyance that Coral had spoken for him, especially when he saw the flash of vindictive amusement in Meredith's eyes. 'Cam, let's go get something to eat after school,' he said. 'Just the two of us?'

'Brilliant. I'll meet you at the gates?'

'Excellent,' said Mark. 'See you then. Bye.'

Imogen and Kerry murmured unenthusiastic farewells as Mark and Coral left the cafeteria. Meredith remained silent until they were gone. 'Well, that was terribly entertaining. Poor Mark.'

'I know,' Imogen laughed. 'Maybe they're off to find where she's hidden his testicles.'

'As if it isn't bad enough being outted to all of south Belfast, now I have to deal with that hipster manatee blubbering all over my life pretending to like me,' complained Cameron. 'This day couldn't possibly get any worse. What am I going to do?'

'Nothing,' declared Kerry, before the other two could say anything. 'Why should you?'

'Because everybody knows!'

'And? Why does that mean that you have to do anything? Princess, it's not your responsibility to deal with these people just because they have a problem with it.'

'Kerry's right,' declared Imogen. 'Why on earth you should have to spend your time worrying about some fuck-ugly peasants riddled with prejudices and pauper cooties?'

'Let me remind you that we are living in the opening month of the Age of Fabulous,' preached Kerry. 'It is not a very fabulous thing to spend your time worrying about the feelings of bigoted others. Actually, I don't even think you *can* have an AOF without at least one out and proud gay man. I mean, I'm sorry, but haven't any of these people watched *Will & Grace* or *Glee* or *Sex and the City*. Gay people exist: get over it! It's not your fault that half the people in this school are stupid. We don't go around apologizing for the fact that Meredith's thin, Imogen's loud or that I have curls that look like they were knitted out of sunbeams by little baby angels, do we? No! You were born this way, Cameron, and we are not beginning the Age of Fabulous by pretending we are ashamed of anything. *Comprende*?'

'Have you been planning that speech?' Imogen asked, admiringly.

'I've been rehearsing it in my head since Assembly,' said Kerry. 'I had a poem, too, but I couldn't get anything to rhyme with "civil partnership."'

Meredith trailed her fingers along the contours of her Diet Coke bottle. 'Kerry is right. Obviously, if we ever find out who told everybody then we will have to punish them, severely...'

'Oh, yes,' said Imogen emphatically. 'Beatings. Beatings-o-rama.'

'... but, there's absolutely no point in acting uncomfortable or unhappy about any of this in the meantime. It'll only make people think that you think there's something wrong with it. Which there isn't. And,' she said, with a supercilious smile that Cameron knew came only from her moments of most unrepentant snobbery, 'everybody knows that this kind of thing isn't a problem for someone like you, Cameron. Homophobia is for poor people.'

Imogen looked positively ecstatic at Meredith's supremely intolerant tolerance mantra. Kerry looked less certain that 'Homophobia is for poor people' was an entirely appropriate motto in terms of political correctness, but figured that now probably wasn't the time to air her doubts.

Cameron sat lost in thought for a moment, before nodding. 'You're right, aren't you? Everyone important in my life, apart from my parents, already knows and they're fine with it. Plus, half the people in school have apparently thought I've been gay since first year.'

'Exactly!' said Imogen. 'The difference now is that they *know*, but they also need to know that you're not embarrassed about it. The only thing that's going to change is that you're not going to feel upset if they call you gay anymore, because now you know it's true! Screw it, Cameron. Screw them and their smelly proletariat B.O.'

Kerry clapped her hands in delight. 'Yay!'

Nine months earlier, Cameron had told Mark that without these girls his life at school would be hellish and he knew now, more than ever, that he had been right.

'Are we done with this?' Imogen asked, shifting forward in her seat excitedly.

'Yes,' Cameron replied decisively. 'Why?'

Imogen exhaled deeply and held up her hands in excitement. 'Daddy said he'd buy me a Mercedes if I pass my driving test!'

◇◇◇

There was a long list of potential culprits who could have outed Cameron and Blake. In Cameron's mind, Meredith, Imogen, Kerry, Catherine, Blake, Mark, Peter, Anastasia and even Charlotte were not totally exempt from suspicion, although he was inclined to think that whoever had talked had done so accidentally. As far as Blake was concerned, there was only one logical suspect and at break time that day, he tracked her down to the corridors near the school swimming pool.

It was a fairly empty part of Mount Olivet, particularly during recess, and Catherine was only there because she was still on her mission to show

Niall everything and anything to do with his new school, merrily disregarding that Niall himself would much rather have been allowed to spend time with his classmates and possibly make some friends. Blake took grim satisfaction in seeing Catherine nearly trip over her own two feet in panic as she realized he was coming towards her.

'Blake. Hi.'

'Hello, Catherine,' Blake extended his hand to Niall, who shook it. 'Hi, I'm Blake Hartman. I'm in Catherine's grade. Are you new?'

'Yeah. I'm Niall.'

'Good to meet you, Niall. Would you mind if I spoke to Catherine in private for a minute? It won't take too long.'

'No, that's alright,' Niall quickly replied. 'I need to go find some of the guys from my class. I should go.'

'Wait! Don't you want me to show you the way to the Latin classrooms?' Catherine asked as Niall sped away from her.

'No, that's cool. I remember. Thanks, Catherine. See you at Granny's.'

Abandoned by Niall, Catherine turned to look at her ex-boyfriend, her face a picture of trepidation and unhappiness. Her hands were clasped in front of her, but her fingers were fidgeting restlessly with one another. Blake steeled himself not to feel sorry for her – a task he could only manage by trying not to look at her.

'I realize that what I did to you was terrible and you have every right to hate me,' he began, 'but you should know that I never, at any point, meant to hurt you. What you did was different. You deliberately set out to hurt me. And Cameron.'

'I don't understand.'

'Everybody knows, Catherine! The whole school is talking about it. They think I was cheating on you with Cameron the whole time we were together.'

'No! That's impossible. There's no way they could know about you. Maybe about Cameron. Maybe that's what you heard and you got confused? He told us at the leavers' ball. Right at the very end. But he didn't mention you. I was there. I promise. They only know about him.'

'No! They know about both of us. Do you have any idea what this is going to do my brother? Do you?'

'Do you really think I'd tell people?'

'Before I wouldn't have, because I thought you were nice, but now that I know you knew about me and Cameron since February, Catherine, to be perfectly honest I'm not exactly sure what you're capable of.'

'I didn't know since February,' she stammered.

'Yes, you did; Meredith told me.'

Catherine's mouth opened to say something, before she realized that she daren't contradict Meredith, even in absentia. She felt miserable as she realized that everybody must be laughing at her for dating a gay guy for so long.

'I would never tell people what you told me, Blake. It's not just you who's embarrassed by this, you know. Everyone's going to be laughing at me and it's totally humiliating for them all to know that you prefer Cameron to me. He's not even that nice, Blake! He's not really a very nice person, at all. He can actually be really, really mean sometimes. And, okay, maybe I did know about you and him back in February, but that happens to lots of people, it doesn't mean that all of them are gay! You'd asked me to be your girlfriend and you were so sweet and so nice and stuff that I thought maybe it was just like a onetime thing with Cameron. A mistake. I kept hoping and hoping it was and then you dropped that great bomb of awfulness all over my head and made me feel rubbish about myself and now you think that I went and told everyone about it. Seriously? I would, like, never do that! I haven't even told Kerry or Imogen what you said to me. Why would I? Why would I even mention you and Cameron to them? It's totally embarrassing!'

'I'm in love with him, Catherine.'

'Well, that's too bad, Blake, because he's not in love with you. He's not in love with anyone but himself. There!' she finished, barging past him. 'Now we're both having a rubbish first day back!'

◇◇◇

Catherine entered the girls' bathroom to wash her hands moments after leaving Blake. As the door swung close behind her, she heard the one sound that no girl at Mount Olivet wanted to hear upon her arrival in any room – sudden silence. Three girls in Catherine's year were huddled together by the sink and they all ceased talking the moment she entered the bathroom.

Cristyn Evans, who had sat next to Catherine in Spanish all of last year, smiled brightly. 'Hey, Catherine! How are you?'

Catherine knew what that tone meant; after all, she used it herself on a near-weekly basis. It was the tone that cunningly tried to cover up the fact that the speaker had just been talking about the new arrival by seeming thrilled to see them. 'I'm fine, thanks.'

Standing next to Cristyn, Fiona Merton shifted uneasily at the sudden awkwardness of finding herself in Catherine's presence; her best friend, Gemma March, looked at Catherine like she would at a limping three-legged puppy – her eyes brimming with sympathy and confusion as to why the poor mongrel hadn't been put out of its misery.

Catherine smiled back weakly and reached for the soap dispenser. She pressed. No soap came out. Catherine pressed again; still no soap. So she pressed again. And again. And again. Finally, she slammed the lever as aggressively as she could and one tiny bubble of foam landed on her outstretched palm. She felt her lip quiver and the silence from the three girls behind her had become positively deafening.

'How could he be gay?'

'Babes!'

Catherine spun round and threw herself into Cristyn's solicitously outstretched arms. Fiona began rubbing her back in calming circular motions; Gemma hovered nearby, uncomfortable and intrigued all at the same time.

'It's got absolutely nothing to do with you,' Cristyn said. 'You didn't turn him, babes. You couldn't have. Remember that old Lady Gaga song? He was born this way.'

'Well I wish he wasn't! He was so hot. And I loved him!'

Fiona cleared her throat nervously. 'Is it true that him and Cameron Matthews were...'

'No!' Catherine gasped, lifting her head from Cristyn's shoulder in a sudden jerking motion. 'No! It isn't. I've never been cheated on.'

'Well, believe us, hun, no one thinks any less of you,' Cristyn soothed. 'It was just a totally uncool thing for Blake to do. He should never have asked you to be his girlfriend. If someone knows they're gay, they just shouldn't do something like that. It's so mean.'

Catherine nodded and averted her gaze. She would be dragged across broken glass before she would ever admit that she too had known. After a moment, she sniffed and turned back to the mirror.

'I'm just so embarrassed. Why did he have to do this to me?'

9
Mad Men & Loose Women

Three days after the first day back, Kerry and Catherine were walking into school together with Kerry taking every opportunity to advertize how delightful her hands looked in her new cerise cashmere mittens. However, it was Catherine who was getting the lion's share of the attention and for all the wrong reasons. Initially, Kerry thought people might be staring because of the ridiculous bow Catherine was wearing in her hair, but it soon became clear that the stares were still Blake-related. Between the entrance gate and the lobby, they had already encountered four looks of embarrassed sympathy and two sets of giggles.

'Guess what?' Kerry said, hoping to distract her.

'What?'

'You're the first person I'm telling this to, so don't tell the others until I do.'

Catherine brightened at this unexpected elevation through the group's pecking order. 'Oh my gosh. Okay. I promise I won't. What is it?'

'I've decided what theme to have for my birthday party this year.'

'OMG,' breathed Catherine excitedly. 'What is it? This is *so* exciting.'

'The 1950s,' Kerry announced.

'Oh my please! That is *so* fabulous!' Catherine said, grabbing Kerry's hand. 'That's an amazing idea, Kerry. Like, oh my gosh.'

'I know. Isn't it? It's going to be utterly delightful. Maybe I'll learn how to jitterbug...'

'Kerry, this is going to be so good and plus, it'll be so much easier for people to do than last year's theme.'

'Are you saying you didn't find last year's delightful?'

'No! No. I did. Obviously. I'm just saying this one's.... it's so good, babes!'

'What's this?' asked Meredith, as she and Imogen swung through the double doors of the school lobby.

'Kerry's having a 1950s theme for her birthday party!' squealed Catherine. 'How fun is that?'

Kerry turned to stare at Catherine in speechless outrage, as Imogen pursed her lips so hard in jealousy at Kerry's theme that she practically swallowed her own chin.

'That's fabulous, Kerry,' Meredith conceded.

'Thanks,' smiled Kerry. 'It's going to be so much fun planning it. All. On. My. Own. Which will be nice, since I didn't get to announce it all on my own. Did I, Catherine?'

Catherine blanched. 'Oh, whoops! I'm sorry. I just got carried away.'

'Speaking of getting carried away, Catherine, what's with the bow?' asked Meredith.

◇◇◇

A hand snaked around Cameron's waist in the boys' locker room and a strong masculine body pressed up against his back. 'Fancy seeing you here,' the voice purred in his ear.

'Hello, Peter.'

'How's it hanging, squire?' laughed Peter, disengaging himself and leaning against the row of lockers next to Cameron's.

'Not too bad,' Cameron answered. 'There's so much more work than last year, though. It's really annoying.'

'I was hoping you and I might partake of some hot and heavy homosexual intercourse later this afternoon?'

From the far corner of the room, two guys in the year below looked over in shock at Peter's ribald banter. Peter winked cheekily at Cameron. 'Your place or mine?' he said, loudly.

'Fuck up,' laughed Cameron. 'You know, people are actually going to start to think there's something going on between us if you keep carrying on like this.'

'They'll be as jealous as fuck, little man.'

'Well, "lover," I'm going to go to class. What have you got next?'

'Free period,' Peter said. 'You?'

'Drama.'

'Ah, right. Well, enjoy yourself and,' he picked up his volume again, for the benefit of the others, 'I'll be thinking of the ride with you, hot stuff.'

Cameron smiled at Peter's gumption and turned to walk out the door.

'Oh, I love to watch you go, baby!' Peter cat-called after him. 'Shake it for me!'

Cameron burst out laughing, just as Blake walked through the door. Blake froze, like a deer caught in the headlights, and the smile was instantly wiped off Cameron's face. Swooping in with what he hoped would rescue the awkward situation, Peter swung his arm around Cameron's shoulder.

'Well, Blake, how're things?' he asked jocularly.

'They're alright,' Blake answered. 'Thank you. How're you guys?'

'We're doing pretty well. Aren't we, Cameron?'

'I have to get to class.'

As Cameron tried to leave, Blake grabbed his right arm, just above his wrist. For a moment, it looked like he was about to say something. There was an imploring look in his eyes that Cameron forced himself to ignore. He firmly removed himself from Blake's grip and walked out the door, without a backward glance.

Peter clapped Blake sympathetically on the shoulder and then turned to walk towards the toilets.

◇◇◇

Kerry set back some embroidered notepaper on the ground floor of the House of Fraser and checked over her shoulder to where Catherine was rifling through some glitter pens.

'I spent a fortune in here when I was doing the invitations,' Kerry informed her. 'Well, Mummy did. Mucho dinero.'

'They're so beau. How's everything going for the party?'

'Delightfully, delightfully,' muttered Kerry, moving along the aisle. 'Well, the party planning is going delightfully, but the guests are stressing me out. I don't mind the organization of the actual festivities, but I don't understand why people seem to think I should sort out every tiny detail of their night for them. Like arranging their lifts. It's ridiculous.'

'What are you going to do about Mark Kingston?' asked Catherine.

'I don't know,' admitted Kerry. 'I worry that not inviting him will cause a fuss and I worry that if I do invite him, I'm going to have to give a reason why I'm not inviting Coral Mandrews.'

'I suppose we could just invite her too?'

'No. Under no circumstances will that little beastlet be stepping into my house. Just because she's trapped

Mark into dating her does not mean she gets invited to our parties, Catherine. We hate her. Remember?'

Catherine nodded dutifully. 'No, I know. I didn't mean it that way.'

'Well, what way did you mean it then?'

'I don't know.'

'This party is already very stressful, Catherine, and the last thing I need is to even imagine Mandrews in my house. Oh my goodness, have you ever seen anything more delightful than this notepaper? It's pink and it's rose-scented!'

◇◇◇

By the time the Thursday before the party had been reached, Kerry's patience with her guests was wearing perilously thin. The moment anyone on the guest list approached her with so much as a questioning look, she instantly began glowering at them. On Wednesday afternoon, she took to ostentatiously rejecting the incoming phone calls of people who had previously irritated her with their queries, demands or confusion. It was in that frame of mind that she finally decided she wasn't inviting Mark, because she couldn't be bothered facing any more difficulties.

'I think Kerry's about to have an aneurysm,' said Imogen, tapping her shoe on the desk leg in the back row of the Italian classroom. They had lost the first fifteen minutes of the lesson to a lecture from Miss Flanagan, who had encouraged them all to get involved with an anti-bullying campaign created by Rosie Prentice, a new girl who had transferred in from Lecale Grammar at the start of the year. Meredith, who found Rosie insufferable, had spent the time deciding what colour of nail varnish to wear to Kerry's party.

'Let's just hope it's not another FIB,' grimaced Meredith. 'Last year's was unholy.'

'I know. It was only when you declared war on her vajayjay that she snapped out of it. Great theme, though.'

'I know,' nodded Meredith. 'Next year, if we want to beat her, we have to do a theme.'

'Meredith?'

'Yes?'

'I feel bad.'

'Why? What have you done now?'

'Nothing – and that's part of the problem.' Imogen paused as she mentally braced herself for the ice storm that was about to come her way. 'I know he's the devil, but don't we feel just a little bit bad about what's happening to Blake?'

Meredith's swivelled in her chair to regard Imogen with scathing incredulity. 'Pardon?'

'Meredith, it's not even teasing anymore. It's outright bullying. I used to think you and I were truly terrible human beings, but it turns out we're just deliciously badly behaved. It's these other fuckers who are actually monstrous!'

'He brought this on himself, Imogen.'

'No, he didn't. Obviously, what he did was wrong, but they're not doing any of this to him because of what he did; they're doing it to him because he's gay. Don't you think that's wrong?'

Meredith tutted. 'You always do this. You always get shrieking mad at someone and then you feel bad and forgive them.'

'That is not true! I just don't hold a grudge as long as you or Cameron. But then, who does?'

'Cameron is more than justified holding a grudge this time, Imogen. Yes, I think what they're doing is wrong in principle. If it was to anybody else, I'd probably say something, but it's not anyone else: it's Blake. And need I remind you that screwing over Blake Hartman was partly your idea in the first place? You wanted to punch him in the penis, Imogen.'

'I wanted to punch him, not castrate him.'

'What are you talking about?' asked Meredith impatiently, refusing to acknowledge the pointed 'be quiet' stares coming from their Italian teacher.

'I wanted to punish him, not ruin his life! He isn't being bullied over what he did to Cameron, Meredith. He's being tortured because... because...'

'Because they can,' finished Meredith. 'There's no easy way to say that and not make it sound awful, I know. They're doing it to Blake because they can get away with it with him and they know they can't get away with doing it to Cameron, because Cameron is one of us.'

'And that doesn't make you feel just the tiniest bit of sympathy for him?'

Meredith hesitated, then suppressed her qualms. 'No. It doesn't. I told Blake at the end of last year that he couldn't expect help from any of us. We're not breaking rank on this one, Imogen. Safety in numbers, remember? Blake got himself into this mess; he can get himself out.'

Bowing to the dictates of pragmatism, Imogen sighed and changed the topic of conversation. 'What's your outfit like for Kerry's?'

'Gorgeous. I've tried to model it on a cross between Jacqueline de Ribe, Princess Margaret and Grace Kelly. I look very thin in it.'

At that stage, Miss Flanagan had obviously had enough and rapped her desk with a ruler. 'Ragazze, calma por favore!'

◇◇◇

It was a rare thing for Catherine O'Rourke to be totally right about anything, but she had certainly been correct in saying that this year's theme for Kerry's birthday was much easier to get right than last year's. Given that last year Catherine herself had turned up dressed like Little Bo Beep with a makeshift wig made out of toilet paper and talcum powder, she knew more than anyone how fiendishly difficult the Marie-Antoinette theme had been. This time, everybody had stuck to the theme and every possibility of the 1950s seemed to have been incarnated by the attending Mount Oliveteans. Peter Sullivan had turned up as a bulkier version of Danny Zucko from *Grease* and spent the night teasing and flirting with Catherine, who came as one of the Pink Ladies. Kerry looked like a picture perfect housewife in a pink dress, with a single rope of pearls around her neck; Imogen turned up looking like a 1950s movie star in a floor-length silver lamé dress with a ribbed bodice and white evening gloves reaching just past her elbows; Meredith had been true to her word and looked like she had just left a cocktail party on the Côte d'Azur *circa* 1957, in a tight fitting white dress with two streams of loose white fabric streaming from her shoulders. She had edged the outfit up a bit with a pair of white Louboutin heels, but the rest of her was period accurate, with her nails painted a deep red, gold bangles and bracelets on her wrists, and one enormous knuckleduster of a yellow diamond ring on the fourth finger of her right hand. Like Imogen, her lips were a bright red; unlike Imogen, who had worn her hair up, Meredith had swept hers sleekly over to the side. Cameron, who had much less room for manoeuvre than the girls when it came to the Fifties, had decided to come as Meredith's aristocratic playboy husband in a tailored suit, with a pair of his father's old sunglasses and a cravat. Punch bowls, pink lemonade and enlarged cut-outs of 1950s advertisements had been strategically dotted throughout the house by Kerry and her mother. Sound systems were placed in every room on the ground floor, disguised as juke-boxes.

The first hiccup of the night came when Peter Sullivan attempted to talk to Kerry, to clear up the animosity that had started on the night she saw him kissing Tangela Henton-Worley. He found her replenishing the punch bowl, with her left heel held out aloft behind her in what she imagined to be a delightfully authentic 1950s pose.

'Happy birthday, Kerry,' he said, tapping her on the shoulder. 'Great party.'

'Yes, Peter; it is,' she said coldly. 'How's your tooth?'

Peter laughed. 'Since you tried to knock it in? It's fine. That was pretty funny.'

'Hilarious.'

'Ah, Kerry, come on now. I know you're pissed off about me hooking up with Tangela, but I didn't even know you were interested. I didn't hear anything from you after the ball, so I thought...'

'I'm the girl, Peter! I don't have to make the effort.'

'Okay. Well, just because I'm a boy doesn't mean that I'm a mind-reader. I am sorry if I upset you, though. If I'd known there was a chance of you and me happening, I wouldn't have gone anywhere near Tangela.'

'Go near her all you want, Peter. I know she's obsessed with you. It really isn't any of my business.'

With that, Kerry flounced away from him, leaving Peter to raise his eyebrows and puff out his cheeks.

◇◇◇

Meredith was sipping a martini at the foot of the stairs, enjoying a conversation with Anastasia (dressed as a debutante) and Lavinia (a pre-alopecia Edith Bouvier Beale), when Imogen waltzed over shivering.

'You know if this party stuck to its theme, we'd be allowed to smoke inside.'

'I know,' Lavinia sympathised. 'It's so brr outside.'

'So brr,' agreed Imogen. 'By the way, have you seen Catherine?'

'She's making out with Quentin Smith,' Meredith said, rolling her eyes. 'I'm not even kidding. I hate the way she kisses people in public.'

'Quentin Smith?' Lavinia asked. 'But he's stunning. A&F-model-hot. How did this happen?'

'Catherine is actually very pretty,' Anastasia announced languidly. 'You just forget that because she's so retarded.'

Meredith and Imogen nodded. 'She is naturally pretty,' Meredith agreed.

'She's boy-pretty,' Anastasia continued. 'Boys find her pretty because she's unthreatening.'

Imogen agreed. 'Yes. She's safe-pretty. She must be plastered to have gone anywhere near Quentin without peeing herself in fright.'

'Apparently they were talking at your birthday,' Lavinia said.

'Oh please,' replied Meredith. 'That has nothing to do with it. The only reason they're kissing now is because Quentin's probably drunk and Catherine makes it so pathetically obvious how keen she is that he knows he won't have to work that hard. It's so embarrassing.'

Cameron slid into view beside them. 'This music is amazing! Hey, where's Freddie?'

'I left him outside,' Imogen said dismissively. 'He's talking to Titus. He'll be fine.'

'Someone come dance with me,' Cameron asked. 'It's so much fun.'

'I'll dance,' said Meredith, draining the last of her martini. 'I may not be able to move very much in this dress, but I'll do my best.'

Cameron smiled and offered her his hand, twirling her on to the centre of the room. Imogen looked over at the drinks table to see Peter Sullivan playing an intense game of beer pong with four of the other rugby guys, one of who was definitely on the precipice of vomiting.

'Potential whitey victim,' Imogen said, nodding in the poor guy's direction. 'A tenner says he vomits before midnight.'

'I'll take that bet,' smiled Anastasia. 'I think he'll make it past midnight.'

◇◇◇

As it turned out, Matthew Kilbride did not make it past midnight. Imogen was richer by ten pounds and Kerry's rockery was stained with beer-induced vomit, all of which had been captured by Peter on his mobile phone for youtubing purposes. In the midst of the digestive disaster, Cameron found Kerry standing like an icon of repressed Fifties domesticity in her laundry room, with a glass of wine resting on the tumble dryer, silently crying to herself.

'Kerry?'

'My beautiful party,' she cried. 'This is not the kind of party you vomit at. Everything was supposed to be pretty and delightful this evening. This is the Age of Fabulous and now someone has been sick in my garden!'

Cameron patted Kerry on the shoulder. 'There, there, princess. It's alright. Nobody really cares.'

'I care! That brute is never coming to any of our parties again. Do you hear me?'

'It wasn't really Matty's fault, in fairness. It's just the bad luck of beer pong.'

'And who started that? Whose stupid idea was it to start that stupid game? It was Peter Sullivan's, wasn't it?'

Cameron shrugged and swayed a little on his feet. Beer pong had definitely been Peter's idea, but given that the last time Kerry had been angry with him he'd ended up needing an emergency dentist appointment the next morning, he theorized that telling her so was a bad idea.

'Right,' said Kerry, mid-sob, 'I have guests to look after.'

She held her head up bravely and walked past Cameron to the door, imagining that she was walking back out to her party as the apotheosis of a perfect hostess. In reality, her eyes were blood red from crying and the occasional sob was still escaping from her body. Following her out into the corridor, Cameron noted with dread that Peter was approaching, cackling hysterically at Matthew's recent vomit attack. Kerry held up her hand at Cameron, indicating that she would not be responsible for her actions if Peter came anywhere near her. Moving quickly to prevent a FIM (Fury Induced Meltdown), Cameron stepped in front of Peter before he could reach Kerry.

'Pete? Fancy a walk outside?'

'Coming on to me?' Peter winked, flinging his arms around Cameron's shoulder. 'Only a matter of time, my friend. Alright, let's go for a "walk." Here, Kerry – I wouldn't go picking any flowers tomorrow! Matty's fertilized them pretty badly.'

Cameron picked up his speed as Kerry spun round with a face like the Donegal banshee. By the time she had been surrounded by a comforting Imogen and Catherine, Cameron had managed to steer Peter out the back door and into the garden.

'I'm just trying to channel my inner-goddess and be a good hostess,' Kerry said, tremulously taking Catherine's hand and trying to look stoical. 'It's my birthday.'

'And it's fabulous, Kerry,' Imogen said emphatically. 'Remember, even vomit cannot undermine the AOF. Nothing can.'

Kerry nodded. 'You're right. Nothing can. Fabulous!'

10
THE PERSONAL PURGATORY OF BLAKE HARTMAN

Mark was sitting in the Sixth Form Centre with Peter on Monday morning, flicking pennies into an empty coffee cup when Coral walked in, looking extremely angry.

'Mark, can I talk to you for a minute, please? Alone.'

'Eh... sure,' he said.

The minute she was sure nobody could hear them, Coral launched into her tirade. 'You tried out for the rugby team?'

'Well, yeah. I told you I was going to.'

'And I told you how I felt about it! The only reason I found out that you lied to me is because there's a sheet up on the notice board saying you're on the squad. How do you think I felt finding out that way, Mark?'

'I got on the team? Seriously?'

'That's not the point,' she snapped. 'I told you how much I hate the culture of rugby and you still went ahead and did it anyway.'

'Coral, I'm not the kind of guy who feels the need to clear my extra-curricular activities with my girlfriend before she "allows" me to do them.'

'You just can't wait to be part of that crowd, can you? So cliquey and so loud and so stupid. You know you're a lot more like Cameron Matthews than you think.'

Coral stormed out of the centre, leaving Mark to walk back to Peter in a towering temper.

◇◇◇

Two days after their first fight, Mark and Coral were still not speaking to each other. Rather than sit with her at lunch, Mark had gone up to the school's computer suite to start work on his first Theatre Studies essay of the term: -

Critically assess the differences between "Dangerous Liaisons" and "Cruel Intentions."

'What's this for?'

He swivelled round in his seat to see a curious Meredith standing over his shoulder. 'Theatre Studies,' he answered.

'If I'd known Theatre Studies set questions like this, I might have considered doing it.'

'You know *Dangerous Liaisons*?'

Meredith looked at him with a sarcastically amused expression and Mark laughed. 'Right,' he said. 'Of course you do. Well in that case, you're probably better equipped to answer this question than I am. As far as I can see, they're basically the same story.'

'Same storyline,' Meredith corrected, sitting down next to him, 'not the same story.'

'What?'

'They have the same storyline, but they're not the same story. *Cruel Intentions* is set in New York in the 1990s, but the original was set in Paris in the 1700s. The original characters lived in a world where the stakes were much, much higher than they are in *Cruel Intentions*. Everything that happens in *Cruel Intentions*

– the seduction, the deceit and the scandal – may be embarrassing, but people can find a way to live with it. In the eighteenth century, you couldn't live without your reputation. You had to keep it, no matter what. If you were a man, it meant that you couldn't let anybody get away with laughing at you; they had to respect you and fear you. So if somebody did disrespect you, you had to fight duels with them to prove your honour, like Danceny and Valmont did. If you were a woman, it meant you had to be pure, beautiful, proper and live within the rules. When Reese Witherspoon ditches the silver ring in *Cruel Intentions*, it's not that big a deal, but when Madame de Tourvel and Cécile get seduced in *Dangerous Liaisons*, they've basically destroyed their lives and brought shame on their families. They're different stories because everything in the original is played to a higher stake. Like Merteuil says, in *Dangerous Liaisons* it's win or die. Kind of like Malone.'

'I think this is the longest you and I have ever spoken to each other without shouting.'

'*Dangerous Liaisons* is one of my favourite stories. Anyway, I've got to get down to the cafeteria. Good luck with the essay.'

'Thanks.'

'And congratulations about getting on to the Firsts,' she said as she reached the doorway. 'That's amazing.'

'Thanks, Meredith. I really appreciate that.'

Meredith smiled and walked out the door, almost colliding with Coral who was standing outside, glaring at her. Meredith did a quick flick up and down with her eyes, before smirking and walking away.

◇◇◇

'Mark? Coral's here to see you.'

In a pair of grey sweats and a black t-shirt, Mark walked down the stairs on hearing his mother's voice.

Coral was sitting in his living room, politely refusing Jennifer Kingston's offer of tea, coffee, water, juice, lemonade or something to eat.

'We're okay, Mum,' Mark said. 'Thanks.'

'Well, let me know if you two need anything.'

'Thanks.'

'How did you get here?' Mark asked, as soon as his mother had left.

'I got my brother to give me a lift,' she explained. 'Do you not want me here?'

'No, it's not that,' he shrugged, still not sitting down. 'You just could have called, that's all.'

Mark regretted it almost as soon as the words had left his mouth. Coral looked upset and then angry. He did have homework, though, and she should at least have called or texted before turning up unannounced at his house.

'Worried I might interrupt you and Meredith?' she said angrily. 'I'll go then. I'm sorry. I shouldn't have come. Clearly.'

Mark put his hands on her arms as she tried to walk by him and he steered her gently back to the sofa. 'No, stay. I'm sorry. I didn't mean it that way. I just have a lot of work this week and I was surprised to see you – that's all. I thought you still weren't speaking to me?'

'You haven't been speaking to me, either,' she said, looking up at him fearfully. *Why hadn't he denied the point about Meredith?*

'I know. I'm sorry. But, Coral, you have to admit that you completely overreacted about the rugby thing. You should have been happy for me. I told you how much I wanted to do it. I'm not asking you to come to every match or suddenly become best friends with the lads on the team, but you had no right to storm into the Sixth Form Centre and start yelling at me just because you don't like the game.'

'I wasn't yelling,' Coral said unhappily. 'But you're right; I should have been more supportive. It's just that I think you're incredible, Mark, and I was afraid that once you became part of the Firsts you'd want a "popular" girlfriend and you'd break up with me.'

'Coral, don't be silly. I love being your boyfriend.'

'Really? You wouldn't rather have somebody like Meredith?'

'What is it about you and Meredith? That's the second time you've mentioned her tonight. No! I really, really would not rather have her as my girlfriend.'

'That's not what it looked like today in the ICT room.'

'What?'

'I saw you, Mark! I saw you and her chatting in there over lunch.'

Mark laughed. 'That! She was just helping me with my drama essay.'

'Meredith Harper doesn't help people! And she certainly doesn't help you. You two are supposed to hate each other, remember?'

'You know that for Cameron's sake we try to be civil to each other and I think that's best. I don't have a major problem with Meredith anymore and, yes, okay, I hate the way she treats people and I wish she was a better person, but she's been a really good friend to Cameron. She's never let him down. I'm trying to do the best thing for a mate here, Coral. It doesn't mean I fancy Meredith Harper. Believe me.'

'Really?'

'Really.'

Coral nodded and placed her hand in his. She looked pacified and reassured. 'That's all I needed to hear, thank you.'

'Why are you so jealous of her?' he asked, pulling her back so her head rested on his shoulder.

'Because she's so beautiful and she has everything and she can't have you.'

'I thought you didn't think she was beautiful?' Mark half-joked.

'Look at her.'

Mark nodded and they sat for a moment in silence. Now that they had resolved their fight, Mark did feel better and he snuggled his girlfriend in closer to him. He felt bad that she felt threatened by Meredith Harper. It was also less than reassuring to have yet another person close to him suggest that he had romantic feelings for Our Lady of BT9.

'I'm friendly to her for Cameron's sake,' he said eventually. 'I'm not friends with her.'

'Why is it so important to Cameron that you two get along?'

'Because he loves her and part of me is grateful to her.'

'Grateful? To Meredith?'

'Last year, when he was going through all that stuff, me and him weren't speaking. Meredith was there for Cameron when I wasn't. I used to think she was only friends with him because he fitted into her little Malone Road bubble, but she stuck by him when I didn't. So I have to be grateful to her for that. I can't imagine what it would have been like if Cameron had gone through all that on his own. Like Blake is this year.'

'Poor Blake,' Coral said stroking her fingers along Mark's. 'It's just awful what they're doing to him. It's so backward.'

'Yeah. No one came over to speak to him to tell him they'd still be friends with him, did they?'

'No.'

'Do you think I should maybe get in touch with him? Hang out with him or something? The poor guy. I mean, I know what he did to Cameron and Catherine was wrong, but everyone makes mistakes and he hasn't got anybody else. I feel really bad for him.'

Coral took her head off his shoulder and looked at him. 'You want to hang out with Blake Hartman?'

'Yeah. I feel like I should. We were quite friendly last year before everything kicked off and...'

'How do you think Cameron's going to feel about that?'

'I'd check with him first obviously, but even Cameron can't want him to be this miserable.'

'You already have one gay best friend, Mark. You don't need another.'

'Excuse me?'

'Some people already wonder about you and Cameron. Do you really want to start getting friendly with Blake as well?'

'People wonder what about me and Cameron?'

'A lot of them think that you're gay together.'

Mark began to get flustered. 'That's bollocks. He's my friend. He's my best friend. Not my...'

'*I* know that, but sometimes I wonder if other people do. Sometimes I even wonder if Cameron does. Deep down.'

'He doesn't feel that way about me,' Mark said. 'I asked him once and he said no.'

'What else could he have said?' Coral asked, sympathetically. 'Think about it, babe. He's gay, you're a guy, you've known each other for years and no one looks out for him like you do. If you had a friendship with a girl like that, how would you feel about her? I'm not saying it makes Cameron a bad person or that he's trying to jump you at the first available opportunity. All I'm saying is, you're in a difficult situation and maybe you should be careful before you start campaigning for gay rights or become Blake Hartman's number one defender, as well as Cameron's. I don't care, obviously.

I just don't know how all your new friends on the rugby team would like being in the changing rooms with you if they thought you were gay. But you know more about it than I do. It's completely up to you and I'll support you no matter what.'

She settled her head back on to Mark's shoulder and waited two minutes before changing the topic of conversation.

◇◇◇

If Blake Hartman had been Catholic, he would have described the three months in his life between September and December of Lower Sixth as purgatorial. However, since he was a Protestant, he recognized them quite simply as being hellish. Some days were better than others, although even the best was marred by the fact that his brother Jack seemed to veer from embarrassment to truculence around him. It was a change in the brothers' relationship which their father noticed but couldn't get to the bottom of; any attempt to question either of the boys inevitably resulted in evasion or aggression. Robert Hartman had still, thankfully, not found out about Blake's sexuality, but he could see that his eldest son had become morose, withdrawn and deeply unhappy.

In the seven weeks since term had started and the story about him and Cameron had become public knowledge, there was a group of boys in the year below who had started making exaggerated effeminate sounds when Blake walked past in the corridor. In his own year, some of the guys had taken to whispering things *sotto voce* like 'Watch your arse, lads! Hartman's about!' when he entered the room, or co-ordinating turning their backs against the wall when he walked by. Copies of the front cover of *Attitude* and photos of half-naked men had been left stuck to the front of his school locker; condoms smeared with moisturizer had been dumped in his schoolbag when he wasn't looking and one of the rugby players, Harry Irwin, had threatened to 'beat the shit' out of Blake if he ever again came into the changing rooms when he was getting changed.

What made it even worse was that Blake felt there was nothing he could do to stop it. He was too mortified to actually go to any of the staff, in case they contacted his father. Every now and then, some of the teachers would upbraid a student if they heard them being openly cruel towards Blake, but that was like plugging a cork in the side of the *Titanic*. Some of the male teachers silently allowed the bullying to carry on under their noses, leaving Blake with the indelible impression that they either found what was being said funny or they thought he had brought the whole thing on himself. His middle names were Joshua and Elijah, but when his name was posted as "B.J. Hartman" in the Technology roll call, their teacher Mr Turner had unsuccessfully attempted to hide a grin when some of the other pupils began catcalling Blake and banging the table in amusement at his initials. When Blake had tentatively pointed out at the end of class that he had a third name, Mr Turner had replied, 'So do a lot of other people, Blake. It doesn't mean we have to change the entire register for them.'

In numerical terms, the students actively bullying Blake amounted to less than one in ten of the school's population. Those actively defending him, however, formed an even smaller ratio. Peter Sullivan tripped up one of the fifth-year boys who was taking verbal pot shots at Blake in the corridor; a few others told people to shut up when they started making fun of him. But the vast majority stayed silent. Like Mark, many of the guys feared being tarred with the brush of being called gay if they defended Blake too much; some of the girls either fancied the guys doing the bullying or were so outraged on Catherine's behalf that they felt Blake deserved this humiliation. The Christian Union, who ordinarily could have been counted upon to intervene, were in a quandary because they felt that defending Blake would be an implicit endorsement of homosexuality. It never seemed to occur to them that not saying anything was an implicit endorsement of bullying. The popular girls, like Imogen, were still ignoring Blake's very existence under combined pressure from Meredith, who refused to budge on the issue of helping him, and Kerry, who seemed to think he was a potential torpedo in the side of her beloved Age of Fabulous.

By the end of October, Blake had therefore taken to avoiding the cafeteria entirely to work in the library, which meant that his grades had improved greatly (the semester's only silver lining). He was pouring over his Spanish homework one afternoon when he was interrupted by a polite cough from the other side of the table; he saw a girl from his form class standing opposite him with a smile on her face, holding a large cupcake, topped with blue icing and an unlit candle.

'Hi!'

'Hi,' he stammered. 'It's Rosie, right?'

'That's right,' she beamed, pulling out a seat and sitting down. 'Rosie Prentice. I'm in your house. We sat next to each other on the first day of term. Remember?'

'Yeah,' Blake nodded. 'Sorry I wasn't very talkative that day. I had a lot on my mind.'

'That's okay! Don't worry about it. Sometimes I get like that, too. Anyway, happy birthday!' She proffered the cupcake, widening her smile into a grin. 'I couldn't light the candle, because I'm just about hoping they won't notice I've smuggled food in here, but I'd probably be chancing my luck if I started a small fire. What's a birthday cake without a candle, though? Even if you can't light it!'

Blake stared speechlessly at the cupcake and then glanced up at Rosie's face, in question.

'It is your birthday, isn't it?' she asked. Her smile didn't falter. 'We're friends on Facebook and it came up on my feed that today was your birthday, so I thought I should bring you in a cake to celebrate.'

Blake smiled with gratitude and reached out to take the cupcake. 'Thank you. That's really kind of you. I appreciate this, Rosie. A lot. Nobody else remembered.'

'That's because people here are being really awful to you, Blake. They've been socially conditioned into thinking this kind of behaviour is acceptable, but it isn't. You need to remember that you've nothing to be ashamed of and that most of the people doing this to you are probably just really paranoid and unhappy on the inside.'

Blake said nothing. The last thing he wanted to hear right now was someone trying to make him feel sorry for his bullies. As far as he was concerned, they could burn for all eternity on Satan's barbecue before he would ever worry about their feelings and insecurities.

'Look. I know what you're going through,' continued Rosie. 'At my last school, everybody hated me and I went to a really dark place. Metaphorically. That's why I started the anti-bullying initiative when I transferred here. Not a lot of people have joined so far, but it's a good idea, don't you think?'

'Yeah... I'm really sorry to hear you had a hard time at your old school,' said Blake, sympathetically. 'It sounds awful.'

'It's in the past,' smiled Rosie. 'Try the cupcake. It's homemade!'

◇◇◇

Rain lashed against the windows of the Sixth Form Centre as Imogen nursed her second coffee of the morning. Kerry was flicking indifferently through a celebrity gossip magazine.

'Anything interesting?'

Kerry shrugged. 'Not really. The bitch we hate has adopted another baby and they're cancelling that American show Catherine likes so much.'

Imogen laughed. 'Funny how all the men in Catherine's life end up leaving her.'

Kerry hummed a sound of non-committal agreement. Over the last few weeks, she had been getting on better with Catherine, but there was no point in interrupting Imogen mid-rant.

'Remember when she threw herself at Mark Kingston last year and he ditched her for Heather Blount?'

'Hmmm. I'd forgotten about that thing with her and Mark.'

'How? It was right before she tried to steal Peter from you. Although he's such a flirt I'm sure anyone could have done that. I used to think he had a thing for Meredith. Weird.'

'Well, he doesn't,' Kerry snapped. 'She's not his type. And he's not hers.'

'No. She has Francesco,' sighed Imogen. 'Can I say something about that, though? And don't tell any of the others I said it.'

Kerry's eyes sparkled with interest and she leaned in closer. 'Surezies.'

'Don't you think it's weird how she never really talks about him? *We* have to ask before she'll say anything about their relationship and even then, her answers are always really short.'

'I know! How often do they even see each other?'

'He's coming over for her godmother's birthday,' Imogen said, 'apparently. But she could easily go over and see him more often than she does. The flight's, like, an hour. If that.'

'Has she said anything to you about it?'

'God, no. I just have this feeling that she doesn't like him as much as she thinks she does.'

'Or thinks she *should*,' posited Kerry.

'Right.'

'Has Cameron said anything to you about it?'

Imogen shook her head and glanced around for someone to give her empty coffee cup to. The bin was at the far side of the room and she detested effort. 'Everything about that relationship is perfect. Except the actual relationship part. Trust Meredith to have something like that for her first romance. Cristyn, hi! Could you put that in the bin for me, please? Thanks.'

◇◇◇

'Quentin Smith is texting me!'

Imogen, Kerry, Meredith and Cameron all turned to look at Catherine in undisguised shock. They were sitting at their table in the cafeteria and Kerry had been busy extracting the blue sweets from her packet of Smarties, because blue sweets displeased her.

'Quentin Smith is texting you?' Imogen asked. 'The captain of the rugby team is texting *you*?'

Catherine nodded and grinned. 'How beau is that?'

'That's not how you use that word,' groaned Meredith. 'It means something is beautiful, not scientifically improbable!'

Since she didn't entirely understand Meredith's jibe, Catherine smiled and ignored it. 'Yeah, he got my number at Kerry's party and he was texting me, like, all day yesterday. Can you believe it?'

'No,' Kerry answered brutally. 'Quentin Smith? Are you sure it's not a prank?'

'No!' Catherine beamed. 'Definitely not. Seriously, he's so nice and his texts have been really flirty. I definitely think he's going to ask me to be his girlfriend.'

Imogen stared at Catherine with jealous dislike. 'I thought Quentin was fooling around with Cecilia Molyneux?'

'Not anymore!' Catherine shot back, all traces of merriment suddenly wiped from her face. 'She's lives in Manchester now. I can show you the texts he sent me!'

She handed her phone to Imogen, who snatched it from her. Kerry huddled in to look at the messages and earned a vicious elbowing from Imogen when she announced, 'Those are actually really promising, Catherine.'

Imogen kept reading. This could not be happening again. How did Catherine keep landing these stunning specimens as her love interests? Alright, the last one had been gay, but still *extremely* attractive. Now, Catherine had managed to nab the equally good looking and undeniably heterosexual captain of the rugby team, whilst Imogen was stuck dating a guy whose life seemed to be divided between his boring old surfboard and his stupid books. Cameron looked across the table at Meredith and raised a conspiratorial eyebrow. Imogen's seething silence made the whole thing a lot more interesting than Catherine's happiness.

'Hey babe!' Freddie swooped in from behind Imogen and kissed her on the cheek. His friend Titus stood behind him, waving politely to the group. 'What are you reading?'

'Texts from Quentin Smith and Catherine,' Imogen replied sourly, tossing the phone back across the table. 'Apparently it's quite the love fest.'

'Oh my god, Imogen. Shut up. That's so embarrassing,' preened Catherine, who had never looked less embarrassed by anything in her entire life.

'Quentin?' Titus asked tactlessly. 'I thought he was hooking up with Mariella Thompson?'

Freddie turned to him and mimed for him to be quiet, but the group had scented gossip like a limping gazelle on the Serengeti. A stunned look smacked on to Catherine's face and a correspondingly euphoric one lit up Imogen's like the sun appearing from behind a cloud. 'What? What!' she gasped. 'Quentin and Mariella?'

'It's not anything official,' Freddie explained. 'It's just... Quentin doesn't like things to get too serious with girls. Not too quickly, I mean...'

'Freddie, don't interrupt,' Imogen commanded, rubbing his arm. 'Titus was speaking! Quentin and Mariella, you say?'

Titus shrugged uncomfortably. Catherine was gazing at him as if he had stolen Christmas from her. 'That's what I heard. It's probably nothing. I also heard that he might be going on dates with Jordan Morris, too. *But,* I'm pretty sure he's stopped seeing that girl from Saint Gregory's, so... that's good? I don't really know Quentin that well. We just have Chemistry together. I feel really awkward right now.'

'Quentin takes his time making his mind up,' Freddie said, moved to pity by Catherine's facial expression. 'I wouldn't worry too much, Catherine. If he's texting you, he obviously likes you.'

Catherine nodded. 'Yeah. Yeah. You're right, Freddie. Thanks. Yeah, that's a really good way of looking at it, isn't it, guys?' Kerry diplomatically avoided her gaze, whilst Imogen almost gave herself whiplash with the speed at which she spun round to look at Freddie in thwarted fury. 'You're right. I'll just talk to him later. I'll text him now, actually. What should I say? I should probably keep it casual, shouldn't I? Guys, help me decide what to type! Okay, I'll start with "Hey."'

◆◇◆

Blake and Rosie Prentice were sitting together on the steps near the library, eating the sandwiches they had bought for lunch.

'Do you still love him?' she asked.

Blake paused. 'Yes. I do. At least, I think I do.'

'Think?'

'I haven't spoken to him in months,' he smiled ruefully. 'There are times when it feels like being that close to him was a dream. How can you know if you're in love with someone who you were close to for four months, then stopped speaking to for nine?'

'You know,' Rosie decided. 'You still are. I can tell. Can I say something? And I'm only saying it because I love you.'

Touched but a little surprised at how quickly she had moved from casual acquaintanceship to intense friendship, Blake nodded for her to continue.

'I don't think it's right that he's let you go through all of this alone. You just said you haven't spoken to Cameron in months, but that also means he hasn't spoken to you in months. Okay, two months of those were the summer holidays, but you've had such a hard time since September, Blake, and Cameron has done literally nothing to help you or even let you know he's thinking about you. I'm sorry, but I think that's wrong.'

'Wrong?'

'Wrong as in immoral, not wrong as in incorrect,' she clarified.

'Cameron's going through the same thing,' Blake said quietly.

'He isn't and you know he isn't. Nothing really bad has happened to him since everybody found out. Nothing compared to what's happened to you. I think if he was worthy of your love, he would have found a way to let you know he cared about you and that he was sorry for how you were being treated.'

'What I did to him was terrible, Rosie.'

'What he's doing to you is worse.'

Blake took a bite of his sandwich and looked down. He hated to admit that part of him agreed with what Rosie was saying. It had now been over two months since the scandal about his sexuality had broken over Mount Olivet and through it all – through the humiliation, the self-doubt, the crisis of confidence, the teasing, the taunting and the name-calling – Cameron had not offered him one tiny sign of recognition, let alone of comfort. Moreover, Rosie was right in saying that nothing like what had happened to Blake seemed to be happening to Cameron. The Malone girls and the BT9 boys seemed fundamentally indifferent to the issue of his sexuality. Cameron was, first and foremost, part of the club created by privilege and nothing would be able to detonate him out of that. As far as the Malone crowd were concerned, there was a lot of truth in Meredith's (half) joking mantra that 'Homophobia is for poor people.' Every now and then, when he looked at his life and then looked at Cameron's, Blake did feel an acid reflux of anger at the sheer injustice of it all.

'What I did to him was awful,' he repeated. 'I don't expect him to help me. I just hope he forgives me, one day.'

Rosie leaned up and kissed him on the cheek. 'I think you're incredible, Blake. You're such a wonderful guy and I know that one day Cameron will be kicking himself for what he's done to you. Trust me. It'll be him asking for forgiveness, not you.'

◇◇◇

At least once a week, Meredith and her father made a point of going out for dinner. Tonight, she was sitting opposite him in the restaurant of the Merchant Hotel in the city's Cathedral Quarter. He was wearing a suit, but no tie, and Meredith was wearing a new Issa dress that she loved more than she loved several of her closest friends.

'How's the salmon?' she asked.

'Lovely,' he replied. 'Very nice, indeed. I booked your flights to see Francesco in November, by the way. Over Friday afternoon and back on Sunday evening?'

'That's perfect, Daddy. Thank you.'

'Is there anything else I need to book?' he asked, guilelessly.

'A hotel room, please,' she answered immediately, as if her father had just asked her to paddle across the Irish Sea to see Francesco.

'In the centre of Oxford?'

'If that's possible. I obviously won't be staying in Francesco's room,' she declared primly. 'Can you imagine? No, I don't think so. A hotel room, please, Daddy.'

Anthony Harper returned to his salmon with a joyful zest that only a father could understand.

11
NO SUCH THING AS A FRIENDLY GAME

Autumn had well and truly come to Oxford by the time Meredith found herself sitting at a wooden table in a riverside pub, enjoying lunch with Francesco. She wore a blue cashmere wrap to guard against the chill and the sun was no longer bright enough to justify sunglasses, much to her distress. On the other side of the table, Francesco looked snug in his quilted jacket and merino wool sweater. Most of the tables were occupied by Francesco's fellow Oxford students, including a few from nearby Merton College, who Francesco had introduced to Meredith but hadn't invited to join them.

'Oxford is very beautiful, isn't it?' he asked, taking another sip from his half-finished gin and tonic.

'Yes, it really is.'

'Where would you like to get dinner tonight? Some of my friends very much want to meet you, but I really think I would rather spend some time together. Just the two of us.'

Meredith smiled. 'That would be nice. We can meet them for drinks before dinner, or after. To be polite. I don't really mind where we eat. I don't know anywhere that's good for dinner, apart from my hotel – so I'll leave it up to you.'

'There are some great little places up in Jericho,' he said. 'I can't see us needing a reservation. How are your friends, by the way? I haven't really heard you talk about them.'

'They're fine. Kerry detests pretty much every class she's taking this year and she keeps trying to organize parties to distract herself from them; Imogen's still dating Freddie Carrowdale, but I think that's solely down to the fact that he's quite handsome. Any day now, I'm sure, she'll end things with him.'

'Poor Freddie Carrowdale.'

'And Cameron seems to have sailed through the whole coming out business pretty well.'

'It hasn't changed his personality?' Francesco asked. 'It does to a lot of people, I think. Do you know what I'm talking about? Once it's happened, they all of a sudden become a lot more, eh, flamboyant and they talk about it, sex, I mean, or being gay, all the time. Am I making sense? I don't particularly feel as if I am.'

'You are, but that hasn't happened to Cameron,' Meredith smiled. 'He's like us, Francesco. He knows how to behave.'

'That's good to hear.'

'The only noticeable change, I suppose, is that Cameron seems quite a bit more confident in himself, which is a good thing. I don't think he would hold up well in a direct confrontation about it, at least not yet, but he is definitely far more at ease with himself. Apart from that, no real change. Although you're right, it does happen to a lot of people. I don't mind people being effeminate or flamboyant, of course. Why would I? Effeminate and flamboyant doesn't necessarily mean someone isn't good company. I don't particularly care what people are, as long as they're interesting, but when *anyone* is too loud or too annoying, I tend to dislike them. If a girl flounced around like a demented hooker, I'd hate her too.'

'Full equal rights?' Francesco joked.

'Exactly.'

'I found out yesterday that I am definitely going to be able to make it to your godmother's birthday, by the way.'

'Oh good,' smiled Meredith. 'That's perfect. She'll be so pleased and her house is incredible. You'll love it.'

'I can't wait,' he said, reaching across the table to take her hand. 'And I'm very happy you're here, Meredith. I really am.'

◇◇◇

As Meredith was enjoying lunch in Oxford with Francesco, Peter and Cameron were splitting a pizza in Cameron's kitchen and talk turned to the subject of "Mark and Mandrews."

'Does he seem weird with me recently?' Cameron asked, as Peter rolled up a slice and bit half of it off in one go.

'Not really,' he answered. 'A bit quiet, maybe, but he always goes like this once in a while. How do you mean "weird"?'

'I don't know,' Cameron answered. 'He just seems a bit stand-offish or something. Not all the time, just… every now and then. I don't know. It's weird.'

'He's weird,' dismissed Peter. 'He gets these wee moods all the time and he's been shit craic ever since he started going with Coral.'

Partially reassured, Cameron nodded and lifted out a slice of pizza. 'You're probably right.'

◇◇◇

Kerry skipped merrily out of the guest bathroom in Imogen's house and returned to the kitchen where Imogen and Catherine were busy whipping up another round of homemade cocktails. Catherine was sporting a new hair cut, which had involved dyeing her hair to a slightly darker colour than usual. The change suited her and since both Kerry and Imogen were in good moods, they had showered her with praise.

'Have we decided where we're going tonight?' Kerry asked. 'Somewhere fabulous, but nowhere where Peter Sullivan is going. I do *not* like that boy.'

'We can decide later,' Imogen said, as she chopped up some more limes.

'Is Freddie coming?' enquired Catherine, tossing her darkened locks over her shoulder with aplomb. 'Or is it just us girlies?'

'Just the girlies. He's got plans with the boys tonight at Titus's, which is fine by me. He's not really great at club scenes.'

'No, he isn't,' Kerry agreed.

'People can't be good at everything, Kerry!' Imogen shouted. 'It's not his fault he doesn't enjoy loud music.'

'Ehm, okay Psycho Cindy, please don't yell at me just because you've suddenly realized your boyfriend is boring. I warned you about this, but would you listen? No, of course you wouldn't. So now you're stuck with a boyfriend who quite simply isn't fabulous and you're blaming everybody but yourself.'

'Do you want a slap in the face?'

'Catherine thinks he's boring too!'

Imogen rounded on Catherine. 'Is that true?'

'I just don't know if he's the right kind of guy for you to be dating, babes,' she said fearfully.

'Oh, what, not gay enough for you, Catherine?'

'Imogen!' gasped Kerry. 'Too far.'

'I'm sorry,' Imogen said. 'He's just so boring. I mean, he's *so* boring. All he cares about is work, university applications, surfing and golf. He's driving me crazy! I don't even know where to begin. He's so dull! I don't think I can take it much longer.'

Catherine rubbed Imogen's shoulder sympathetically; Kerry happily turned to the freezer and fetched a large tub of ice cream.

'Time for a chat, ladies' she said.

◇◇◇

Mark stood with his red raw hands pressed against the kitchen radiator; his mother boiled the kettle and fished a £20 note out of her purse. A tool belt still hung from Mark's waist; he had been outside doing odd jobs for his mother to make a bit of extra pocket money. Over the last few weeks, his socializing expenditure seemed to have doubled. He had to find money to take Coral out, drink with the rugby lads and see all of his regular friends.

'Mum, I really think I'm going to need to get a proper job,' he said as she poured him a cup of tea. 'There's only so much I can do around the house and I really need the money.'

'Mark, your father would have a fit if he thought you had a job near the exams.'

'Well Dad doesn't live here, does he?'

'No, he doesn't, but that's not the point. He's still your father. If you really need the money and need to get a job, then sign on to a temping agency. That way, when it's time for the mocks and the exams, you won't be contracted to work if you don't want to.'

'I wouldn't do anything to risk my grades, Mum,' he said. 'You know I wouldn't.'

'Then we'll take you into town tomorrow and get you signed on to an agency, love. Here's your tea.'

◇◇◇

The following weekend, there was a friendly rugby game between the First XVs and the rival squad from Belmont Grammar. Belmont won 10 – 8 thanks to a drop goal right at the end of the game and the disappointment was written all over Mark Kingston's face as he returned to the changing rooms a defeated man after his first game for Mount Olivet. However, it was the games being played off the pitch that provided more interest for Kerry, Cameron and Meredith. First of all, there had been a hilariously awkward encounter between Catherine and Mariella Thompson, the popular girl in the year above who Titus had insinuated was also involved with Quentin Smith. Mariella seemed unaware that Catherine had a problem with her, but Catherine had done her level best to throw her dirty looks for the majority of the match. She had only stopped when Quentin did anything even remotely competent on the pitch, at which point Catherine either applauded or leapt to her feet with a scream, as if someone kept sending an electrical shock through her seat. Secondly, and even more amusingly, Coral had turned up to watch her boyfriend's first official game as a member of the squad.

She sat three rows behind Meredith's clique and four behind the other rugby girlfriends, none of who made any attempt to include her. Joanne and Paula had accompanied her and poor Paula couldn't have looked more terrified to be in the midst of a rowdy crowd of sports enthusiasts. For Cameron, the best bits of the afternoon came when major developments happened on the pitch, since Coral was so ignorant of the rules of rugby that she kept looking around in her in confusion to see what everybody else was doing.

'Look who's trying to fit in now?' he whispered maliciously to Meredith. She smirked in cruel agreement.

Imogen had enjoyed herself much less than her friends. Under normal circumstances, the sight of both Catherine and Coral making fools of themselves would have kept her entertained for hours, but she was too irritated by the fact that she had to sit in the row behind the squad's girlfriends. Last year, that had been her. She had been sitting up there, smiling and cheering proprietarily. It didn't occur to Imogen that even if she had stayed with Stewart, she wouldn't be sitting in that row today because he had transferred to another school. All she could feel was sorry for herself.

She was bored by her life again. If she had to listen to one more story about Freddie's application to Cambridge or his love of surfing, then she was going to have to kill herself. And him. It was almost a relief that she wasn't helping to organize the Our Lady of Lourdes ball this year, because that meant she wouldn't have to bring Freddie along as her plus one. That wasn't fair. He'd look very good in a tux.

Her gaze floated past the girls in front of her and on to the players. When did Oran Cahill get so good looking? And why in the name of goodness was someone as hot and tall as Colin Ferris dating someone like that mousy little fifth-year in front of her?

Her bad mood had still not alleviated after the game, when Catherine bounced over to talk to them in the car park.

'Quentin's having a party at his house tonight and he asked us to come!'

'Why's he having a party?' Imogen asked. 'They lost. What's there to celebrate?'

'It was only a friendly,' Catherine stammered.

'There's no such thing as a friendly game in rugby, Catherine. Trust me.'

'What's wrong with you?' Cameron asked. 'Who cares why he's having the party? Let's just go. It's not like we have anything else planned for tonight. Meredith?'

'We may as well,' Meredith agreed. 'Find out the times, Catherine.'

Catherine nodded obediently and began texting Quentin. Imogen sighed and tossed back her head. 'Fine! Ugh. God, it's so exhausting being popular.'

◇◇◇

Quentin Smith's party turned out to be one of those unplanned house parties that somehow organically became one of the biggest events of the term. Everyone who mattered in Mount Olivet was there. The house was packed and Quentin had managed to lay his hands on three or four kegs for his guests.

Separating from the girls in search of drinking utensils, Cameron weaved his way through the crowded kitchen. He stopped for a minute to say hi to Mary-Elizabeth and Kirsten, his sister's friends, who were standing together by the cooker, and asked them if they had seen the match that afternoon. It turned out that Kirsten had a crush on one of the fly-halves, who had invited her here this evening and she was very excited. Cameron wished her luck and continued in his quest, bumping into a few people, some of who were already pretty inebriated. He apologized to a girl he didn't recognize when they collided near the centre of the room, but she smiled and indicated that she wasn't offended. As he turned away from her, he accidentally nudged into Harry Irwin, a 6'2 eighteen-year-old with dark hair and brown eyes, who usually played fullback for the XVs. Years earlier, he had dated Anastasia Montmorency, who now loathed him more than any other human being currently alive.

Harry pushed Cameron back aggressively. 'Watch the fuck where you're going, you little faggot.'

For a moment, nobody in the immediate vicinity seemed to believe Harry had just said those words. After stumbling slightly from the surprise of Harry's shove, Cameron was looking up in the elder boy's red-rimmed eyes and wondering if he was about to receive his first ever punch in the face.

'Don't you ever fucking touch me again, do you hear me?' Harry snarled. 'Think you can grind up against me and I won't notice, faggot?'

From behind him one of his team mates looked apologetically at Cameron and laid a hand on Harry's shoulder. 'Mate, stop that. C'mon. It was an accident.'

'Was it fuck an accident! He was trying to get a feel of my dick. Weren't you?'

'No!' exclaimed Cameron.

'"No!"' mimicked Harry. 'Get the fuck away from me.'

Cameron turned and barged his way through the crowd. He could feel a blush spreading across his face and he seemed to have forgotten to breathe. How had this just happened to him? In front of basically everyone he knew. He had to get out of here, get upstairs, call a taxi and leave at the first available opportunity. By the time Harry announced, 'See? He's got nothing to say for himself when those three bitches aren't here to protect him,' Cameron had already made it through the kitchen doors and was halfway up the stairs, where he encountered Imogen, deep in conversation with Kerry.

'Princess, where are our glasses?' Kerry asked. 'We still don't have any.'

Cameron rushed past them, muttering, 'I'm going home. I just need to... use the bathroom.'

Recognizing a mid-party bathroom meltdown when they saw one, Kerry and Imogen followed him. The last thing Cameron wanted was for anyone to see him like this, but he didn't really trust himself to start speaking, so he kept quiet and continued walking. Imogen and Kerry were going to follow no matter what he did. He didn't even bother to lock the door as he stepped into an empty bathroom; he sat on the edge of the bath, holding on to it with his hands.

'Cameron, sweetie, what's wrong?' Imogen asked softly. 'Has something happened?' 'I need to go home.'

'Why?'

Cameron shook his head. 'I don't feel well.'

Kerry bit her lip. She knew Cameron was lying, but she was nervous about pressing him too far for details in case it resulted in an explosion of bad temper.

'I don't feel well,' he repeated. 'I want to go home.'

'We can call a taxi,' Imogen assured him, 'but it'll take at least half an hour, maybe longer. It's a Saturday night, Cameron. Remember? So, in the meantime… what happened?'

'Nothing!' he shouted. 'Please. I'm serious. Just leave me alone.'

'Something obviously happened and please don't shout at me.'

'I don't want to talk about it! Nothing happened. Okay? Just leave it. Nothing happened. I don't feel well. I want to go home. You can't make me stay here.'

'I know we can't. But why are you…'

'Imogen! Seriously! Just forget it. Nothing happened!'

Kerry screamed in fear as the bathroom door flew open and Peter Sullivan stormed into the room.

'What the fuck did he say to you?'

None of them had ever seen Peter like this before. He was absolutely livid, his fists were clenched and he was breathing heavily. Nor had they fully appreciated just how brawny Peter was. You could actually see the muscles in his arms bulging as a result of his anger. Cameron shook his head mutely.

'I am not messing around here, Cameron. What the fuck did Harry Irwin say to you?'

'Harry Irwin?' Kerry asked. 'What did he do?'

'I don't know,' Peter replied, still staring at Cameron. 'I saw you bump into him, I saw him push you and say something, you ran out and now you're up here, hiding in the bathroom. Matty thinks it was something to do with you being gay. Was it?'

Cameron nodded.

'Right, get up and get downstairs. I will take you down there right now and make out with you right in front of him. Do you think I'm joking? I swear to God, I will. We're going downstairs! You do not let anybody speak to you that way! Do you hear me?' Peter roared. 'We are going downstairs, now!'

By this stage, both Imogen and Kerry were staring at Peter as if they had never seen anyone more attractive in their entire lives. He was like a medieval knight, a civil rights activist and a cage fighter all rolled into one.

'I'm not going down there.'

'I wasn't asking!'

Cameron shook his head. 'I'm not going. I want to go home.'

'Cameron, what did he say to you?' Peter asked, slightly more gently than before.

'He called me the f-word.'

'Fat?' gasped Kerry, her hand flying to her chest in horror.

'No. Faggot.'

Initially, nobody spoke. Imogen's lust-filled thoughts of Peter vanished and she instantly turned to regard Cameron with the one emotion he hated receiving the most – pity. Kerry stood still, with her hand still pressed to her chest, unsure of what to do or say and Peter fell silent before he said, 'Right.' He turned and ran out the door, thumping it as he left.

'Oh, shit,' panicked Cameron, leaping to his feet and rushing after him. 'Peter! Don't!'

An ecstatic Imogen grasped Kerry's hand and squeaked, 'Fight! *Fight*! The AOB is going militant. Grab the camera. Grab it! Let's go, go, go!'

It was magical how fast Imogen Dawson could move down a flight of stairs in high heels when in pursuit of scandal and even more amazing how quickly Kerry Davison could be moved when dragged along behind her. Cameron was ahead, dangerously clearing the stairs two or three at a time, but he hadn't been able to catch up with Peter, who not only had a head-start but was also taller, fitter and taking the stairs four or five at a time.

By the time the threesome hurtled into the kitchen, it was too late to stop Peter moving his way through the party towards Harry Irwin with rugby player-like efficiency. Peter's crowd-clearing tactics, however, were as nothing compared to Imogen's, who practically bulldozed twenty-five people out of her way in order to reach the centre of the excitement, occasionally using Kerry as a battering ram. One of the people she nearly toppled was Meredith, who spun round when she was shoved into Anastasia and Lavinia Barrington.

'Imogen!' she snapped. 'Am I invisible? You just pushed me. What is going on?'

'Fight,' Imogen said feverishly. 'Fight! Did you hear about Cameron and Harry Irwin? Fight!'

'Yeah, I heard he pushed him and I've been texting all of you to see what happened.'

'Harry pushed him and called him the f-word and now Peter Sullivan's going to go kick the crap out of him!'

'Move, Kerry, move!' squealed Meredith.

'If one of you pushes me again, you will die,' vowed Kerry.

'Just go!'

The three of them scythed their way through the crowd and hurtled into the centre of the room next to Cameron, just in time to see Peter walk over to Harry Irwin and shove him hard on the chest with both his hands.

'Oi, dickhead!' he yelled. 'What the fuck did you say to him?'

When Harry didn't immediately answer, Peter shoved him again, knocking him into the keg on which a terrified Catherine was perched mid-conversation with Celeste Fitzpatrick. Both girls screamed at seeing the 6'2 wall of muscle that was Harry Irwin fly towards them and Catherine ran in a blind panic to her friends, slamming into Imogen, who contemptuously tossed her out of the way in her zeal to see all of the drama unfold. Catherine toppled to the floor, but immediately sprang back up like a jack-in-the-box, with a floor welt on her forehead, announcing, 'I'm fine. I'm fine. I tripped!' Nobody noticed, because everyone was now rooted to the fight unfolding between Peter and Harry. From the back of the room, several of their team mates began elbowing their way towards the two boys, in the hope of separating them.

'What the fuck is wrong with you?' Harry yelled, pushing back against Peter.

'Don't you ever speak to him like that again!'

'Is this about Matthews? Why are you giving off stink about a queer?' Harry laughed. 'Are you shagging him?'

'If I was it'd be none of your fucking business! You touch him again and I swear to fuck, I will beat the living shit out of you, Irwin. That is not a lie.'

Mark moved in front of Peter and tried to push him back. 'Mate, c'mon. That's enough. Nobody wants to see a fight.'

'Eh, yes we do.'

'Imogen, stay out of this. Pete, c'mon. Leave it. Okay? You're both on the same team. Just leave it.'

Peter shoved Mark aside. 'Get out of my way. "Both on the same team." Jesus. When did you turn into such a friggin' hippie, Mark? Did Coral weave you a daisy chain? Get out of my way.'

Mark stepped away, clearly both surprised and affronted by what Peter had just said. Peter pointed a finger in Harry's face, 'Come near him again and I swear, no one will be able to pull me off you.'

'Look, I'm not going to say nothing when some queer tries to make a grab for my dick.'

'You're worried about someone grabbing your dick, are you, Harry? Well, worry about this.' Peter lunged forward before anyone could stop him; he grabbed Harry by the crotch, squeezed hard, punched him in the stomach and had him in a headlock, all in the space of about five seconds. No slouch himself when it came to brawls, Harry recovered quickly and smacked Peter around the back of the head, before wrapping one arm around his waist and proceeding to pummel Peter with his spare hand. Some of the people around them were chanting, 'Fight! Fight! Fight! Fight!' led by Imogen. However, none of the other rugby players were joining in, since a fight between two members of the same squad needed to be avoided as much as possible. A minute later, with Peter suffering from a cut lip and Harry a bloodied nose, the two boys were pulled off each other by Quentin, Oran Cahill and Peter's drinking buddy, Matthew Kilbride.

'That's enough!' Quentin shouted, standing between them both. 'Stop it, the pair of you! Stop!'

Held back by Matthew, Peter did not break eye contact with Harry. 'I'm serious, Irwin,' he said. 'Do it again and I won't stop. That's my mate. You say anything to him and you're saying it to me. Do you hear me?'

Quentin gestured for Matthew to take Peter in one direction and for Oran to take Harry in another. As he was processed past the girls, Imogen smiled mischievously at him. 'That was the single most arousing thing I've ever seen,' she said. Peter winked, before Matthew steered him outside.

'Oh my god,' said Kerry, 'I thought I was going to wet myself during that.'

A very pale Cameron turned to look at Meredith. 'I am mortified,' he whispered.

'Don't be,' Meredith replied. 'What he did was true friendship, Cameron.'

'Absolutely! Cameron, it was magnificent,' said Imogen. 'Deranged, certainly, but magnificent nonetheless.'

'Oh, it definitely was,' agreed Meredith. 'I know I never say anything like this, but does everyone else find Peter freakishly attractive right now?'

'Are you joking? A thousand times yes!' enthused Imogen. 'He is the most attractive man. Ever. Good for him. I think the occasional punch in the groin is a very satisfactory way to solve things. Harsh, simple, brutal, effective. Like a Brazilian wax.'

'And it ends up hurting pretty much the same area,' nodded Meredith.

'Precisely.'

'I should go find him,' said Cameron. 'I'll catch up with you later.'

As soon as he had gone, Catherine shuffled towards them, massaging her temple. 'My head really hurts, guys. But it's no biggy. Wevs.'

◇◇◇

Cameron found Peter sitting on Quentin's garden wall, alone. The cut on his lip looked pretty nasty, but otherwise he seemed fine. Cameron stood before him and cleared his throat.

'You didn't have to do that, Peter.'

Peter patted the place on the wall next to him and Cameron sat down. Peter flung his arm around Cameron's shoulder and pulled him closer towards him, speaking very seriously. 'You know when this all first started, I told Stew that if anyone ever gave you any hassle, I'd sort them out for you. And I meant that. Cameron, do not ever let anyone speak to you that way. If you do, they'll think they can get away with it and then other people will think they can get away with it too. Now, Meredith and Imogen and Kerry are all well and good, but they're not going to be able to do anything against the likes of Harry. He needs someone like him to stand up to him when he's a dickhead and that's what I did. I have three wee brothers and if any of them turn out to be gay, then I hope they'd be honest about it, like you. I hope they wouldn't lie about it. I hope they'd be men about it. I also hope that if they were ever in bother, they'd have a friend there to stand up for them and help them out. So that's why I did it. Because it's the right thing to do and because you're my friend. And, obviously, because you're the best sex I've ever had.'

Cameron laughed at the last point and nudged him. 'Well, obviously. Thanks, Pete.'

'Don't mention it,' he said, ruffling his hair. 'What are friends for?'

12
Broken Hearts & Bromances

Imogen sat facing Freddie in a coffee shop on the Lisburn Road. He was twirling a cinnamon stick around in his hot chocolate and looking heartbreakingly attractive in a grey hoodie, distressed jeans and loafers. His hair was sitting perfectly and there was just the faintest edge of damp in it, thanks to the light drizzle falling outside.

'Freddie, we need to talk.'

Freddie looked up from his drink nervously. 'Okay...'

'This is difficult. Obviously, we care about each other a lot, but I don't feel like we should really be "together" anymore.'

'What? Why?'

Because you're too boring to live. 'Lots of reasons. It's not a great time for me. You've got your A-Levels coming up in May. We have totally different socializing schedules. This wasn't the right time for us to start dating again. I think we're better as friends.'

'We weren't really friends before this, Imogen.'

'Sure we were.'

'No, we weren't. We've barely had a proper conversation since the last time you dumped me.'

'That was two years ago, Freddie. Don't sound so bitter.'

'You dumped me to start dating some slimy polo player you met in Argentina with Kerry!'

'Don't you dare speak about Jesús that way!'

There was a tense silence before Imogen softened and sighed. 'Freddie, honestly, I'm just not having enough fun dating you. That's why I don't think we should be together any more. I'm sorry.'

'You're not having enough *fun*?' Freddie asked. 'That's the reason?'

'We're seventeen, Freddie. It should be fun at this stage. We're not compatible. We don't really have any of the same interests. Summer was fantastic, but it hasn't stayed that way. I think you're a really great guy and one day, I'm probably going to kick myself about this decision, but I don't want to be your girlfriend anymore. I'm sorry.'

Freddie shook his head and snorted slightly. 'So that's it?' Imogen nodded. 'Imogen, why did you want to date me in the first place?'

'I liked you. I thought it would work.'

'It didn't have anything to do with Stewart Lawrence transferring to Imperial, did it? Was I your rebound?'

'Of course not. Why would it have anything to do with Stewart? Him and I broke up in December!'

'Are you still in love with him?'

The question threw Imogen temporarily off track. 'Am I what? No. No, I'm not. He's wonderful, but it didn't... No. I'm not. This has nothing to do with Stewart. It's just about you and me, Freddie, and the fact that it's not working.'

Freddie folded his arms and looked out the window. It was getting dark outside and Imogen really wanted to wrap this up and get home. After a few moments, Freddie spoke without turning his head. 'I think you're making a mistake.'

'I really don't think that I am.'

'Then I guess there's nothing I can do in this situation. You've made your decision and I just have to accept it. I'm obviously not going to make a scene or anything. Just tell me you've thought it through and that you're sure.'

'I'm sure. I'm sorry, Freddie.'

Freddie shook his head ruefully. 'Okay.'

Imogen got up from her seat and began rifling through her handbag for her purse. 'I'm going to go.'

'I'll get this,' he said, waving his hand dismissively.

'Are you sure?'

'It's only a coffee and boyfriends are supposed to pay for their girlfriends. Best to do it right, up to the end, I suppose.'

Imogen nodded and swung her bag up on to her shoulder. 'I really am sorry things didn't work out, Freddie.'

'Me too. I'll see you in school, Imogen.'

◇◇◇

Meredith stepped into a small pub hidden in the backstreets near the city centre. A roaring fire managed to take some of the chill from the icy gale blowing outside. She spotted Cameron at a table in a window alcove with Peter Sullivan.

'Thank goodness you got a place near the fire,' she said, removing her coat and gloves and taking the seat next to Cameron. 'It's freezing outside.'

'Where's Imogen?' he asked. 'I texted her too.'

'She's supposed to be meeting Freddie for coffee in Malone and she was already late when we left the meeting.'

'Where were you tonight, Meredith?' Peter asked, draining off the last of a pint of a Guinness.

'Imogen and I are helping with the Poppy Appeal this year and we had a meeting about a fundraiser we're doing for it.'

'Ah, you Protestants,' ribbed Peter. 'You do love your Poppy banter.'

'Peter, I'm Catholic.'

'Are you?'

'I say hello to your father after Mass every Sunday!'

'I did not know that,' Peter laughed. 'No offence, Meredith, but if someone was to write down the stereotype of a Protestant woman, you'd be it.'

'That's not offensive,' Cameron teased. 'That's a compliment.'

'I should probably go get a drink,' Meredith decided. 'Does anyone want anything?'

'Nah, your money's no good here,' said Peter, rising to his feet and pulling his wallet out of his back pocket. 'What can I get you?'

'Are you sure?' Meredith asked, since in the entirety of her time at Mount Olivet no boy, bar Cameron, had ever offered to buy the millionaire's daughter a drink.

'Course I am. What'll you have?'

'They're not IDing, are they?'

'This is Belfast, Meredith,' Cameron reminded her.

'Right. Could I get a gin and *slim line* tonic, please? Thanks.'

'You know they're serving hot whiskey tonight?' said Cameron.

'Yum! Could I have that instead, please, Peter? Thank you.'

'No bother. Same again, Cameron?'

As Peter sauntered over to the bar, Meredith turned to Cameron. 'Don't tell anyone yet, but Imogen's breaking up with Freddie right now.'

'Seriously?'

'It was inevitable. He's so boring you can practically see her Horcrux every time he speaks. The only reason she hasn't ended it before now is because she didn't want to admit Kerry was right.'

'I'll text her later to see if she's alright. Who does she have her eye on now?'

'No one that I know of,' Meredith said, removing a black cashmere beret and fluffing out her hair. 'Which is unusual for Imogen.'

'Which is unheard of for Imogen,' corrected Cameron. 'I still think that she wanted to get back together with Stewart and she was only filling time with Freddie until Stewart got jealous enough to try and win her back.'

Meredith looked dubious. 'If she really wanted to get back together with Stewart, she could have. He still lives in the same place and it's not as if no one from school has ever dated an Imperial boy before. If Imogen wants something, she gets it, Cameron. She therefore obviously does not want Stewart Lawrence.'

'I think her ego's dented because he left in the first place.'

'A nuclear bomb couldn't dent her ego. I think she thought Freddie was good looking, which he is, and hoped he was interesting, which he isn't. It's got nothing to do with Stewart. Speaking of which, how is he by the way?'

'He's fine. He was supposed to come here tonight, but he couldn't get a lift home. So it's just me and Peter.'

'Yes, about that,' Meredith smiled. 'This thing between the two of you is the most unexpected bromance I've ever encountered. When did you become so close?'

'Well, he's a great friend and ever since Stewart left school and Mark started spending so much of his time with Fugo McHipster, Peter and I are kind of the only two left.'

'And we have incredible sex on a fairly regular basis,' Peter interrupted, returning to the table and passing out the drinks.

'Yes, I heard that rumour on the grapevine,' Meredith said. 'Thank you for the drink, by the way.'

'No problem. Cameron, don't pretend this is just a normal friendship. We both know that we are friends with incredible benefits. Don't lie about us. Don't do that. Not here. Not in a pub. Not in our holy place.'

Cameron laughed. 'It's true. We do have unbelievable levels of passion.'

'Sometimes I do wonder about you two,' Meredith said lightly. 'I mean, if you were actually fooling around together, this would be the perfect way to throw everybody off the scent. Tell them you're doing it and then they'll never suspect that it's true.'

Peter leaned in across the table and winked. 'Meredith, I'm not trying to throw anybody off the scent. We hook up regularly and it is hot, hot, hot.'

Before Meredith could issue a rejoinder, Cameron spoke up. 'Meredith, I'm telling you now, you won't be able to outmanoeuvre him on this one. He will keep this joke going much longer than you will. He doesn't have an embarrassment threshold.'

'It's true,' nodded Peter. 'I know no concept of shame. Only banter. And those too weak to appreciate it.'

Meredith laughed. 'Well, what is the banter then?'

'Nothing much,' said Cameron. 'Did I tell you about Mark and Coral's big fight? It was a couple of weeks ago.'

'Is this the fight they had about the rugby team?' Peter asked.

'Yes! Apparently Coral threw a complete shit fit when he got on to the squad and they didn't speak for a couple of days. She came over to his house unexpectedly and apologized, but when she did, she kept telling him that she thought he fancied you instead.'

Meredith grinned. 'She saw us in the computer suite a couple of days after he made the team. He was doing that drama essay you had on *Dangerous Liaisons*. I spoke to him about it for maybe two minutes tops, but when I walked out, Coral had been staring at us through the door and she looked *very* upset. But then if I was ugly enough to prove that Darwin was right, I'd probably be pretty unhappy as well.'

Peter roared with laughter.

'The first fight is always a good sign, isn't it?' asked Cameron

'Depending on what it's about. Coral has made a *big* mistake, because she's positioned herself as the enemy of fun by objecting to the rugby try-outs,' reasoned Meredith. 'What did you say when he told you about it?'

Cameron took a drink and looked pleased with himself. 'I took her side. I was so nice about her. When he told me what she'd said, I made sure to agree with it and tried to make him see it from her point of view.'

Meredith bit her lip in amused pleasure. 'Well done, lover.'

'How does that help?' asked a confused Peter. 'Why didn't you point out that she's a banter-hating psychopath?'

'Because if he criticized her then Mark would feel like he had to defend her,' Meredith explained. 'But if Cameron defends her, then Mark becomes more and more angry at her, because no one's supporting his POV. Then, eventually, he'll crack because he won't be able to vent.'

'Is this how you lot operate?' Peter asked, with a grin. 'Are these some of the famous manipulations?'

'Oh, Peter,' smiled Meredith. 'You have no idea.'

'Well, if anyone deserves it, it's Coral,' Peter replied. 'Her shanter makes me sick.'

Meredith tapped her fingers around the edge of her glass and gave a happy little shrug. 'I love it when a new game begins.'

◇◇◇

It was hard for Cameron Matthews to break the habit of the last five years and not make witty yet cruel observations any time Coral was mentioned, but for the next month he stuck exactly to the new plan to sabotage her. Whenever Coral even faintly irritated Mark, Cameron was the first to leap to her defence. He hugged her when he saw her and he reacted with wonderfully convincing confusion when Mark queried why he wasn't getting invited out drinking with Cameron and Peter more often. 'I just assumed you would want to spend the time with Coral,' had been the infuriatingly unanswerable answer.

When things were going well between the couple, Cameron's scheme had no discernible impact, but when they had even the most minor of disagreements, it worked brilliantly. Denied any opportunity to complain about Coral, even to his best friend, Mark began to internalize every tiny complaint he had about her, mulling them over and magnifying them in his head when, if he had just been able to get them off his chest, he probably would have forgotten about them and moved on. He began to resent how much time he was being forced to spend with her and, when they were fighting, he could convince himself that she was taking over his social life.

Coral too, unintentionally, was undermining her own relationship. By giving voice to her jealousy of Meredith, she had encouraged Mark to start directly comparing the two girls. For years, Mark had scoffed at school rumours that suggested he was romantically interested in Meredith Harper. However, looking at her through the spectacles of Coral's insecurities, he could at last admit to himself that there was something which made Meredith attractive. He could see why his girlfriend was jealous and had it not been for Meredith's own actions at her godmother's birthday a few weeks later, she might have continued to silently drive a wedge between them. As it was, she behaved so insensitively that she ended up undoing all of Cameron's good work and driving Mark back into the arms of his girlfriend.

◇◇◇

Meredith stepped on to the gravel that surrounded her godmother's home, twenty miles outside Belfast. The manor house's cool white walls shone majestically in the autumnal moonlight and nearby there was a small garden with a low red-brick wall. The house's other gardens consisted of rolling lawns, a lake and a belvedere that could be seen peaking through the trees on the far side of the water. It had been in the family for over two hundred years and Victoria, Meredith's godmother, had been a young woman of twenty-four when she married into it, sixty-six years ago. Her husband had passed away when Meredith was nine and technically the house now belonged to their son Edward, a man Meredith had always looked upon as a kind of uncle. Uncle Edward, still working in New York at the age of sixty-three, was seldom at home and rather than bring out the dust covers, he preferred to let his mother stay in the house she loved so much.

From her magnificent home, Lady Portlester continued to live a life that the rest of the world hardly recognized anymore – she invited people to tea; she wrote gushing thank you letters to house guests; she invited the local vicar to walk with her in the gardens at least once a month; she liked to stroll around the grounds and chat to the local boys hired in to do the gardening for the estate. When she spoke of "the Glorious Twelfth," she meant the start of the grouse hunting season; she had friends to supper at least three times a week and she would occasionally dispatch handwritten notes to people she had read about in the newspaper or heard on the radio, telling them she found them 'frightfully interesting' and would they like to come for lunch some day next week. Tuesday, perhaps? At two o'clock. How lovely. She dressed for dinner, she wrote long letters to friends she had kept in touch with since boarding school, and she drank a lot of gin. She also refused to believe that cigarettes caused cancer, despite fifty years of medical proof on the subject, and claimed to believe it came from people using lighters, rather than matches. Today was her ninety-first birthday and she seemed as sprightly as ever.

Meredith glanced behind her as her father and her boyfriend alighted from the car. She caught Francesco looking up at the house in evident approval. He looked wonderfully handsome in his bespoke suit and he was freshly shaved for this evening.

'I told you it was lovely, didn't I?' she said.

'Yes,' he smiled. 'I wish you had worn a coat.'

'I'm only walking from the car to the house. A wrap is fine,' she replied. She noted her father smiling at Francesco's concern. Meredith had been prone to headaches and chills throughout her childhood and there were constant mini-battles waged within the Harper household when Anthony tried to persuade his daughter to wear a coat and she did not feel said coat went with her outfit.

'You've met Victoria before, haven't you, Francesco?' asked Anthony.

'Yes, Mr Harper. At Meredith's birthday in August.'

'She's a wonderful woman,' he said, approvingly. 'A very great lady. The last of her kind, I'm afraid.'

The doors to the manor house were opened for them by Lady Portlester's butler, a spry and efficient man in his late forties, who smiled as he greeted them.

'Good evening, Miss Harper. Mr Harper. And you must be Signor Modonesi?'

Francesco nodded as he and Anthony stood back politely to allow Meredith through the door first. The butler helped remove her shawl and then took Anthony's coat. 'Her ladyship is upstairs with her other guests, if you would care to follow me?'

'No, no, Stephen,' said Anthony, with a wave of his hand. 'I'm sure you're very busy this evening and we know our way well enough by now. Thank you, though.'

'Thank you, sir.'

'Stephen, there is a cake for her ladyship outside in our car,' said Meredith. 'I didn't want to bring it in just now, in case she spotted it, but would it be possible for you to send someone to bring it into the kitchens later? If it isn't too much trouble? I'll come to the kitchen to fetch it after supper.'

'That's absolutely no trouble at all, miss. If you give me a nod, I can take care of bringing it out for you when it's time.'

'I have a few candles and things I'd like to put on the cake myself.'

'Of course, miss,' nodded Stephen. 'We have hired in a few people to help with serving this evening, so I'll let them know to expect your visit.'

'Thank you,' she smiled, taking Francesco's arm as they crossed the thick carpets of the entrance hall. A burning log crackled in its cavernous fireplace as they walked by; they proceeded up the staircase to where Lady Portlester was entertaining the guests who had already arrived. Twenty or so people were milling around, all with champagne or cocktails in their hands. The men were dressed in suits and most of the women in floor-length gowns. Standing in the centre of the room was Lady Portlester, with a double martini, talking to one of her nephews and the county's Anglican bishop. She wore a white gown with a glistening matching jacket. Her hair was swept up and styled in a way that reminded Francesco immediately of Queen Elizabeth. Jewels shone from her wrist, fingers, ears and throat. Spotting the Harpers, she made her excuses and crossed over to greet them. Francesco was impressed to see that, despite her age, she apparently had no need of a cane. Her face bore many wrinkles, but it was still a fine one. There was an alertness and intelligence there; there was a sparkle in her eyes and, strangely, even a kind of youthfulness.

'How utterly and impossibly lovely to see you,' she enthused, kissing Anthony and then Meredith on both cheeks. 'And Mr Modonesi, it's really too kind of you to come all the way from Oxford for an old lady's birthday.'

'It is not every day a great lady turns thirty-five,' Francesco said, with a slight bow.

'Ah, yes, thirty-five!' she laughed. 'I had such fun being thirty-five that I decided to make it last seventy-two months. But that was back before Confucius invented the abacus, so it's hard to say. We must make sure you all have a drink. Now, tell me Mr Modonesi, which college are you at?'

'Corpus Christi, your ladyship.'

'How wonderful! My late husband was a Saint Peter's man – a fact which I like to think must have come in terrifically handy at the Pearly Gates. It's always useful to know someone on the doors. Meredith, my dear, you look absolutely charming. What a beautiful dress.'

'Thank you,' she smiled. 'I know you like the colour.'

'I adore it. It's too lovely for words. Now, come along,' she said, taking Meredith and Francesco's arms and smiling. 'I want you to meet the bishop. He's terribly worthy.'

◇◇◇

Over the dinner table, Lady Portlester had somehow managed to flatter one of her guests (who owned a small airline) by saying that aircraft *were* a wonderfully convenient form of travel, before then paradoxically announcing that all the glamour, grace and charm had gone out of long-distance travel the moment luxury liners had been replaced by aeroplanes.

Meredith watched with touched amusement at how often Francesco was nodding at Lady Portlester's pronouncements. Given how he felt about the world before the 1960s, everything she was saying was like music to his nostalgic ears. Meredith smiled and bent her head down to look at her plate. If she had ever worried about finding a boyfriend who would fit in to her life, then Francesco was a fantastic form of reassurance. This was the world they both belonged to and, as such, it logically followed that they belonged together.

As Uncle Edward began to regale the table with the story of how his late father had proposed to his mother on the deck of the *Queen Mary*, Meredith glanced across the table at Francesco. He subtly winked back at her and picked up his wine glass.

Half-way through the final course of the evening, Meredith slipped quietly out of the dining room and turned right, passing down the corridors that led to the kitchens. As she walked, she fidgeted with her necklace. It was the same one she had worn to her seventeenth birthday party and the clasp was, once again, giving her trouble. Tomorrow, she would have to make sure it got left in somewhere to be mended, regardless of what Francesco said. There were two kitchens near the back and from the one closest to her, she could hear a flurry of noise and activity. Correctly assuming that Stephen would have left the cake in the quieter of the two so that she could arrange the candles in peace, Meredith passed by the first kitchen and turned towards the second one. She pushed open the swing door and stepped inside. One of the cater waiters Stephen had mentioned was standing with his back to her on the far side of the kitchen. On the table between them was the birthday cake, matches and a box of candles.

'Good evening. I've just come to collect the cake,' she explained, before her face froze as Mark Kingston turned to face her.

'Meredith?'

Meredith's eyes took in his black bowtie, white shirt and dark trousers. Mark was a cater waiter. He was the hired help. At her godmother's ninety-first birthday party. And she was standing opposite him in a floor-length gown with a diamond necklace around her throat, a diamond bracelet on her wrist and her beloved Mount Blanc studs in her ears. If she had been thinking clearly she might have been able to make some witty observation about "upstairs/downstairs," but as it was she simply looked like she had seen a ghost. A poor ghost.

'What are you doing here?' she eventually asked.

'I'm working,' he said. 'It's uh... a temping agency thing. What are you doing here?'

'I'm Lady Portlester's goddaughter,' she answered. 'I'm here to... I'm here to fetch the cake.'

'Oh. Right. Okay. Do you need any help?' he offered, stepping awkwardly towards the table. He placed his hands in his pockets, then took them back out again and finally left them hovering.

'No, it's fine,' said Meredith, looking down to avoid eye contact. She walked over to the table and began removing the candles from their container. 'I just need to get it ready myself.'

'I'll get you a tray.'

Meredith could feel herself beginning to blush. To steady her nerves, she focussed with great concentration on removing each of the candles and placing them neatly but firmly on to the cake. Then, she lifted the cake from its box and set it down on the table. It looked perfect. Her godmother was going to be so pleased.

Turning round to fetch a tray, her ribs crashed in to the one Mark had come up behind her with. She doubled over in the pain; the clasp of her necklace finally gave way and it fell to the floor.

'I'm so sorry!' said Mark. 'I was just getting a tray for you and...'

'Look what you did!' snapped Meredith, hunkering down on the ground to retrieve the jewellery. It was hard to do in her dress and Mark knelt down next to her. Their hands touched over the necklace.

'I said I was sorry,' he said quietly. 'Did I hurt you?'

'You mean when you slammed a tray into my ribs, Mark? Oh, no, not at all,' she said sarcastically, snatching the necklace from his grip and standing up. She spun back to the table and set the cake on to the tray. There was an awkward silence, which Meredith felt compelled to break after a few seconds. 'Why are you even here anyway?'

'It's my job... I need the money,' he answered. A blush was now beginning to spread in his cheeks too. 'Coral and I want to go to a couple of concerts in the spring. She's really keen about them and I'd like to be able to buy her ticket, as well as my own, so I thought I'd maybe get a part time job to p...'

'Mark, I'm really not interested in the mating rituals of the lower-classes,' interrupted Meredith, haughtily. 'I need to get back to the party.'

Leaving Mark both humiliated and infuriated, she picked up the tray and nudged open the swing door, sweeping out into the corridor and away from their conversation.

◇◇◇

In the corridor next to the dining room, Meredith slowly lit the candles and wondered what to do about her necklace. She had stupidly left it sitting on the kitchen table, but she couldn't face the idea of going back, in case she saw Mark again. The outfit was practically ruined now that the necklace was broken and all she wanted to do was go home. Her ribs hurt a little, too. She would make a point of telling Stephen she had left the necklace in the kitchen. She could come back and get it tomorrow.

What is wrong with you? hissed a self-critical voice in her head. *You're actually leaving one of your favourite pieces of very expensive jewellery in there, rather than going back to face Mark Kingston?*

Meredith breathed in, silenced the voice and picked up the cake, now aglow with light. She temporarily balanced it on one hand to knock on the door, which was opened for her by a solicitous Stephen, waiting on the other side. She stepped in, smiling. Francesco, her father and several of the guests applauded, as Lady Portlester gasped in touched surprise and stood up to receive the cake Meredith was carrying towards her. She set it down on the table in front of her and the two women kissed on both cheeks. Jewels flashed a little in the candlelight as they did so. Meredith Harper, the girl who had everything, smiled and clapped as Victoria, Lady Portlester, who seventy-four years earlier had been called the same thing, bent down and blew out her candles.

13
THE DEMISE OF DÉTENTE

It was rare to see Meredith without her friends during the school day, so it was either a piece of luck or fate that Mark managed to find her on her own at the vending machines on the morning after Lady Portlester's birthday party.

'This is yours,' he said, tersely. In his hands was the diamond necklace she had left in the kitchens the night before.

Meredith's eyebrows nearly hit the ceiling when she realized what it was. 'Did you carry that around in your schoolbag?'

'Yes. I didn't realize you cared about it so much when you ran out and left it on a kitchen table.'

'I didn't run.'

'No, that dress was too tight.'

'I had a birthday cake in my hands.'

'Something you said last night really bothered me.'

'I'll try not to cry.'

'For someone who prides herself on being so well-mannered, you're actually pretty rude a lot of the time, Meredith. We've been getting on much better this term and I know it's mostly for Cameron's sake, but I thought we'd at least agreed to be civil to each other. Last night, you were really weird with me and I don't exactly know why, but I really don't think it was fair of you to say that thing about me and Coral being members of "the lower-class." You basically tried to make me feel ashamed about needing to get an after-school job and that was a really shitty thing to do. Most people we know have jobs to get their spending money, Meredith. Not everyone can be like you and rely on their parents. I don't know why you were as bitchy as you were last night, apart from the fact that that's your go-to position, but it was really uncalled for and I didn't appreciate it.'

Meredith pressed the button on the vending machine and a Diet Coke landed with a thud in the serving area below. She turned back to look at Mark. 'Is this because of what I said about Mandrews?'

'No, it's not just what you said about Coral. And stop calling her that.'

Meredith picked up her drink and stepped past Mark. 'Mark, I'm sorry if anything I said last night really upset you,' she said patronizingly, 'but I'm not going to apologize for not all of a sudden pretending to like your hideous she-hippo of a girlfriend just because some synaptic misfire in your brain has persuaded you to start dating her. Even you could do better than Coral. She's vile.'

'Why do you care?' he shot back.

'I don't. I have a boyfriend, remember?'

'Ah, right, yeah. Tell Giuseppe I was asking about him.'

'Francesco.'

Mark shrugged. 'Oops. You're welcome for bringing the necklace back by the way.'

For a split second Meredith looked like she would like nothing more than to find a particularly sharp Louboutin heel and stab it through Mark Kingston's hateful, smug, fugly neck. Since none were currently at hand, she drew herself up to her full height, spun on her heel and swept away.

'Always a pleasure, Meredith!' Mark shouted sarcastically at her retreating back. He clenched his hand into a fist and lightly punched the front of the vending machine with it, before making his way in the general direction of the Sixth Form Centre.

◇◇◇

Over those months between September and the start of the Christmas holidays, Kerry, Imogen and Meredith infrequently returned to the question of who had blabbed about Cameron and Blake at the start of term. It was a question that had no satisfactory answer. Try as they might, none of them could ever quite figure out who it had been. For a long time, Anastasia Montmorency remained the prime suspect because she had been there on the terrace at Stormont when Cameron officially "came out" back in June. Furthermore, she was one of the very few people who had known about Blake's involvement in the whole thing as well, and, as Mexico had demonstrated, she had at the very least passed the news on to her brother, Sasha. However, Meredith had eventually exonerated her by confessing that Anastasia had actually known for months before Cameron's big announcement, because over dinner in March Meredith had confided in her about the boys' kiss. Kerry had huffed for three days upon discovering that even Anastasia had known before her, but she had eventually calmed down when Meredith bought her a conciliatory froyo. Like Imogen and Meredith, Kerry agreed that with Anastasia having known since March, it was highly unlikely that she would have waited until summer to break the news.

Depending on what mood they were in, both Imogen and Kerry had a tendency to suspect different people at different times. If he had particularly irritated her that day, Kerry would vehemently insist that it must have been Peter Sullivan. The timing admittedly did work for her hypothesis, because Cameron had only told Peter he was gay at Meredith and Imogen's joint birthday – or the

"We hate Kerry party," as Kerry had taken to naming it in retrospect. That left just about enough time for Peter to tell someone and for that someone to tell someone else and so on and so forth until half the school knew by the first day back.

Meredith remained unconvinced by all the suggestions. Initially, she had agreed with Cameron's charitable assessment that whoever spilled the secret had done so accidentally, but her instincts eventually told her that somehow one of the popular girls were involved. The news had spread so rapidly and so mysteriously that it seemed impossible that it could have happened without at least one of the senior school socialites helping it along. If Meredith's intuition was right, it changed everything, because surely no one could have been stupid enough to reveal such a huge secret to one of Mount Olivet's gossip queens without knowing that it would go viral in a matter of days.

'The more I think about it, the more I'm certain someone did it on purpose.'

Kerry looked up from her plate of chips. The two girls were dressed casually and hanging out in a diner at the top of the Malone Road. It was already dark outside and they were planning to head back to Malone Park to watch a movie at Meredith's. Meredith was currently wearing her hair up in a pony tail, jeans, boots underneath and a blue and white fitted sweater. Kerry had donned a gilet to protect against the cold and she was contemplating buying a matching headband.

'Who would do that, though?'

Meredith shook her head and looked out the window. 'I don't know.'

'It could have been Mariella Thompson,' opined Kerry. Mariella was an insatiable gossip, with little-to-no moral qualms about how she got her information or who she had to screw over in order to spread it. 'Anastasia could have told her by mistake?'

'No. Anastasia wouldn't do that and I was there when Mariella found out. She was genuinely stunned and very, *very* angry that she didn't know sooner.'

'Yes, well, some of us can understand that feeling.'

Meredith looked at her wearily; Kerry shrugged defiantly and sprinkled more vinegar on her food.

'You don't think it could have been Charlotte, do you?'

Meredith raised her eyebrows. 'No.'

'Not intentionally, obviously, but she could have let it slip in conversation to one of her friends and then *they* told everyone. That would explain Celeste Fitzpatrick.'

'It always comes back to Celeste, doesn't it?'

Kerry nodded. 'Yes. She's always the last person you can trace it to. Literally, half the people I've spoken to heard it from someone who heard it from someone who heard it from Celeste. But then Celeste says that she just heard it on the grapevine and so did Mary-Elizabeth O'Neill. I don't know.'

Meredith sighed and helped herself to a chip. 'I've gone over and over the list in my head and I cannot think of anyone who definitely knew about Cameron who'd be stupid or cruel enough to deliberately spread the story. It just doesn't make any sense.'

'Imogen thinks it was Catherine.'

'That's because last week Catherine accidentally spat orange juice in Imogen's face and Imogen wants to see her die for something. It wasn't Catherine.'

'I know, I know.'

'I can't figure out who told. It's so frustrating!'

◇◇◇

The weather the next Friday night was dire – a real December evening in Belfast, with heavy rain and icy winds. Cameron wanted to stay in by the fire and read. He was tired and irritable and he felt no great desire to attend Celeste Fitzpatrick's first official house party, but he was slowly crumbling under combined pressure from his sister and from Kerry, who had her heart set on *en masse* group merriment that evening.

'Cameron, don't be ridiculous,' she barked down the phone. 'Celeste is in your sister's group of friends and she's delightful. You have to come.'

'I just don't really feel like it, Kerry.'

'What's that got to do with it? You're coming. It's the Age of Fabulous; this is a party; everyone's going; therefore you have to go. It's going to be lots and lots of fun.'

The line went dead and Cameron groaned in defeat, dragging himself in the general direction of the shower to start getting ready.

◇◇◇

By eleven o'clock, Cameron knew he had made the wrong decision. Trying to force himself into having a good time, he had joined in four or five drinking games, but they hadn't worked and he knew it was time to call it quits. Someone had already spilled their drink on him, the smell of smoke was making him sick, he hadn't spoken to any of his friends in the last half hour and so he decided to just leave and text them afterwards to let them know he was alright. Kerry was currently riotously drunk and sequestered in a far corner holding Celeste's hands in a pose very reminiscent of a television agony aunt. Apparently, in her tipsy state, Kerry had decided that Celeste was her newfound best friend who could not possibly have been the source of the Blakeron scandal (as it was now known). Imogen and Meredith were locked in conversation with Peter Sullivan and

Charlotte was upstairs taking twenty-five minutes to help Mary-Elizabeth reapply her make up.

Slipping out quietly and walking quickly down Celeste's driveway, Cameron regretted not bringing a coat. The weather outside was absolutely freezing. *Well, it is December, moron*, he reminded himself. For a moment, he toyed with the idea of ringing for a taxi. It was at least a ten minute walk from Celeste's house in Adelaide Park to Cameron's in Malone Park, but that would equate with a less than two minute taxi drive and he worried the taxi people might judge him for his laziness. Furious at Kerry for dragging him out to a party that he hadn't wanted to go to in the first place and then ditching him when he refused to participate in her stupid "Age of Fabulous"-themed shenanigans, Cameron dug his hands into the pockets of his chinos in a vain attempt to keep them warm. He decided to take the Lisburn Road route home, rather than the Malone Road, since it would be quicker that way and if he didn't move fast, he might lose one of his fingers to frostbite. He turned left and was hit by a strong gust of wind which made him suck in his breath and curse.

Cameron's head was bent down against the breeze, meaning that he didn't notice the three boys standing at the corner where Adelaide Park ends with a large police barracks and merged on to the Lisburn Road. Ordinarily, he would have surreptitiously looped back on himself to take the Malone Road route home, but by the time he noticed them he was too near to get away with his usual exit strategy. He was also tired, cold and slightly drunk. What were these people doing outside on a night like this in nothing but tracksuits and hoodies? He hoped that they weren't one of his greatest pet hatreds in life – Maloners who decided to dress this way on purpose and pretend they were gangsta. They didn't dress this way when their parents took them to the golf club, did they?

'Here, will you see my mate?' one of them asked as Cameron walked towards them.

'Pardon?'

'Will you give my mate a blowie? He fancies you.' The other boys sniggered. 'Does that give you a woody, nancy boy? You fancy my mate too?'

'I'm sorry,' Cameron replied icily. 'I don't get aroused by people whose only achievement in life is an ASBO.'

The next thing Cameron knew, his face had collided with the pathway of Adelaide Park and a kick had been aimed at his side by the leader. 'You fucken wee prick!' he roared. 'Who the fuck do you 'hink you are?'

No matter the state of his spiritual conscience, Cameron would always believe that what happened next had been an act of God. The moment he saw one of the boys move towards Cameron for the first push, Blake Hartman leapt out of his car, but left it running. He managed to reach the boys just in time to intercept the third kick.

'Get off him! Cameron, go and get in the car.'

'What...'

'Get in the damn car!' Blake yelled, before turning his attention to the guy who had pushed and kicked Cameron. 'Leave him alone.'

'He your boyfriend, Yankee Doodle?'

Blake was outnumbered three-to-one. Cameron, having clambered up from the ground, was now hovering behind him, paralyzed by indecision and fright. 'Didn't I tell you to go and get in the car?' Blake said to him. 'I wasn't kidding, Cameron. Go. Look, we don't want any trouble with you guys.'

'Well, you've got it. Your wee mate wasn't very nice to us, alright? So now we're going to kick the shite out of both of yous.'

Blake nodded slowly. Cameron sat in the passenger's seat of Blake's Clio. In a split second, Blake shoved the leader as hard as he could and slammed him into one of his cohorts, who fell over on impact. Blake turned and ran back to the car, jumped into the driver's seat, closed the door and pressed down on the accelerator. They sped round the corner on to the Lisburn Road and were past the fire station when their opponents ran into view behind them. By the time Blake passed Marlborough Park, their pursuers had evidently given up the chase.

Cameron glanced over at Blake, who had slowed down to within the speed limit now that the danger had passed. His jaw was set very tight and he looked far angrier than Cameron had ever seen him. From the way his muscles had tensed the whole way down his arms, Cameron knew he must have been gripping the steering wheel like a vice. The radio was still playing and after a few seconds, Blake reached out and turned it off. For the next two or three minutes, they sat in silence. Cameron laid his head against the car window and a couple of tears trickled down his face. He was pale and still shaking from what had happened. It wasn't until Blake tried to turn into Malone Park and found himself confronted by the erected bollards that Cameron broke the silence.

'You can't get in this way,' he said, ejecting his seatbelt. 'But it's okay. I can walk from here.'

Before Cameron even had a chance to open the door, Blake reversed the car slightly and drove up to the traffic lights. Cameron quietly refastened his belt as the car turned left on to Balmoral Avenue.

'What did you say to them?' Blake asked. His voice was very low and very dangerous.

'Nothing,' Cameron lied. 'They just... pushed me.'

'I saw you Cameron! I saw you stop and say something to them. What did you say? Are you an idiot?

What would have happened if I hadn't been leaving Rosie home? If I hadn't been there, they'd... Are you really that stupid, Cameron? Do you really think you can behave like that out in the real world? The whole world is like high school and you can say whatever the hell you like and get away with it? Just mosey on by, launch some funny comment and people will take it? Do you really... I mean, is that what you actually think life is like? What did you say to them?'

'I just... They asked me if I would like to kiss one of them and then they started calling me gay...'

'Oh, that must've been really awful for you, Cameron. I have no idea what that must be like! Hey, here's an idea: why don't you try biting your tongue like I've had to every day for the last three months? But why would you do anything that sensible? You're Cameron Matthews! You're Cameron Matthews and you can do whatever in the hell you like!'

'That's not the way I think.'

'It is.'

Cameron put his hand up his face and felt the warm stickiness of blood running out of his nose. As a child, he had fallen on the stile of his grandparents' country house in Donegal, banging his temple on impact. Ever since then, random bumps could lead either to bad headaches or nosebleeds. He wondered what he must look like right now; it was not a comforting thought. Pale and shaking, with blood and tears smeared across his face, his hair and clothes soaked from the rain and his teeth chattering from the cold was not exactly how he had imagined looking during his first proper conversation with Blake Hartman in months. He tried to brush the blood away with the back of his hand, but more kept coming and he resigned himself to letting it drip down his lips and chin and on to his sweater. This night was a total write-off in terms of dignity anyway.

Blake took a left and then another left and drove under the enormous trees which lined Malone Park. Lights glinted through the rain from the large houses looming behind well-trimmed hedges, electronic gates and long driveways. He drove through the gates Mr and Mrs Matthews had left open for their children returning home and stopped the car near the house's side entrance. Blake turned off the ignition and turned to look at Cameron.

'You're bleeding.'

'It just started. It's okay. It happens sometimes.'

'It happens to everybody sometimes,' Blake snapped, opening the driver's door. 'Get out.'

Cameron obediently got out and walked over to the back door that led into a little corridor behind the kitchen. Blake had seen lights on upstairs and he assumed Cameron's parents were in, but right now his main priority was to make sure someone took care of Cameron's nosebleed. Knowing Cameron, he would try to sneak up to his room and eschew medical aid rather than have a potentially awkward conversation with his family.

Cameron opened the doors into the kitchen and turned on the lights. It was warm inside, but Cameron was still shaking from a combination of shock and the frigid weather. 'Do you have ice?' Blake asked.

'Yes. It's in the freezer. It looks like a cupboard, over by the AGA. But I'm fine, you don't have to...'

A look from Blake silenced him and Cameron sat down on one of the chairs by the island as Blake retrieved a bag of ice from the freezer. He made Cameron tilt his head forward and pinch his nose, waiting for the right moment to apply the ice.

'Cameron?'

Blake turned to see Cameron's father, Alistair Matthews, standing in the kitchen's other doorway, wearing a diamond-patterned sweater, jeans, moccasins and carrying a tumbler with some scotch whiskey in it. 'Blake! We haven't seen you around here for a while. Good evening, squire.'

'Good evening, Mr Matthews,' Blake replied, taking Alistair's firm handshake. 'Sorry to barge in.'

'Not at all. What happened to you?' he asked, pointing the question at his blood-spattered son.

'I fell,' he explained.

'Fell drunk?'

'No. I just fell over my own two feet in Adelaide Park. Blake was driving by and he offered me a lift home. It really isn't that bad, Daddy.'

'Well, I'm sure part of that's true, Cameron, but I can also smell the wine,' he laughed, ruffling his son's hair. 'Are you sure you're alright?'

Cameron nodded. 'Yes. It doesn't even really hurt.'

'Alright, but the next time you're like that, call me or call a taxi. I'm not going to shout at you and I always want you to come home, no matter what state you're in, but falling on your face because of drink is a step too far, kid.'

'I told you, I -'

'Cameron.'

'Okay. Sorry.'

'Alright. I'll leave you two to it. Your mother's up in bed. Is Charlotte still at the party?'

'Yeah. She's sharing a taxi home with the girls later. I texted her.'

'Alright.'

Alistair clapped Blake affectionately on the shoulder as he left. 'Thanks very much for bringing him home, Blake. Are you sleeping here tonight?'

'No, sir. Thank you. I'll have to drive home pretty soon. I was just leaving my friend Rosie home for the night and I think my dad's going to start worrying about where I am.'

'Well, it was nice seeing you again.'

Alistair left and Blake tilted Cameron's head forward again. 'I said, pinch your nose.'

'It's basically stopped.'

'When it completely stops then you can stop pinching, okay?'

'Yes.'

Cameron kept his head tilted forward, as Blake wandered away slightly and leaned up against the sink. 'That was a really stupid thing you did tonight, Cameron.'

'I know.'

'Guys like that are just looking for an excuse to beat the crap out of you and you basically handed it to them.'

Cameron took his hand away and lifted his head to look at Blake. It was surreal to be standing in a room alone with him again. After months and months and months of thinking about nothing but him and wondering how it had all gone so wrong, it was as if he had forgotten that Blake was actually real. He found it simultaneously enraging and comforting to be this close to him. He'd forgotten how much he missed him and how another part had never wanted to see him again. It was the months of silence that hurt the most; the lack of contact. At times, it had all seemed wantonly cruel and Cameron had struggled to reconcile that side of Blake with the side he had known before – the good guy, who was loyal and protective and funny.

'Why didn't you get in contact?' he asked, wondering what answer Blake could possibly give – if any.

'You told me not to.'

'No, I didn't.'

'After the letter, you did.'

'What letter?'

'I wrote you one at the start of summer and I gave it to Meredith to give to you,' Blake said, stupidly.

Cameron stared at him in disbelief – like he had just suggested telling Kerry he hated her hair. 'You gave it to Meredith? You gave it to Meredith! Why would you do that? She's probably stuffed it up a voodoo doll version of you and burned it by now!'

'She never gave it to you?'

'Of course she didn't! Blake, it's only because of the prison system that she didn't murder you. Did you really think she'd pass on your mail for you?'

'I... I don't know. No... I didn't know.'

'Oh, well that's true of pretty much everything you've done over the last year, isn't it? Is there anything that you are capable of doing without messing it up?'

'Hey! Don't yell at me because your best friend didn't give you a letter addressed to you and then lied about it!'

'You shouldn't have written it in a letter. You should have said to my face.'

Blake's mouth opened to respond, but stopped when he accepted the validity of Cameron's point.

'After everything you did, you shouldn't have put it in a letter, Blake. Did you choose a letter because you were afraid I wouldn't speak to you if you tried?'

'Yes. No! I can't remember. I don't know.'

'Of course you don't know! The full extent of what you don't know, Blake, could fill south Belfast.'

'Cameron, I am trying!'

'No, you're not. You're blaming Meredith because she didn't give me a letter. What's that got to do with it? Even if she had given it to me, it wouldn't change what you did. You just said you wrote it at the start of summer, but you stopped speaking to me last December!

Do you have any idea what those first few weeks after my birthday were like? After you vanished?'

'I didn't van...'

'You may as well have! I sent you texts *begging* you to just pick up the phone. I e-mailed you. I Facebook messaged you. I left you about a million missed calls. I made a complete fool of myself trying to get you to talk to me. And you wouldn't. You wouldn't even respond. You even hung up on me once when I tried to call you on New Year's Eve. You told me we were friends and you promised that we'd always be friends no matter what. And then you cut me out. I have never in my life felt pain like that. When I was alone, I couldn't stop crying and all I thought about was you. I was so upset it felt like I was ill. That sounds like I'm exaggerating, but I'm not. It was awful. And then, and *then*, you started dating Catherine O'Rourke! There are six hundred girls in Mount Olivet, Blake. Why did you have to pick her? Heartbreak wasn't enough; you had to add humiliation in as well? Why, Blake? Say something!'

Blake shook his head and two streams of tears spilled slowly down his face. 'Actually, it's not even a question of why you did it,' Cameron continued. 'I know *why* you did it. What I don't understand is how. I was terrified, as well, you know; you weren't the only one dealing with coming out. But I know that no matter how scared or angry I was, there is absolutely no way I could ever have done to you what you did to me. And to yourself! I just don't understand. Why are you crying?'

'Seriously?'

'I've never seen you cry before.'

'Well, I've never had to stand in front of the man I'm in love with and hear him tell me that I broke his heart. Maybe that's why!'

Blake reached up with the back of his palm and angrily wiped his face. Under any other circumstances, the sight of him crying would have moved Cameron to pity, but after nearly a year of pent-up fury, he felt nothing but irritation at Blake's grief. Where had all these tears been twelve months ago? Where had the guilt been when he sashayed into Meredith's Valentine's Day party with Catherine O'Rourke on his arm? Even Blake's declaration of love, which Cameron had unconsciously spent months hoping and waiting for, only seemed to rile him further.

'You don't love me.'

'Yes, I do!'

'No, you don't. It's just one of those things that you say to sound good. I bet you said it to Catherine.'

'I never said it to Catherine. I have never said it to anyone before. I mean it. Stop doing this! Stop it.'

'If you loved me and you still managed to do all that to me, then God only knows what you're capable of when you hate someone.'

'Cameron, please, stop or I'm going to put my fist through a wall.'

'Well, you'd better go then.'

'What?' Blake asked, startled.

'Get out. Isn't that what you do best, Blake? Leaving? This'll be a first for me, actually. It'll be the first time I get to ask you to fuck off, rather than letting you pick the time to exit.'

'Do you really want me to leave?'

'Yes. I do. Get out.'

The conversation had changed direction so quickly that Blake gave Cameron a few seconds to calm down and retract his sudden edict of eviction, but Cameron did not back down. Blake nodded slowly and walked towards the door. Cameron looked away and Blake left. Ten minutes later, once Cameron thought he had gathered himself, he left the kitchen and walked out into the main entrance hall of his family's house. His father was exiting from the study, the room directly opposite their kitchen.

'Hey, sport. Has Blake left?'

Cameron looked at his father and croaked out, 'Daddy.' And in that moment, Alistair Matthews knew that everything he had wondered about his son since he was twelve-years-old was true. He crossed over to him, setting his scotch down on the telephone table and wrapped him in a hug. Cameron started sobbing again, like he used to when he was a toddler. Pitiful sobs shook his son's body as he cried into Alistair's sweater.

'There, there, son,' he soothed, patting Cameron on the back. 'Your first love is supposed to be the hardest.'

◇◇◇

Mark Kingston found Blake Hartman walking out of the changing rooms used by the school's football, tennis, cricket and basketball teams late on Monday afternoon. He had been looking for an opportunity to talk to Blake all day, ever since Cameron had told him about nearly getting beat up on Friday night. Earlier in the day, he had seen Blake talking to Mr Cavan, the head of the PE department, and subsequent enquiries revealed that Blake had been persuaded to take up a place on the school tennis team.

'Blake?'

'Hey, Mark.'

'Congratulations on the tennis thing. Mr Cavan says that you're incredible.'

'I used to play back in the States,' Blake said, modestly. 'Coach Cavan found out from my dad and asked me to try out. It's cool. I didn't realize how much I missed it until today. I haven't done as much gym as I did last year.'

Mark cleared his throat guiltily. 'Yeah... I wanted to say thank you for helping Cameron on Friday night.

If anyone needed rescuing from that kind of situation, it's him.'

'I'd help Cameron any way I could,' he said shortly. Blake didn't particularly like the way Mark had felt the need to thank him, as if helping Cameron had been a favour Blake had done for Mark or because Mark hadn't been there to help Cameron himself. It seemed like a benign form of egotism and after three months of nothing but the occasional awkward nod in the school corridors, Blake wasn't particularly in the mood to indulge Mark's Messiah complex.

'Right, right, of course,' Mark nodded, oblivious to Blake's bristling. 'Listen dude, I just wanted to say that I'm really sorry for everything that's happened to you this term.'

'Don't worry about it. You weren't the one who told people and, anyway, I guess they had to find out eventually.'

'It still wasn't right though and I feel like I should have done something.'

'There's nothing you could've done, Mark.'

'So where do things stand with you and Cameron now?' Mark asked. 'Are you thinking about maybe...?'

Blake regarded him analytically and couldn't figure out if Cameron had told him about the rest of their discussion on Friday.

'I dunno. It's difficult. Maybe if we'd been able to talk back in September, things might be easier. I should have gone to talk to him myself, but I didn't and he's very angry about that.'

'Why didn't you?' Mark asked, exasperated.

'Because I was a coward and because I was an idiot. The coward bit is because I didn't step up to the plate like I thought I would in a situation like that and the idiot bit is because I trusted that Meredith Harper might actually put her friend's happiness above her own scheming.'

'Meredith?'

Blake picked his school bag out of the racks and swung it on to his left shoulder. 'I wrote a letter to Cameron back in June explaining everything and I asked her to give it to him. She didn't, but she e-mailed me and told me that she had. She then told me that Cameron was so angry that he never wanted to speak to me again and if I had any respect for him, I'd just leave him alone. So I did and then on Friday I found out that everything she told me was one great, big, fat lie.'

Mark looked like he was suffering from the first signs of shell shock. 'Is that true?'

'Yeah. Welcome to Malone, I guess.'

Mark shook his head. 'But she...'

'She's Meredith Harper,' Blake finished. 'You shouldn't be surprised. You always thought she was capable of this kind of thing. Me, on the other hand... well, I'm just a fucking moron. See you around, Mark.'

◇◇◇

Mark stood on Meredith's doorway fifty minutes later, nervously preparing himself for what he had to say. His left foot was tapping away in agitation and he reached up to ring the bell for a second time. Almost immediately, the heavy front door swung open. Mark had expected the Harpers' housekeeper, Pauline, to answer, like she had the last time he was here. However, it was Meredith herself who stood facing him, still in her school uniform.

'Can I talk to you for a minute?' he asked, instead of a greeting.

'Come in,' she said. She had no idea why he was here or why he seemed so agitated; they hadn't spoken since the day he returned her necklace to her, but she was careful not to betray any signs of surprise or uncertainty before she could find out what he wanted. 'You remember the way to the library?'

Mark spun back to face her half-way across the hall. She had just closed the front door, but Mark couldn't wait.

'I know about Blake's letter.' Meredith froze at his words. 'And so does Cameron.'

'Oh?' she asked calmly. Even in the midst of his anger, he had to give her credit for her self-control. She didn't seem even remotely surprised or panic-stricken at his announcement. 'He hasn't said anything to me about it.'

'Well, I'm saying something about it.'

'Off crusading again, Mark?'

'How could you do that to him?'

'Do what?' Meredith asked, impatiently.

'You had no right to keep that from him.'

Meredith rolled her eyes. 'I'd completely forgotten about it until you barged into my house and brought it up. The epistolary endeavours of Blake Hartman aren't something that keep me up at night, Mark.'

'You expect me to believe that you just forgot to give it to him?' Mark half-laughed. 'Really? That's the best you've got?'

'I expect you to believe it, but I don't care if you do or you don't.'

'For months, those two have been wondering why the other one hasn't said anything and they've been blaming themselves or blaming each other. But it turns out that the person they should have been blaming all along is you! Cameron is supposed to be your friend, Meredith. How could you do this to him? And Blake does not deserve the shit he's gone through! One word from Cameron or from any of you and half that bullying would have stopped. One word! But you did absolutely nothing to help him. Instead, you did what you always do – sit back and watch people suffer.'

'And what exactly did you do to help him?' Meredith shot back, infuriated at what she considered to be Mark's self-righteous posturing. 'You're the "Mr Nice" of the whole school, aren't you? You're Mark Kingston, the good guy. That's what everybody thinks and, even more pathetically, that's what you think as well. Strangely though, I haven't heard you defending Blake at any point this semester. Which is odd, because this is the kind of thing you usually live for – getting to swoop in, rescue everybody and in the process remind them all of how wonderful you are. But this time round – nothing. Total silence from Mount Olivet's self-appointed peacekeeping force. Now, why could that be? I think I have an idea. You know, sometimes, when Cameron hugs you in front of other people, I can see you flinch. Just a little. Did you think no one had noticed? Could it be that you didn't do anything to help Blake because you were worried what people would think? Friendship with one gay guy is okay, but if you leap in to start defending another one then people are really going to start to wonder about you. Correct me if I'm wrong. Go on. Correct me, Mark. No? Nothing to say? Well then, I wouldn't be so quick to start pointing fingers when your own conscience seems to have taken a convenient vow of silence for most of the term.'

Mark's face had flushed with the devastating accuracy of her jibes. Stay calm. This is what she does, he reminded himself, she sneaks inside people's mind and messes with them and that's how she wins an argument. Even if she had a point and he could, or should, have done a lot more to help Blake, he hadn't done anything to actively ruin his life like she had.

He saw that she was pleased; she knew her observations had hit home. 'Oh poor Mark,' she cooed.

'Wanting everyone to think you're so tolerant by having a gay best friend, but then hoping to God they don't think you're the same way.'

'I don't think about him that way!' Mark yelled. 'He's my friend. He's my best friend and I don't think of him that way.'

'Of course you do. Every time you look at him, I bet you wonder how you could possibly have missed that he was gay for all those years. Well, don't blame yourself too much, Mark, like most "nice" people you're so staggeringly self-obsessed that analyzing or noticing anything about other people, except what they think of you, was never going to be your strong point.'

'You're going to lecture me on being self-obsessed?' Mark retorted. 'Seriously?'

'The difference between you and me, Mark, is that I know my faults. You don't have a clue about yours.'

Blood was pounding in Mark's ears. She was standing in front of him like the old Meredith Harper, magically reincarnated – the one he had always hated. Cold, perfect, cruel, unnaturally beautiful. This was what she was and what she had always been – a snow queen who played with other people like a mean kid with ants and a magnifying glass. He knew she was lying about just "forgetting" to give Cameron the letter from Blake, because if she had been telling the truth she would at the very least have reacted with confusion or surprise when Mark mentioned it. She hadn't. Instead, she had cunningly tried to flip the argument into one about Mark's actions, rather than her own. She was as guilty as sin and Mark hated himself for ever having believed for a single second that she was anything other than the vindictive ice maiden he had always known her to be.

'You know what, Meredith? One day you're going to push someone too far and that person is going to stand up to you. And when that day happens, you won't have a clue what to do. There are rules, Meredith. Rules for how you should treat people and what you did to Cameron and Blake broke pretty much all of them. You can't keep getting away with stuff like this.'

Meredith looked at him like he was hopelessly and irredeemably stupid. 'Of course I can. Mark, I'm probably the richest person you're ever going to meet and I'm more intelligent before 9 a.m. than most people are all day. When are you going to realize that all these rules and regulations you're talking about don't apply to people like me? They apply to people like you. You know – B Listers; people who have to try. Now, get out of my house and if you come back uninvited again, I'm going to call the police. Run off to your fat little heifer of a girlfriend, plat each other's back hair and have a feelings-fest about how awful I am. I understand that to people like you, I'm usually the main topic of conversation.' She opened the front door. 'Goodbye.'

With great effort, Mark walked to the doorstep. 'One day, Meredith, you will lose.'

'No, I won't.' She smiled and slammed the door in his face.

14
BY THE PRICKING OF MY THUMBS

At break time on the last day of term, Catherine O'Rourke bounced over excitedly to her group's table in the cafeteria. As was traditional for the last day of term, it was a non-uniform day and Catherine had opted for a sea blue merino wool sweater, a Burberry skirt and high heels. Her favourite handbag hung over her left elbow as she dropped into her seat opposite Kerry and Imogen.

'JMJ, you guys. JMJ!' She grinned, clapping a little as she did so.

'What's JMJ?' Imogen asked.

'"Jesus, Mary and Joseph!"' Catherine explained, happily. 'It's the Irish OMG. Today is signup day for the Social Committee elections!'

'I have been dreaming of this day since first year,' Kerry sighed. 'Now, remember, I'm putting my name down for chairperson of designer events. It's basically party planning, which means it's mine. *Mine.*'

'I still think you should be going for treasurer and I should be going for chairperson,' said Imogen, 'but whatever. I suppose it's been decided now.'

Cameron walked over with a bottle of Diet Coke in his hands and sat down. He was joined a few seconds later by Meredith; neither of them had yet acknowledged their respective confrontations with Blake or Mark, but although none of their friends knew why, they could sense the tension between Meredith and Cameron and it made them uneasy. Any questions about the group's confusing temporary dynamic were avoided when Anastasia Montmorency walked over to their table, flanked by Natasha Jenkins and Lavinia Barrington.

'The signup sheets have been posted on the notice board,' Anastasia announced. 'Have you all decided what you're going to nominate yourselves for?'

'Yes,' replied Meredith. 'Cameron's going to go for vice-president, Imogen for treasurer, Kerry for chairperson and Catherine will get entertainment manager.'

No one bothered to ask what position Meredith would be running for. Given that for the last six years the most popular girl in sixth form had run totally unopposed for the presidency, there didn't even seem to be much point in bothering with an election, let alone questions about it. However, the formalities had to be observed and so the signup sheet was ready for Meredith to grace with her signature.

'It technically needs to be done by the end of the first week back,' Anastasia informed them, 'but obvi there's no rush.'

'We'll do it now and get it out of the way,' Meredith ruled, rising from her seat. 'Are you ladies going out tonight?'

'It's the end of term. We may as well.'

'We'll see you later then. Happy Christmas.'

The two groups exchanged holiday greetings as the three heiresses shimmied off towards their own table and Meredith, Kerry, Catherine, Cameron and Imogen left the cafeteria. As they walked down the corridor, Catherine waved politely to Mark and Coral, who were standing holding hands in an alcove two hundred metres from the office. A malign smile flashed across Mark's face as Meredith passed by.

Catherine reached the signup sheet before anybody else and she squeaked loudly, with what Cameron initially mistook for excitement. He realized how wrong his diagnosis was when Catherine turned around to look at them, her mouth opening and closing like a slow-dying fish out of water. From further down the corridor, Mark pulled Coral closer in towards him and shouted, 'Hey, Meredith! Good luck with the elections.'

Imogen, Kerry and Meredith turned to look over their shoulders at him in irritable bewilderment. Their confusion, like Imogen's periodic vows to give up drinking, was extremely short-lived. Plucking a pen out of her Birkin and walking towards the board, Meredith came to an abrupt halt.

MOUNT OLIVET GRAMMAR SCHOOL SOCIAL COMMITTEE
NOMINATION SHEET FOR SPRING TERM ELECTIONS
POSITION: President of the Social Committee

NOMINATED
Coral Andrews

All five of them stared at the board in total and complete shock.

'Sweet Virgin Mary Mother of God conceived without the stain of Original Sin, what the hell is this?' hissed Imogen.

For a second, you could see the absolute agony of indecision on Meredith's face as she realized that her name would have to appear below Coral's. The pen hung limply in her unmoving hands before she steeled herself, stepped forward and signed her name. She then took a step back to look at what had just happened.

Kerry shook her head and whispered fearfully, 'Oh, no.'

◆◇◆

'What the hell was that?'

Mark closed his locker and turned to look at a livid Cameron. 'What?'

'Don't pretend you don't know what I'm talking about.'

'It's an election, Cameron, not an empire. Other people get to nominate themselves for it once in a while.'

'I know this was your idea,' he said accusingly. 'I saw the way you looked at us when we were walking up to the notice board. You persuaded that bunch of circus freaks to stand against us. Didn't you?'

Mark was beginning to lose some of his cool certainty in the face of Cameron's fury and he stumbled slightly over his next sentence. 'We were... talking. At Coral's. And we thought it might be, y'know, a good idea if Meredith didn't just get the presidency like she expected.'

'But it's not just Meredith, is it? You've put someone up against all of us, Mark!'

'Cam, it wasn't just my decision and, plus, if you think about it, I did it to help you!'

'Are you on crack? How in the name of Holy God did you do this to help me? Standing against Callum Quigley is supposed to be, what, my birthday present this year? Why didn't you just stick to your usual tactic and not get me one?'

'Blake told me about the letter that Meredith was supposed to give to you. She can't keep getting away with stuff like this, Cam. She needs to be taught a lesson.'

'Tell me you didn't.'

'Didn't what?'

'Tell me you didn't speak to Meredith about the letter?'

'Of course I did!'

'What! Are you... What! Mark, you had no right to do that! I hadn't even told you about it. I did not mention that letter to you! I didn't ask for your help or your advice. So explain to me why you thought you had a right to speak *for* me about it to one of *my* friends?'

'You're my best friend. I look out for you, Cam. That's what I do.'

'Like you did at Quentin's? Funny how you're much better at standing up to people like Meredith than you are to people like Harry. She can't hit you, I suppose. And do *not* pretend that you are doing any of this to help me. If you are, then why is that evil little freak running against me? Why, Mark? Have you any idea what it will do to my reputation if I lose to *Callum Quigley*? You're not doing any of this for me. At least be honest about it! You're pissed because you're obsessed with Meredith, you can't have her and you never will. You have completely humiliated me and my friends in front of the whole school, because of some stupid obsession that you've had for years but won't admit to. I warned you that if you didn't at least acknowledge it, you'd end up doing something crazy. And I was right! And what's worse about all this is that you don't even have the balls to admit that you care more about Meredith's misery than you do about my happiness! Some best friend.'

When Mark reached out to grab his shoulder, Cameron swatted his hand away aggressively. 'Do not follow me.'

◇◇◇

Years later, when her own mother passed away after a long and happy life, it would be difficult to say if Kerry took that tragedy with more or less tears and wailing than she did the news that Joanne Sexton was standing against her in the Social Committee elections. Surrounded by Catherine and Imogen, Kerry was currently sitting on the top floor of a Subway in the city centre, having demolished her first meal deal and moved on to a multi-pack of cookies. Imogen was sitting opposite her with a refillable drink, apparently too angry to eat, and Catherine was morosely picking at a sub she had yet to bite into.

'Chairperson of designer events,' Kerry sobbed. 'That means organizing the spring charity fashion show and looking good! I have devoted my entire life to looking good and she's spent her whole life looking like... deliberately trying to look like, like, like a...'

'Like a fat little piglet stuffed in a condom,' Imogen finished.

'Exactly! I mean, what the hell's she going to do for fashion week? March a couple of ugly hipsters down the runway in a set of kaftans and some accessories she bought from the reduced-to-clear bin in *Fresh Garbage*?!'

'Doesn't matter,' Imogen shrugged. 'Won't happen. She'll be dead by then. We have to kill her now. That's it. They've left us no choice.'

'I've wanted a position on that committee since first year,' Catherine announced, sadly.

'Catherine, you're getting that position,' Imogen replied. 'Understand?'

'But what if Coral wins?'

'Don't be stupid. The only thing she'll ever win in life is a pie eating contest!'

'On her own, she couldn't win,' Catherine answered. 'But she's not on her own, is she? Mark's helping her. Mark's her boyfriend. Coral will get all the unpopular and the anti-popular votes and Mark will persuade a lot of the rugby team and all the normal people who don't want to be our friends to vote for them too. That's like over half the year.'

Imogen looked like she would very much like to punch Catherine square between the eyes for daring to regale her with such monumentally unwelcome facts, but her thoughts about whether or not to twist her ring upon impact were interrupted by a furious slamming of the table from Kerry.

'Why is Mark doing this?'

'Because of the letter,' Imogen answered.

'Are you serious right now?'

'What letter?'

'Trust me, Catherine, you don't want to know.'

'Tell me!'

Imogen rolled her eyes and twisted to face her. 'Fine! It's a letter from your big gay ex-boyfriend to one of your best friends telling him in great detail why he'd rather have sex with him than you.'

Given the look on Catherine's face, it would have been kinder for Imogen just to have gone with her initial instinct and punched her. 'I... he... wait... Blake wrote him a let...'

'Catherine, shut up, today isn't about you,' Kerry snapped, cradling her head in her palm. 'That stupid letter! How does Mark even know about it?'

'Blake told him and he also told Cameron. Cameron didn't say anything about it to Meredith, but Mark did and told her if she didn't apologize, he'd sabotage her.'

'How is this any of his business?' Kerry roared.

Imogen shook her head and looked back out the window, pursing her lips in rage. 'I hate him.'

Kerry stuffed another cookie into her mouth. 'So do I!'

'Blake really wrote Cameron a letter?'

Imogen tutted. 'Yes, Catherine, he did.'

'But why?'

Cookie crumbs sprayed out of Kerry's mouth in frustration as she answered. 'Because Cameron is a man, Catherine. Because he has a penis!'

'Just like the one located directly in the middle of Mark Kingston's forehead!' seethed Imogen.

'Blake gave the letter to Meredith and she never gave it to Cameron and now, apparently, our lives are being ruined because Mark Kingston thinks this is somehow his concern!'

Catherine lowered her head as her lips quivered. 'I just can't believe Blake did that.'

Kerry had swallowed the cookie. 'Look, what do you care more about? Some stupid ex-broken-hearted thing or getting a position on the Social Committee?'

'The Social Committee, obviously!'

'Exactly!' exclaimed Kerry, tossing her arms up like Evita. 'Imogen, get Meredith on the phone! We are sorting this letter nonsense out, tonight. She is going to give it to Cameron and then we are going to plan how to get our lives back. You realize that this is just how the French Revolution started? Ugly bitches trying to ruin the lives of people prettier and more fabulous than them. Seriously, you guys, I'm like the Second Coming of Marie-Antoinette right now.'

Imogen lifted her phone out of her blazer pocket and began dialling. 'I know how to make petrol bombs and I know where Coral lives.' The other girls looked at her in horror. Imogen shrugged and placed the phone to her ear. 'I'm just saying.'

◇◇◇

Meredith was shown up to Cameron's bedroom by his mother. From across the landing, she could hear the sounds of Charlotte and her friends preparing for a big night out to celebrate the end of term and she remembered that, this time last year, her friends had been doing exactly the same thing. All of them standing one week away from the party that changed everything. Every disaster of the last year could somehow be traced back to Cameron's sixteenth birthday and largely because Meredith had buckled under the pressure of having to deal with Mark Kingston. At the time it had looked like Meredith was winning. Breaking up Stewart and Imogen, temporarily ruining Cameron and Mark's friendship, blackmailing Catherine, outwitting Kerry and sidelining Blake – they had all seemed like victories. However in the wake of today's social catastrophe, she was now forced to acknowledge the unsettling possibility that she had mistakes.

As she stepped into his bedroom, she saw that Cameron was standing in the doorway to his bathroom, freshly showered, shaved and dressed in a white and blue shirt and new jeans. A blazer was slung over the bedpost, ready for later, and the scent of Tom Ford cologne wafted across the room towards her.

'You're dressed,' she said, by way of greeting.

'I thought we'd be pre-gaming,' he answered.

'Not yet. Imogen and Kerry said they'd meet us here once they're ready.'

Cameron nodded and then gestured perfunctorily towards one of his two overstuffed blue and white armchairs. 'You can sit. If you like.'

Meredith sat and crossed her legs elegantly. 'I brought you the letter. Do you want it?' Cameron hesitated. 'It's alright to admit you want it, Cameron.'

'I'm quite aware of that.'

'You're angry.'

'Yes. And embarrassed.'

'Embarrassed?'

'I was always under the impression that I came across as an intelligent person...'

'Cameron...'

'I haven't finished. I was always under the impression that I came across as an intelligent person, but apparently I was wrong. Two of my best friends think I am so indescribably stupid that I shouldn't even be consulted on any of the issues pertaining to my life.

I didn't tell Mark that I knew about Blake's letter and yet bizarrely he felt it was his prerogative to go to you personally and upbraid you for keeping it from me. Six months ago, you were given a letter, addressed to me, which I have absolutely no doubt you have since read and you decided I didn't deserve to even know about it. Blake left; he gave me no choice about accepting that. Mark went to you to start a fight about me and he gave me no choice about that, either. You withheld that letter; you didn't give me any choice. Do you spot the theme?'

Meredith paused for a moment before answering. 'Cameron, it has nothing to do with you being stupid. I don't know what Mark's reasons are for his behaviour; they may have something to do with him being the Anti-Christ's dim-witted brother. Who can say? The reason why *I* didn't give you the letter is not because I thought you were too stupid to handle it, but because I didn't think you deserved to. Let me finish, please. You don't know what it was like in the weeks after Catherine's birthday. You don't know what it was like watching it. You fell completely apart and it was because of how Blake treated you. I had never seen you like that before and I don't want to, ever again. When he gave me the letter, yes, I read it. I even re-sealed it, in case I one day had to give it to you and lie that I hadn't read it...'

'I wouldn't have believed you.'

'You might have pretended to and that's all that matters. When Blake gave me the letter, I was worried that you would forgive him for everything he had done. But what if he did it again? I know he was having a hard time coming out, Cameron, but plenty of people do and they don't ruin the lives of everyone around them in the process. What if you forgave him a second time and he threw it back in your face again? I kept it from you, yes, but not because I think *less* of you.'

She fished the letter out of her handbag and handed it over to Cameron. He walked over towards her and took it. As he looked down, a smile passed over his lips for the first time that evening. 'You messed up.'

'Pardon?'

'You re-sealed it in Smythson stationery, Meredith. Somehow I don't think the Shepherd of Judea Baptist Church has a huge amount of it.'

Meredith smiled, too. 'Evangelicals are disgusting in their choice of letter-writing accessories, aren't they?'

Meredith's phone buzzed in her hands. 'It's Imogen,' she announced. 'She says they're coming over now to start pre-drinks.'

'Cool,' said Cameron, opening the letter.

'Do you want some privacy?' Meredith asked.

Cameron shook his head. The letter was written on lined paper, torn out of a file block. Blake's handwriting was messy, like it had always been.

Dear Cameron,

Um, I don't really know how to begin this or what to say, which is probably why I actually started a letter with the word "um".

Anyway, by the time you get this (or if you get this – I haven't decided yet), I won't be around anymore. I've decided to go back to New Canaan.

Basically, before I go, I wanted to apologize to you, but right now I just don't have the balls to do it to your face. After everything that's happened, I realize that what happened at your birthday should have been the start of something wonderful and that night at Catherine's was so special, but both times I ruined it and hurt you a lot. I'm so, so, so, so sorry Cameron. And if it makes any difference I haven't been truly happy since that night. Not really.

Dating Catherine and lying to everyone, including myself, is probably the most terrible thing I've ever done and I know now that there's nothing I can do to make it better. So I think it's best that I just leave. I might come back, but I'm not sure. I understand that you probably never want to see me again and a couple of your friends have made it clear that I'm not welcome here. I'm not mad at them, or upset, because honestly I deserve their hatred.

Um ... (there's that um again! No surprise why I don't do so well in English!!!!...) this letter is becoming seriously self-pitying and that's not what I wanted at all! It was supposed to be about you – or actually, about me and you. I know that people think that they fall in love at sixteen all the time and everyone says it's just hormones, but if I'm sure of anything anymore it's that I did do love you. And I hurt you, a lot, because after that first kiss I got so scared. All of a sudden we were going to have to make these big decisions and our lives would completely change and I couldn't handle it. I kept thinking what everyone in my family would say and I panicked. I've never panicked like that in my life, Cameron. That's obviously no excuse, but it is a reason. I was frightened.

This letter's getting so messy and I definitely haven't structured it as well as I could have, but for once I just wanted to be honest and say whatever came into my head. People always say that if you fall in love, that person has the power to change you. And I always assumed that it would be for the better, because love is good. But I loved you and it changed me for the worse and that's not your fault. It's mine. & now I've blown it. Forever. Haven't I?

I suppose I should end this by saying that I will always remember you as the first person I ever loved and despite everything that's happened, I just hope that one day you'll be able to forgive me.

I love you.

Blake.

The door swung open to reveal Imogen and Kerry. Imogen was carrying a bottle of champagne and both were still clearly seething about Coral's attempted Social Committee coup.

'Dies Irae, bitches,' Imogen announced, sweeping into the room. 'Dies. Irae.'

'This is a disaster of unprecedented global proportions,' said Kerry, without a trace of irony.

'I actually cannot believe today has happened. I thought pigs would grow wings and Coral Andrews would win the Rose of Tralee before something like this could occur!'

Cameron gently placed Blake's letter in his desk drawer and then leaned against it, with his arms folded across his chest. 'I spoke to Mark today. I'm very angry at him.'

'You should be,' Imogen said. 'Any pretence that he's doing this solely for your benefit has been blown out of the water by the fact that he's placed that four-eyed mutant to run against you.'

'I know.'

'We are going to be the laughing stock of BT9 unless every single one of us beats every single one of them.'

Kerry and Meredith nodded their agreement, as Cameron reached over to uncork the champagne. While he was pouring, Imogen continued her rant. She looked sensational tonight, Meredith noticed approvingly. She had gone to get her nails done, re-styled her hair and pulled out the dress she had worn for results night. She smelled sensational, too. Kerry, whose face wore the expression of a woman preparing for battle, had pushed her curls to a new zenith of excellence and was perched on one of Cameron's chairs, wearing a light pink swing dress. All in all, an excellent effort on the girls' behalf to remind everyone who was out partying tonight which clique had the hotter half of Mount Olivet's impending civil war.

'From now on, we have to be on the top of our game,' said Imogen.

'We will be,' agreed Cameron.

'The Age of Fabulous is over,' declared Kerry. 'It's time for vengeance. We'll still look fabulous, obviously, but we're going to have to be just a little bit psychotic.'

'A little bit? It has to be savage,' Imogen continued. 'No mercy. They want a fight? Fine! We'll give them a no-holds-barred fiesta of manipulation, treachery and deceit. It'll make the time we kicked Lisa Flaherty out of the group look like a Sunday School excursion. Those evil little hipster cretins humiliated us and Mark Kingston helped them do it. We are *not* letting them get away with it.'

Kerry raised her glass. 'I feel like we should have a toast.'

'What to?' asked Meredith.

'To next term,' replied Imogen.

The four of them raised their glasses and a silky smile danced across Meredith's lips. 'Well then, here's to the Age of Vengeance, everybody.'

15
AND THE TRUTH SHALL SET YOU FREE

The island of Ireland is a spectacularly beautiful place and any child born there will always carry that beauty with them in their hearts, wherever they may go in life. Depending on where they grow up, there will be some site near to them that establishes a hold over their unconscious, be it mountain, sea, river, forest or glen. No matter how many times they go there, and it may be hundreds, they will never become completely jaded to it. Its beauty will always have the power to move or soothe. For Cameron, that place was the coastline of North Down. In summer, its beaches were golden and chock-full of families; the waters of Helen's Bay glistened in the sunshine and the smell of barbecues floated tauntingly through the lazy evening air. In winter, the wind would rush in off the sea, waves would pound the rocks, the trees were stripped bare and the whole area became infused with a kind of wild and savage grace. Cameron had been coming here longer than he could remember and he loved it.

'Did you really have a beach house here?' Blake asked him.

'Yes. Right over there,' he pointed.

'It's fifteen minutes from where you live.'

'Twenty-five,' corrected Cameron. 'But, yes, that is eventually why Daddy was persuaded to sell it. He'll buy another one here though, one day, when Mummy lets him again. He loves it here. So do I.'

They had left Blake's car in a small car park and wandered down the hill to the gates of Crawfordsburn Country Park. The path would take them through the trees, along the coast and past the beaches. The wind was not too forceful, but it was cold and Blake had a strong urge to take Cameron's hand. He repressed it when he saw an elderly couple up ahead. They were walking their King Charles, who looked mightily unenthusiastic to be outdoors in such weather. Cameron and Blake smiled at them as they walked by; the couple beamed approvingly at the young men's manners and said hello.

'Are you still mad at Mark?' asked Blake.

'Yes. Wouldn't you be? I know this Social Committee stuff probably seems stupid to you, but it's important to us and Mark knew that. He didn't care that he was making my life difficult as long as he could get back at Meredith.'

'On our behalf,' said Blake. Cameron glanced up at him. *When did he get two inches taller than me?* He caught the wry tone of Blake's voice which suggested that he too believed they were the cover story for Mark's rage against Meredith, not the actual cause. Cameron had told him all about it on the ride up.

'Because we need protecting,' joked Cameron. 'I'll call him tomorrow or the day after. I'm not mad enough to have another falling out like last year's. It's just really, really annoying that he always seems to put our friendship in second place to his obsession with Meredith.'

'And then he accuses you of doing the same.'

'Exactly! Last year, right before you and I... y'know... he started yelling at me because *she*'d upset him. Every fight we've ever had has been about her. Literally, I cannot remember a single argument that he's started that wasn't in some way about Meredith. It's exhausting.'

'Well, he's kind of doing the same thing with Coral now. I know you don't like her...'

'That's an understatement.'

'... but he's her boyfriend and that still hasn't stopped him from putting her in Meredith's metaphorical crosshair, because he knew that nothing would annoy Meredith more than being in direct competition with Coral and that's all he seems to care about.'

'I don't know why he can't admit how he feels about her.'

'Because he doesn't like what it says about him that he's attracted to her. If he likes her for her money or her looks, then he's shallow; if he likes her for her personality, then he's condoning everything he's criticized for the last six years.'

'He's an idiot. Sometimes.'

'I feel sorry for him, in a weird way,' Blake said. 'I don't think he has any idea what he's started.'

'No,' replied Cameron, firmly. 'He hasn't.'

Blake cleared his throat and changed the subject. 'So, we've danced around it for forty minutes, but I have to ask: why did you call me this morning?'

'Disappointed to hear from me?' Cameron jibed.

'Now, you know that's not true.'

'That was sweet.'

'You know me – sweet like a candy bar.'

'That was embarrassingly unfunny, Blake. How awkward.'

'Shut up,' grinned Blake, nudging him. 'We weren't too sweet to each other last time we spoke.'

'Well, at least we managed to reach the crazy-angst quota for our first reunion in months, right?'

'Right! I mean, you've got to admit,' Blake smiled, 'it was pretty cool that I managed to save your life. As dramatic re-entrances go, I did good.'

'Saved my life is a bit of an exaggeration.'

'I don't think so. I think it's an accurate and factual assessment of what happened.'

'You're right. You're my hero.'

'I'd look good in armour,' Blake replied. 'All I'm sayin'.'

'Are we flirting?'

'I hope so. Otherwise that armour comment will have seemed pretty dumb.'

'Did we do this before? When we were just friends?'

'Flirt?' clarified Blake.

'Yes?'

'Yeah, we did. Looking back on it, we absolutely did. We went on a date to Gourmet Burger Kitchen, Cameron. We went out, for dinner, to a restaurant, just the two of us for the express purpose of getting to know each other.'

'And we didn't realize?'

'We did not.'

'Blake... I hate to say this, but, are we stupid?'

'You are,' teased Blake.

'Pardon?'

'I am. I am stupid and you are wise.'

'Smart move.'

'For someone who's stupid?'

'Right,' Cameron smiled.

'This place is really beautiful,' Blake said. 'I've never been before. My dad would love it.'

'I read your letter. That's why I called you this morning.'

'My letter?'

'Yeah.'

'Meredith gave it to you, then?'

'Yes. Last night. She kind of had to once she knew I already knew about it. Even she couldn't think of a way of winning that one.'

'Of course. You're not mad at her?'

Cameron shrugged. 'I know she may seem like a manipulative sociopath, but she is my best friend and she did have reasons for doing what she did. She doesn't always, but I believe her this time.'

Blake nodded and dug his hands further into his jean pockets. The closer they got to the water, the cooler it became.

'What did you... think of it?'

'Of the letter?'

'Yes.'

'If I'm honest, I still wish you'd said it to my face.'

'Yeah. Me too.'

'I'd have said yes.'

'To what?'

'To...' Cameron seemed to think twice about how to end his sentence. He looked at the ground for a few seconds, gathering his thoughts. 'I talked to Dad about it, when I got home last night.'

'Does that mean you've come out to your Dad?'

'Yeah.'

'I didn't know that. When?'

'The night you left me home. I kind of started crying after I kicked you out and Dad looked after me.'

'Is he mad?'

'No. My parents are incredible.'

'They know what I did?'

'Dad does. I told him you'd written me a letter about it and he asked me how it made me feel.'

'How did it make you feel? Apart from frustrated that I'd apparently forgotten how to speak to you face-to-face.'

'I don't really know. Lots of things, obviously. But for most of the time, I just felt quite sad when I was reading it. That's probably the best way to describe it.'

'Sad?' Blake angled his head to look at Cameron, but they kept walking.

'For you.'

Up ahead, they saw Tangela Henton-Worley out for a walk with an earmuff-wearing Mariella Thompson. Mariella nearly had some kind of on-the-spot aneurysm when she realized who she was seeing, together. As the two duos passed each other, they exchanged hellos and Mariella could already be seen scrambling for her phone from the bottom of her bag.

'Do you think they might start a rumour we're gay?' whispered Blake. It was the first time he'd ever directly joked about his sexuality and Cameron giggled.

'God, I hope not,' replied Cameron. 'That'd be awful.'

'Don't worry. I'll just start dating Catherine O'Rourke again and everything'll be fine.'

'Blake, I will only be able to laugh about that in the year 2049.'

Blake nudged him affectionately and they lapsed into an easy silence that lasted until they reached a lone bench, staring out over the grey waters of the bay.

◇◇◇

'That letter wasn't supposed to make you feel sorry for me,' Blake said later.

'How could it not, though?'

They were sitting next to each other on the bench. Over the last year, Blake had started to lose some of the prettiness he had at sixteen. He was taller, better built and he hadn't shaved in a couple of days. There was faintly perceptible stubble on his face that Cameron found extremely attractive. Blake, slightly hunched over and with his hands clasped together, had his leg touching Cameron's and he remembered, suddenly, when its arm brushed past him, how soft Cameron's sweaters always were. He had forgotten that. Cameron was also wearing the same Tom Ford scent he'd worn on the first night they'd had dinner together.

'You didn't think I deserved much sympathy when we were at your house on Friday, Cameron, and you were right.'

'I made you cry. I shouldn't have done that.'

'How many times have I made you cry?'

'I needed to shout at you, but that doesn't mean you have to keep beating yourself up about it for the rest of your life. I don't want that part of my life to follow me. It was bad enough living through it the first time without you, me and everyone we know carrying it with them afterwards. Just because I was angry doesn't mean that you don't deserve sympathy. I had friends, Blake. They weren't saints, obviously, but they had my back. You went through all of this completely alone.'

'We could have gone through it together, though.'

'Okay. Stop. You're just annoying me, now.'

Blake stared out across the bay and exhaled. 'I still don't know how I did it.'

'Pardon?'

'You said in your kitchen that you knew why I'd done it, but you didn't know how. I couldn't answer you then and I still don't know if I can now.'

Blake parted his hands slightly, so that Cameron's could fall in between them.

'It was manic,' he said. 'The whole thing was manic. It's the only way I can describe it. It was like my brain wasn't working properly. When I left Imogen's house after you and I kissed for the first time, I was buzzing, Cameron. I can't remember a time when I was that happy. But when I woke up the next morning, everything was different. It was like a crash. Everything in me went into overdrive. I couldn't breathe properly. I was agitated. I felt sick. It was like my whole body had tinnitus. Even though I know you can only get that in your ears. I don't know how to describe it, Cameron. All I wanted was for it to stop.'

Cameron squeezed Blake's hand. He squeezed back and continued. 'I started to re-write my own memories. I became convinced that the only reason I felt this way was because of you – that when I was with you I was unsure of myself, but when I was away from you, I could be myself again. And myself, of course, meant heterosexual. Because what else matters, right?'

Cameron was taken aback at the self-loathing bitterness in Blake's voice, but again he didn't interrupt.

'I was running myself ragged trying to prove to everyone around me that I was straight. No one asked, but I felt that I somehow had to let them know. I started changing my behaviour and my mannerisms and my way of speaking. I made a complete fool of myself trying to act like some kind of frat star. I honestly was like a really bad parody of a straight guy. Any innuendo I could make; any comment about a good looking girl, I just blurted out. I must have sounded like a pervert. I started swaggering and I don't do that. I'm from Connecticut, Cameron! I don't even know how to swagger. Everything in my life was about proving you "wrong". Everything was about proving I wasn't gay. But I never blamed you, Cameron, honestly. I never hated you. That's probably no consolation, but I really want you to know that.'

'There were times I definitely thought that you did.'

'No. Never. The only time I ever got mad at you was when you stopped trying to contact me. I hadn't responded, I hung up on you, I ignored your messages and even then I was upset that you'd stopped. It was awful. I should never have stopped talking to you, Cameron. I'm so sorry.'

Cameron chose to remain diplomatically silent. It seemed the best option since he didn't quite know what to say. His impulse was to murmur the usual 'That's okay,' or 'It's fine,' but it hadn't been either of those things and to say so would be an outright lie.

'There were times when I could almost convince myself that I was happy without you,' Blake continued, 'even though there was a nagging little voice in my head that kept telling me that what I was doing was wrong. Every time I saw you, I felt horrible. It was like I was running and as long as I didn't stop, it'd be fine. When I competed for Track and Field back home, I could reach a point during training where I could keep going on adrenalin alone. Your body gets so tired that it doesn't even register it's tired. That's what it was like. Tired, all the time, but never stopping to thinking about it.'

'And now?'

'I'm gay. That sounds so obvious and so stupid, but I spent so much time and energy trying to do everything I could to make sure I'd never have to say those words. Then one day, I realized that I didn't want to keep going. I got sick of it; I didn't want to live the rest of my life like that. It's so liberating not to be afraid of the word 'gay' anymore, Cameron. To be able to think of it as an adjective, rather than an accusation – it's just incredible. It's like a weight's lifted off that you always knew you were carrying, but you didn't know what its name was. I dunno. I love you and I'm sorry. I suppose that's my conclusion. I guess it's that simple. Weird, huh?'

There was a long silence and Blake noticed that Cameron hadn't reciprocated. He hadn't said 'I love you.' But he hadn't let go off his hand, either, and he was still sitting here, next to him. After a few moments, Cameron spoke.

'Last night, all I could think about was your letter, even when I was helping Imogen krunk three of Coral's friends off the dance-floor in *Box*, and I realized that if I was thinking about your letter, then I was thinking about you. I know that a lot of bad stuff has happened and that we've both messed up, but I don't believe I was wrong about you for all those months that we were friends. I still think you're a good guy. I know that it's not going to be easy, but I don't want to mess up again. I don't want us to miss the chance of being together because we couldn't let go of what happened a year ago.'

'Together? As in... you want to be my boyfriend?'

'Yes. That's what I would have said yes to. In your letter. But then I realized that you hadn't actually asked me. You just said you were sorry, you didn't ask me to... you know.'

'I didn't think I had the right to, after what happened.'

'I suppose.'

'Do you wanna?' asked Blake.

'Do I wanna?'

'Yeah, I probably could have phrased that better.'

'After everything that's happened, that's how you ask me?' laughed Cameron.

'Dude, you just told me that the moment you realized you finally wanted us to be together was when you and Imogen were ghetto-grinding three hipsters off a dance-floor.'

'I regret nothing.'

'You still haven't answered my amazingly-phrased question.'

'Yes, I do. Very much.'

Blake sighed deeply and smiled. He tightened his grip around Cameron's hands and pressed his forehead up against his.

'Wow. Just like that.'

'Yeah, twelve months, a fake relationship and two nervous breakdowns later and here we are.'

'Easy as,' smiled Blake.

'We are stupid.'

'At least we have each other.'

'Truezies.'

'We'll never be able to walk through Belfast holding hands,' said Blake. 'We're only holding them now because there's no one else around. We probably won't be able to kiss on the lips in public while we live here. There'll be a lot of clubs and bars where we can't kiss or dance together. People will think they have a right to tell us what they think of our private lives and my father is a Baptist pastor. It is not an ideal situation, by any stretch of the imagination.'

'I know,' whispered Cameron.

'But we have the truth. We know the truth now, Cameron, and that's worth a lot.'

'I'm sorry that you were in pain,' Cameron said. 'I'm sorry that we both were, but I'm still glad I met you.'

Blake leaned in and kissed Cameron very softly. The wind kept blowing in off the bay, the cries of seagulls could be heard in the distance and Cameron's hand tightened around Blake's. The world was still turning.

Author's Note

They say that the path towards your second book, particularly if it's the second in a series, is never easy. Well, *The Immaculate Deception* was certainly a case in point and so perhaps the first person to thank properly is Saint Jude. Seriously.

The decision to start a master's in medieval history at exactly the same time as I was due to start writing this sequel may not have been the wisest move. I should thank, or apologize to, Dr James Davis, who put up with my editing mania on a field trip to Cumbria, and Ciarán Noade, Sarah Mawhinney, Laura McCosker and Ruth Cowden, who kept me distracted.

To everyone else, who kept the faith and encouraged me to keep going, a huge thank you. Your support and persistence means more to me than I could possibly say. To all those who read *Popular* and then got in touch to say how impatient you were for the sequel, that meant a great deal and your comments were very much appreciated. Especially from the students and staff at Friends' School in Lisburn, Hunterhouse College, The Rainey Endowed School in Magherafelt, Sullivan Upper School in Holywood and Saint Edward's School in Oxford, who invited me in to speak about writing and *Popular*. To the team at the Belvoir Players' Studio in Belfast, who helped bring *Popular* on to the stage in

2011 and 2012, thank you for an incredible summer and spring in a fantastic venue. The cast and crew of both shows brought *Popular* to life in unique and hilarious ways.

So many people helped, prayed and encouraged along the road to *The Immaculate Deception*'s publication that it would be impossible to mention them all, but ungrateful to leave everybody out. I would like to personally thank Laura Bradley, for all her incredible editorial suggestions; Ellen Buddle; Scott De Buitléir; Allan Davison, for listening to me talk about this for months on end; Emerald Fennell; Sarah Houghton; Joanne Law, for the drives; my aunt Pauline; Pamela Mills; Sarah Patterson, for her wonderful song *Today* inspired by the storyline of *Popular*; Alexa Stewart Reid and Amy Weber Reid for years of friendship and all the wonderful summers in New Canaan; the brilliant Tim and Claire Ridgway, without who none of this would have been possible; my delightful gal-pal and muse, Kerry Rogan; my parents Ian and Heather; my sisters Lynsey, Jenny and Ashleigh; Joel Samaha; Lucy Williams; Tom Woodward and, of course, Eric Spies who, throughout the freezing winter nights it took to write this book, kept up a steady stream of contact and support from the other side of the Atlantic Ocean.

Gareth Russell,
The Feast of Saint Jude (weird, right?), 2012

Abbreviations, definitions and banter II: A guide to the vocab in *The Immaculate Deception*

There is nothing I enjoy more than a good fake word or an unnecessary abbreviation and *The Immaculate Deception* is littered with them. So here's a guide to some of the more niche words used by the characters; not just their slang, but also some of the academic/geographical terminology. You may already be familiar with these; you may not. In any case, definitions abú.

Abú an Irish word that translates as 'to victory.' In Malone terminology, it allegedly entered popular vocab courtesy of Rathmore Grammar School and it's used to indicate that a certain quality has triumphed in a specific social situation. For instance, when Mariella says 'Hotties abú' she is indicating that she believes there is a proliferation of hotties at Imogen and Meredith's birthday party. If you were to say 'Bad times abú' or 'Banter abú,' then it indicates that either bad times or banter are triumphant in your life/party. Sounds stupid? You're wrong. It's amazing.

A-Levels a set of British exams taken over the two final years of high school. Students generally pick either three or four subjects and they are then rigorously examined in them in two sets of exams. The first set takes place at the end of Lower Sixth (known as the AS-Levels); the second at the end of Upper Sixth. College/university admission is usually determined by one's final A-Level grades. The leap in difficulty from GCSE to AS-Level is considerable. The A stands for 'Advanced'; Lower Sixth's AS stands for 'Advanced Subsidiary.'

And stuff a true Maloner will always have this on the tip of their tongue, just in case they can't think of another way to end their sentence.

AOB the Age of the Bisexual.

AOF the Age of Fabulous.

ASBO an Anti-Social Behaviour Order.

Banter banter is essentially the English form of craic. It has recently made its presence felt in Northern Ireland. It is often shortened to 'bant.'

Beau Malone abbreviation for 'beautiful,' pronounced 'bee-yah.' It was particularly strong in Victoria College, an all-girls school in Malone. In *Popular*'s storyline, it was created by Meredith Harper.

Betty No-Bant
someone who is the incarnation of anti-banter.

Buck   sex.
(Well, there was no easy way to say that, was there?)

Caoimhe   an Irish girls' name. It's usually pronounced *Keeva*.

Chips   in the UK, French fries.

Chunder   English slang for vomiting.

Cracking   when used as slang: amazing.

Craic   pronounced 'crack.' The origins of the word are debated, but it basically means fun, a good time, a pleasing situation. Questions like 'What's the craic?' are a standard way of starting conversations in Ireland, meaning 'Well, what's going on?' Craic is, by far and away, the most-prized social attribute in Ireland. To be described as 'bad craic' is a sign of apocalyptic social failure.

Crisps   in the UK, potato chips.

Emergencia
    slang from *Popular*. It refers to an urgent social emergency and if you receive it via text, you have to contact the sender ASAP.

Eóin   an Irish boys' name. It is pronounced in the same way as 'Owen' would be in English.

Fancy   slang for having a crush on someone.

FIB From *Popular*, a fabulous-induced breakdown, when one is so overwhelmed by the burden of your own popularity or a dazzling impending social occasion that you suffer a mini-episode and have to take to your bed. The original FIBs were pioneered by Kerry Davison.

Fifth year Sophomore year in American high schools; students are usually fifteen or sixteen.

First XVs when spoken, it's said as "the First Fifteens." They are the school's best rugby team.

Fit it can mean in good physical shape or, in slang, it means the same as 'hot'/good looking.

Form room
roughly equivalent to a home room in American high schools. In most Northern Irish schools, your form room is usually allocated based on which school house you're in.

Garage it can mean the car-storing extension to a house or a gas/petrol station.

GCSE the General Certificate of Secondary Education. Exams taken at the end of fifth year in ten or eleven subjects, moderated by a national examination board, with grades ranging from A* to U. A* to C are classed as passing grades; D to G are Level 1 grades and a 'U' means that the paper was un-gradable.

Go out If used in the way Mark asks Coral, then it implies going steady with or dating someone.

Grammar School Northern Ireland has very few private schools. Grammar schools mostly still use a series of academic tests for their eleven-year-old applicants. The schools usually run from first year (11) to Upper Sixth (18.)

Head Boy in the British school system, a male student in their final year who is either elected by the student body or appointed by the teachers to represent the school at various official functions, organize prefects in their duty rota and perhaps help with various administrative tasks, such as reading out the morning announcements. The head boy usually excels academically and if an election is held, teachers and the principal have the right to veto the result if a candidate is chosen based on popularity rather than aptitude. In mixed schools, there is also a head girl, with similar duties, and usually one or two deputies.

ICT a school subject. Its abbreviation stands for "Information and communications technology." It can also be referred to as "IT" or "computer sciences."

Lads 'lads' or 'lad' can be used in pretty much the same way as 'dude.' It can be used to denote a group of guys or as a form of greeting. However, 'a lad' or 'such a lad' is also a compliment, indicating that someone is good craic/banter, socially confident and prone to doing outlandish things on a night out to ensure that communal banter is had.

Lairy Rowdy, loud or socially aggressive.

Lower Sixth   Junior year in American high schools; students are usually sixteen or seventeen. Sometimes referred to as 'Sixth year.'

Malone   an area in south Belfast that has some of the highest property prices in Northern Ireland. In Northern Irish humour, Malone is often synonymous with wealth, privilege and (depending on your interpretation) snobbery. Its postcode (zip code) is BT9, roughly equivalent to something like Dublin 4 or SW1, and it's often used in the same way as 'Malone' is in conversations.

Mate   used as a form of greeting, mostly between boys; essentially, it's like 'dude.'

Melt   a melt or a head-melt is someone who is so annoying that you feel as if your brain is melting.

Mocks   exams held either before or after Christmas, which simulate the experience of proper exams and try to prepare students for what the real exams will be like in June.

Munters   ugly people.

P.E. Physical Education. Basically, gym class. There is a very specialized and scientific form of it that can be taken as an A-Level subject nowadays, but even if you don't study it, you are still expected to do physical exercise (sometimes known as "Games") for the full seven years of your high school education. In Down High School, this will at some point involve inventing artful excuses to avoid running around the Mound of Down in Noah-levels of a torrential downpour. (Just me? I regret nothing.)

Poppy Appeal
during the First World War, the only flower that was capable of growing in the battlefields was the poppy. Since then, the flower has become associated with the loss and carnage of conflict. Every year in November, the Royal British Legion launches a nationwide fundraising initiative that involves selling paper poppies that people can wear in their lapels to honour those who have died in every conflict since 1918. It culminates in the national minutes' silence on November 11th and again on the Sunday nearest to it.

Prep School
although nearly all schools in Northern Ireland are state-run, some of the older schools still have the right to run a privately-funded junior department. These are known as prep schools and they usually cater for students from the ages of four to eleven.

Pulled English slang for kissing or making out.

Rah   a rich or "posh" person, perhaps with a fondness for pashminas, Jack Wills or yacht clubs. It can get a bit confusing at times, since "ra" was an old code word for referring to the IRA. There's not much crossover.

See   über-irritating slang for hook up/kiss/make out.

Shanter "shit banter."

Sixth Form Centre
a bit like a common room that's set aside solely for the two sixth years. It's a recreational area to be used during free periods. Or during study sessions, if you're clever enough to outwit the study hall supervisor. (When they hand the roll around at the start of the year, just don't sign your name for a couple of the periods.)

Social Committee
called the Formal Committee in some schools, it's the Social Committee's job to organize the end of year ball or the Formal (i.e. prom.) They can do this by organizing a series of fundraisers and even hiring out local nightclubs to generate enough money to fund the formal/ball.

Sozzles I'm sorry. (97% of the time, it is almost certainly a fake apology if they use the word 'sozzles.')

Sweets   in the UK, candy.

Talent   when used as slang, it refers to hot or attractive people.

Theatre Studies
>at A-Level, the study of drama on both a practical and academic basis.

Ulster Schools' Cup Final
>the high point of the Northern Irish school rugby year. It is a match held on Saint Patrick's Day in Belfast between the two best school rugby teams in the country. It has been held every year since 1876 and it attracts huge crowds. Squads have been competing throughout the year, in various stages of competition, until the two most successful teams are left to battle it out in the Final. The prize is the Ulster Schools' Challenge Cup. And, obviously, eternal glory. I'm not kidding. It's amazing.

University Challenge
>a majorly difficult television quiz show that pits teams from Britain's top universities against each other in intellectual combat.

Upper Sixth
>senior or final year; students are usually seventeen or eighteen.

-zies This can be unnecessarily stuck on to the end of any word to make it cooler. For instance, 'Heyzies.'

THE IMMACULATE DECEPTION

ISBN-13: 978-1481138390
ISBN-10: 1481138391

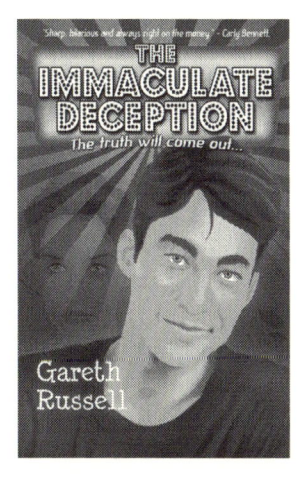

BOOK TWO OF THE "POPULAR SERIES"

As the students prepare to return for another year at Belfast's Mount Olivet Grammar School, a scandalous secret about Cameron Matthews, the popular girls' BFF, is about to blow the lid off Mount Olivet's festering world of tensions and lies.

Who has the most to gain from trying to ruin Cameron's life? Could it be recently-dumped desperado, Catherine O'Rourke? Rising gossip girl, Celeste Fitzpatrick? Coral Andrews, the hipsters' hug-dispensing queen bee? Or could it even be Meredith Harper, Cameron's lifelong friend and the most beautiful girl in school?

Only one thing's for certain – in this school, you have to watch your back...

POPULAR

ISBN-13: 978-1481129244
ISBN-10: 1481129244

BOOK ONE OF THE "POPULAR SERIES"

On the first day of September, 16 year-old Meredith Harper rules over the teen it-crowd of Belfast, Northern Ireland. But beneath the surface, Meredith's complicated web of manipulative lies and self-serving intrigue are slowly beginning to threaten her social position and she finds herself being challenged by handsome Mark Kingston, the only guy in the school who's always hated her.

In a world where nothing stays secret for very long, Meredith and her friends will need all their skills to guess who's in, out, coming out, going up, going down, dating, cheating, lying and trying to cope....

Let the games begin!

◇◇◇

Book Three:

THE AGE OF VENGEANCE - OUT SOON...